Titles by Rebecca M. Hale

Afoot on St. Croix

Rebecca M. Hale

BERKLEY PRIME CRIME, NEW YORK

THE BERKLEY PUBLISHING GROUP
Published by the Penguin Group
Penguin Group (USA)
375 Hudson Street, New York, New York 10014, USA

USA | Canada | UK | Ireland | Australia | New Zealand | India | South Africa | China

Penguin Books Ltd., Registered Offices: 80 Strand, London WC2R 0RL, England
For more information about the Penguin Group, visit penguin.com.

AFOOT ON ST. CROIX

A Berkley Prime Crime Book / published by arrangement with the author

Berkley Prime Crime Books are published by The Berkley Publishing Group.
BERKLEY® PRIME CRIME and the PRIME CRIME logo are
trademarks of Penguin Group (USA).

For information, address: The Berkley Publishing Group,
a division of Penguin Group (USA),
375 Hudson Street, New York, New York 10014.

ISBN: 978-0-425-25195-9

PUBLISHING HISTORY
Berkley Prime Crime mass-market edition / October 2013

PRINTED IN THE UNITED STATES OF AMERICA

10 9 8 7 6 5 4 3 2 1

Cover photo by Rebecca M. Hale; *Rocks* from Shutterstock.
Cover design by George Long.

For Elizabeth Berwanger

"There," said the author, feeling a sense of accomplishment. "I've finally got them reunited with their mother—all five chicks."

The cab driver stroked his chin and leaned forward in his frayed lawn chair. For the last forty-five minutes, he and his colleagues had watched the woman chase the chicks back and forth across the busy intersection.

Shaking his head, he gave the author a sympathetic smile.

"This morning, she had nine."

Introduction

The Goat Foot Woman

TWO CHILDREN—A girl of seven and boy just turned four—played in a gravel courtyard outside the Comanche Hotel in downtown Christiansted. On the ground between them lay a pyramid of empty beer bottles, scavenged from a nearby waste bin. Several dozen pebbles and a few hardened chunks of sun-bleached coral were piled around the base, an effort to prop up the shaky tower.

The children's mother sat at a picnic table about ten feet away, tensely smoking a cigarette. Despite the day's humid heat, the woman wore a dark cloak over her sleeveless silk dress. The black material draped loosely over her shoulders and spanned the length of her body, falling all the way to the ground. Only the open-toed tips of her shoes peeked out beneath the fabric's bottom hem. A scarf made of similar cloth covered her head, leaving the pale oval of her face exposed.

The woman appeared not to notice the encumbrance of the cloak and scarf. Every so often, she glanced across the courtyard to check on her offspring, but for the most part, she kept her focus trained on the sky above the harbor.

GREEN EYES SQUINTING, the young girl wrapped her hand around the neck of a brown bottle and lifted it toward the peak of the unstable heap. The makeshift castle was almost complete—this last topper was all that remained.

The girl's tongue slipped over her upper lip as she concentrated on the bottle's wide bottom rim, trying to balance it on the stack.

One by one, she released her tiny fingers.

The heavy glass teetered, wobbling for a long moment, before clattering to the ground.

"*Ay*, Elena, watch *ya'self*," the mother snapped testily. She rose from her seat at the picnic table, as if she were about to launch into a lengthy scolding, but a distant movement in the sky caught her attention.

Once more staring out at the sea, the woman sucked in another steadying puff from the cigarette, leaving a ring of red lipstick on the smoldering stub. The smoke swilled in her lungs; then she slowly blew out a curling gray plume.

THE GIRL ROLLED her eyes in annoyance. She tossed her head, causing the dark wavy hair tied in her pigtails to swing wildly through the air. Noting her mother's distraction, she picked up a stone and tossed it at her playmate.

"*Ay*, Hassan, watch *ya'self*," she said, her voice a perfect imitation of her mother's.

The boy opened his mouth to protest, but Elena held up a shushing hand. She leaned toward him, a serious expression on her sun-flushed face.

Her words took on a heavy Caribbean lilt as she dropped her voice to a whisper.

"*Wat'ch ya'self, leet-le brother*," she cautioned. "*Special-lee at night. Ya dun wanna bey caught out by duh Goat-foot Wo-man.*"

"Who?" the boy asked, dropping the pebble that he had scooped up to throw in retaliation.

Elena drew in her breath with exaggerated surprise.

"Don' yah know you got-ta wa'ch out for dah Goat-foot Wo-man?"

Hassan shook his head, his expression one of puzzled concern.

Elena slid forward, moving even closer to her brother. Bending to his shorter height, she wrapped an arm around his shoulders and pointed inland over the hotel's steep roofline.

"Dah Goat-foot Wo-man, she lives in duh hills abuv Chris'ted. If you leesen, you can hear hur, creaking through duh trees . . . crackeling een duh branches . . . rust'ling through duh leaves . . ."

The little boy cringed, visibly unnerved, but his apprehension only spurred his sister on. Her eyes gleamed as she continued.

"She's a fright-ful creature, haf hoom-an, haf goat, but you wudd'n know it from seeing hur on dah street. When she comes een-ta town, she hides hur lef' foot een a beeg floppy shoe—so dat no wone can see duh hoof."

Hassan squeezed his eyes shut and clamped his hands over his ears. Elena persisted, increasing the volume of her voice.

"Hur spirit's oldah dan dah jumbies . . . oldah dan dis island . . . oldah dan tyme eet-self."

She strummed her fingertips across her brother's shoulders, tapping out an eerie cadence. He tried to shrug away from her grip, but her hand clamped down, pressing through his shirt.

"She wuz here 'fore dah Danes, 'fore dah French, 'fore dah first Spanish slave tradas. She wuz wit duh Car-ib at Salt Reev-ah when Christ'pher Columbus came a-shore."

Quickly circling around her brother, Elena hunched to her knees in front of him.

"Dah Goat-foot Wo-man, she helped dem Car-ib carve up a man from dat Spanish crew. They strung 'eem up ova a fire an' cooked 'eem on a stek."

Concentrating, the girl crossed her eyes, skewed her face

into its most grotesque contortion, and luridly licked her lips.

"Tha's where she first gut duh taste fer hoom-an flesh."

Elena grabbed Hassan's hand. Twisting his wrist, she turned his palm upward and traced her fingernail across its sweating surface.

"Evah so often, when she gets a hank'ring, duh Goat-foot Wo-man teks a child home an' eats 'eem for dinn-a."

Hassan jerked his arm away from his sister's grasp.

"No," he said, his lower lip trembling as he clenched his fist against his chest. "I don't believe you."

"Oh, Hassan," the girl replied in mock horror, instantly dropping the accent. "Don't say that. Don't ever say that."

Hassan gulped as his sister looked up and across the courtyard at a shadowed figure in an alley about thirty feet away. When Elena returned her gaze to his, her face was darkly somber.

Returning to her hushed tone, she whispered a grim warning. "She's listening. The Goat Foot Woman, she's always listening."

AN ELDERLY CRUCIAN woman crouched in an alley near the Comanche Hotel, watching the children in the gravel court-yard. A thin smile crimped her dusty lips as she listened to Elena's story.

"She's gut it 'bout haf right," the hag said with a raspy chuckle.

Gripping the handle of a rusted shopping cart piled high with refuse, the old woman hobbled through the courtyard in the direction of the harbor. As she limped past the chil-dren's mound of glass and rubble, she resisted the urge to stop and leer down at the awestruck pair.

But when she reached the edge of the boardwalk on the courtyard's opposite side, she heard the girl's voice croak hoarsely to her brother.

"Children ain' nuttin' but an appet-tizah."

Her yellow eyes shining with amusement, the hag turned

to look back at the children. Resting a stiff hand on her hip, she shook her head at the girl's antics.

Just then, the mother crushed out her cigarette on the gravel, scooped up the boy, and grabbed the girl's hand.

Elena got out one last comment before being dragged off toward the hotel.

Hassan shrieked in terror as his sister hungrily smacked her lips.

"Nuttin' more dan a snack."

~ 1 ~

Gedda

A HOT CARIBBEAN sun shone down on the Christiansted harbor, baking the pink faces of the Danish tourists strolling across the boardwalk's warped wooden pier. The motionless heat simmered over the flat water, a dry parching broil. A half mile in the distance, scattered waves broke along a crescent-shaped reef, the refreshing spray a cruel taunt to those sweltering on land.

The weather-beaten walkway curved around the harbor's edge, passing a shabby collection of open-air restaurants, bars, and block-shaped hotels. A few overgrown lots and an abandoned nightclub added to the mix, the unkempt vacancies marring the downtown commercial area like gaps from missing teeth.

Beneath the shade of the nightclub's front entrance, a pair of shirtless West Indians stared listlessly out at the blue horizon. The men's shoulders slumped forward; their scabby limbs hung limply over the edge of the building's exposed foundation. Their bodies lacked any sign of animation—until the Danes approached.

Suddenly, the men sprang to life, calling out to the

blond-headed tourists while wildly gesturing to a pile of green coconuts gathered on the litter-strewn concrete.

"Ay, you dere! Ya gut ta cum see deese feresh coco-nuts. We picked dem jes' fer you!"

Raising the ragged edge of a machete, one of the vendors scooped up a round nut and expertly lopped off its top.

His partner quickly plunked a plastic straw through the opening and offered it to the nearest Dane for a sampling taste.

With an embarrassed grin, the hapless European tried to demur, but the pair persisted.

Gingerly, the Dane brought the straw to his mustached lips and took a tentative sip. After swallowing a small dose of the watery liquid, he glanced up from the straw with a grimace.

The warm juice felt thick on his tongue, but he swallowed his dislike of the drink. The coconut vendors leaned toward him, eagerly awaiting his verdict.

An uneasy shadow crossed the Dane's eyes as his face hardened with disapproval.

We should have never sold this place, he thought to himself. *Look at what the Americans have done to it.*

After an awkward moment of silence, the Dane reached for his wallet.

"Mmm," he announced loudly but in an unconvincing tone. "That is . . . *fan-tastic.*"

TOWARD THE BOARDWALK'S east end, the yellow ochre walls of Fort Christiansvaern gleamed in the sunlight. The signature landmark in a small park commemorating St. Croix's colonial past, the refurbished Danish stronghold was in far better shape than many of the island's modern-day constructions.

Nearby, a barrier of red construction webbing surrounded the Customs House, a structure of similar vintage that was just beginning the updating process. At the far edge of the grounds, not far from a taxi stand and the park's public restrooms, the smaller Scale House stood graying with mildew and rot. The third in line for refurbishments, this building would have a while to wait for its beautifying treatment.

A dozen or so chickens scratched in the dry grass outside the fort's imposing walls, their beaks vigorously pecking for grubs. Hens fussed over their chicks, clucking anxiously to keep them from straying, while cagy roosters eyed one another, puffing out their feather-covered chests and haughtily preening their silky black plumes.

A flurry of loud *squawks* broke the air as an olive-skinned man in a cropped T-shirt, running shorts, and sneakers jogged from the boardwalk's terminus onto the park's open green space.

The birds scattered, jumping out of the runner's path. Unfazed by the avian commotion, the man proceeded toward a white-painted gazebo in the center of the wide lawn and thunked up its wooden steps.

Stooping, the man spread a stack of laminated sheet music across the gazebo's splintered floor, carefully arranging the pages in numerical order. Once he had the papers in place, he stood and turned to face the harbor.

Stripping off his T-shirt, he rolled his shoulders to loosen his joints. The afternoon sun angled beneath the gazebo's roof, splashing across the man's chest to reveal a series of elaborate tattoos depicting scenes from Dante's *Inferno*. The masterpiece of ink art covered his upper torso, wrapped over his shoulders, and crept down his back. Howling demonic figures clawed out from his tanned skin, the images forever frozen in their desperate attempt to escape the torture chamber of searing flames.

The tattoos, it turned out, were a visual aid, meant to inspire the man's vocal performance.

After a few trilling warm-up scales, he began to sing. His voice, wobbly at first, grew in strength and volume as he belted out the opening stanzas of an Italian opera. Throwing his arms wide, his now pitch-perfect tenor floated across the water, a pleasant if strangely incongruous sound.

Seemingly comforted by the music, the chickens settled in around the gazebo and resumed their pecking.

⌒⌒

YET ANOTHER REMNANT from the Danish colonial era dotted the boardwalk at its midway point, well outside the bounds of the fort's sanctioned historical site. The cylindrical base of a windmill once used to crush sugarcane studded the shoreline, its round tower a beacon for arriving mariners with a strong—and preferably indiscriminate—alcoholic thirst.

For the small boats that moored in the Christiansted harbor, many serving as their occupants' full-time residences, it was but a few short strides across the boardwalk's width to the windmill's rustic bartending station.

A counter cut into the curving coral-rock wall allowed beers to be passed from coolers stored in the circular interior to a line of stools ringing the outside. Rudimentary mixed drinks were also available, the most popular being the island's signature Confusion cocktail of flavored Cruzan rum and pineapple juice. The sweet liquid, often chilled with a few chips of ice, was served in the standard plastic cups used for cheap drinks throughout the Caribbean.

IT HAD BEEN a slow afternoon, the flip-flop-wearing bartender thought as he leaned his tall body over the windmill's counter and rested his chin in his hands. The stools on the counter's opposite side were empty, perhaps due to the heat—perhaps due to the overenergetic a cappella performance under way at the gazebo down by the Danish fort. The robust singing could be heard all along the boardwalk.

"Umberto's in rare form today," the bartender mused, tilting his head to listen to the powerful crescendo of Italian.

The bartender didn't mind these daily singing sessions, an opinion that put him in the minority among the boardwalk's regulars.

He found the music cleared his mind—it made him think less about his last cold shower from the rain catchment outside his shack of an apartment, and more about his next day off, when he would spend several hours relaxing on the sailboat his girlfriend captained for one of the local dive shops.

He was a lucky man, he thought as he stared sleepily at the collection of watercraft floating in the harbor. He lived on an island, he had a low-key, stress-free job, and he'd found the perfect girl.

She possessed the two essential features he looked for in a woman: she was attractive, with an island girl's ruffled, sun-kissed mystique, and, even more important, she had easy access to a boat.

THE BARTENDER YAWNED, shaking loose his daydream, as a rusted shopping cart bumped toward his counter.

"Hey there, Gedda," he said softly, nodding at the withered old woman pushing the cart onto the boardwalk from the gravel courtyard behind his bartending station.

He didn't expect a response. Everyone knew the hag's hearing was almost gone. Years of constant exposure to the sun and hard liquor had presumably fried her mental faculties.

She looked like a walking corpse; the calloused surface of her dark skin had toughened into a dingy gray shell. She moved with a pronounced limp, caused primarily by her lame left foot, which dragged stiffly across the boardwalk's uneven planks.

Gedda's heavyset figure was dressed in layers of rags. The loose-hanging folds of cloth obscured the shape of her limbs—particularly her deformed left foot—which she'd covered with an old floppy shoe.

THE HOMELESS HAG was a constant presence in downtown Christiansted, hovering silently around the edges of activity, lurking in the narrow cobblestone alleys leading inland from the boardwalk.

Most nights, she could be found hanging around the Dumpsters behind the boardwalk's busier restaurants. The waitstaff would scrape their best-looking leftovers into foam containers and leave the packages perched on top of the easiest-to-reach refuse heap.

No one ever saw the woman move the containers to her cart, but within seconds, the food always disappeared.

WHERE GEDDA WENT after she left the Dumpsters was anyone's guess, but the bartender suspected that she had been sleeping inside the Danish fort. Twice, he'd seen her hobbling out from behind the corner of its nearest harbor-facing wall. Both instances had occurred early in the morning, before the park service employees had arrived to open the front gates.

Gedda had either stumbled across a secret entrance or, he reasoned, someone in the park service was leaving a back door open for her.

The old woman's digs were probably nicer than his own, the bartender thought with a sigh as the hag left her cart and hobbled toward the windmill's counter.

"You thirsty, Gedda?" he asked, reaching for a plastic cup.

She shuffled the last few feet to the bar as he measured out twice the normal dose of rum and dumped it into the container.

Topping off the drink with a splash of pineapple juice, he gave the woman a conspiring smile, set the cup on the counter, and turned his back to fiddle with a plastic cooler on the far side of the windmill's round room.

GEDDA'S CLAWED HAND immediately reached for the cup. Her grip shaking, she brought the flimsy plastic rim to her chapped lips. Tilting her head back, she took a long gulp, draining half the volume in a single swill.

Her creased eyelids closed as she savored the familiar burn on her throat. She rocked back and forth, relishing the temporary numbness the drink brought to her aching, arthritic body.

But the moment of solace was soon interrupted.

Gedda's bloodshot eyes popped open at the distant buzz of the two-o'clock seaplane arriving from Charlotte Amalie.

She watched the plane putter across the sky above the harbor, circle the soot-stained towers of the power plant on the bay's west side, and descend smoothly toward the water.

As the tiny aircraft made its final approach to the buoy-demarcated runway, the old woman's vision honed in on one of the faces peering out of the plane's oval-shaped windows.

"Char-lee Bak-ah," Gedda said with a crooked smile that revealed several chipped teeth. Her voice cracked with eerie delight.

"Wel-cum back ta San-ta Cruz."

Her grip now much steadier, she lifted the cup as if toasting the seaplane and then downed the remainder of the rum cocktail in a single gulp.

~ 2 ~

The Seaplane

CHARLIE BAKER CLENCHED the armrests bolted to his seat as the seaplane tilted into its last turn above the Christiansted harbor. The sideways motion churned his stomach; the tight rotation skewed his center of balance. He gulped and blinked his eyes, trying to straighten his vision.

As the plane skimmed over the water, Charlie glanced skeptically out the nearest portal, expecting the worst. It was his third trip to St. Croix since Thanksgiving, and each landing had been more precarious than the one that came before.

The pilot steadied the craft for its final approach, leveling the wings. The plane dropped through the air, now in a rapid descent toward the harbor.

Charlie muttered to himself.

"I must be crazy for coming back here."

DESPITE THE PERILOUS nature of his last few arrivals into the Christiansted harbor, Charlie still preferred the seaplane to the commercial airliner that flew between St. Thomas and St. Croix.

The seaplane was far more convenient, with minimal security screening and an abbreviated check-in process. Plus, the plane's terminus points were within a short walking distance of the downtown areas of both Christiansted and Charlotte Amalie.

Up until last summer, a commuter ferry had serviced the route, but Charlie wouldn't have considered that an option even if the boat had still been in operation.

The ferry had been a notoriously unreliable means of transport, frequently canceling its runs due to weather concerns or high seas. In addition, the boat took almost twice as long as the seaplane to traverse the forty-mile distance between the islands. Even on the best of days, the ride had been extremely bumpy, only recommended for those with seaworthy stomachs—a qualification that Charlie did not meet.

Despite having lived in the Caribbean for the last ten years, Charlie was still ill at ease on the water. Earlier that morning, he'd taken a short boat ride from his home base of St. John across the Pillsbury Sound to Red Hook on the east end of St. Thomas. That brief boating session had given him all the bumping and bobbing action he could handle for one day.

Regardless, the St. Croix ferry service had been out of commission since the previous July, when the boat ran aground on one of the cays near St. Thomas. The accident had occurred while the passengers—and apparently the ship's captain—were watching a local fireworks display.

The official investigation into the cause of the incident had been inconclusive as to blame, but the ferry company had so far been unable to raise funds for a new vessel, leaving the seaplane as the main means of inter-island transport connecting St. Croix to its sister Virgin Islands.

A SHEEN OF water sprayed against the aircraft's metal body as its bottom booms skimmed the sea's surface. Charlie stared nervously out the droplet-covered window, his stomach tightening with apprehension.

It wasn't the actual landing he was afraid of—in most instances, a seaplane's transition from air to water was remarkably smooth.

It was the showdown.

As the booms dug into the water, kicking up waves, Charlie spied a small dinghy anchored near the protective reef that circled the harbor. The pilot began to swear, his irate words easily traveling from the front of the plane into the passenger cabin.

"Here we go," Charlie muttered, bracing his shoulders against the back of his seat.

A second later, the seaplane took a sudden jerking turn, sending it skidding outside the marked runway, only partially under the pilot's control.

Holding his breath, Charlie leaned toward the center aisle, angling his head to look out the pilot's front windshield. The narrow view captured a chaotic scene as the plane careened wildly toward a sailboat that had just entered the harbor.

Charlie caught a brief glance of the sailboat's wide-eyed captain, a young woman who worked for one of the Christiansted dive shops. Cursing, she spun the boat's wooden steering wheel, helpless to avoid the oncoming plane.

A second slew of expletives exploded from the cockpit as the seaplane made yet another abrupt evasive maneuver. The plane swung into a sharp curve, this time whipping around to face the marked runway.

There, floating in the middle of the lane, was the obstacle that had caused the plane's initial swerve.

A rogue swimmer raised a clenched fist above his snorkel mask, emphasizing his triumphant gesture with the point of a fishing spear before diving back beneath the water's surface.

The pilot's exasperated howl echoed through the cabin.

"One of these days, I'm just going to run him over!"

CHARLIE SHOOK HIS head, thankful to have survived another landing, as the plane motored toward its dock.

The standoff between the spear fisherman and the seaplane had been going on for months, but the dispute had escalated in recent weeks. The stretch of water demarcated as the seaplane's landing zone had apparently become a prime hunting ground for lobster, and the spear fisherman was unwilling to disrupt his lobster pursuit to accommodate the plane's landing schedule. That the practice was illegal appeared to have little bearing on the matter. In any event, the spear was pointed more frequently at the seaplane than the lobsters, the fisherman preferring to corral his catch into live traps.

As the captain's bitter mutterings continued to spew out of the cockpit, Charlie turned toward the passenger seated beside him, a traveling salesman he'd met before their take-off from Charlotte Amalie.

Charlie gave the man a knowing look, raised his thick eyebrows, and groused cynically.

"Gives a whole new meaning to the phrase *clear the runway*."

~ *3* ~

The Sweepstakes

A FEW MINUTES later, the seaplane pulled into its slip by a metal hangar on the power-plant side of the harbor. A crew member jumped out and secured the plane's riggings to the pier. Turning, the man grabbed a wooden gangplank from a heap of supplies stacked on the dock, and, with a grunting heave, propped it against the plane's open side door.

Charlie Baker was one of the first passengers to unfold himself from his cramped seat and scramble out onto the walkway.

He was a small man, shrunk down in size like a tiny lion, miniature, but not petite. His calloused hands bore a workingman's perma-dirt stain, the irremovable grime that sinks into the grooves of the skin, immune to the cleansing effects of soap or detergent.

Charlie had on his regular work attire of heavy-duty combat boots, cutoff camouflage pants, and a white T-shirt. He kept his unruly dark hair tied back in a ponytail and tucked beneath a worn baseball cap bearing the logo for his construction firm.

He looked as if he were ready to strap on a tool belt and step onto a building site, but this wasn't a business trip. He had no current construction projects on St. Croix—for the past ten years, he had done everything he could to avoid the island.

Despite his physical appearance, this was a personal visit.

As Charlie stomped his feet against the concrete, shaking out the kinks, he gazed across the Christiansted shoreline to the boardwalk that ringed the water's edge.

The rest of the passengers started to file past as Charlie stood there on the landing, staring at a place that was both familiar and yet strangely foreign, the landscape of a recurring dream that had gradually morphed into a nightmare.

It was here where his first ill-fated Caribbean odyssey had led him, just over a decade earlier.

This was the place where his life fell apart.

�begin{center}~~begin{center}ᴄ~~end{center}

IT HAD ALL started up in his home state of Minnesota.

Born and raised in the Midwest, Charlie had worked through his mid-thirties to build a thriving construction business in a little lakeside town not far from the Canadian border.

With financial success came increased marital eligibility. The once-solitary bachelor met and soon after married Mira, a delicate beauty, generally considered the most attractive woman in their sprawling rural community.

(She was also one of the most pampered and spoiled females in the region, but Charlie managed to overlook that trait during their brief courtship and engagement.)

Two children came in quick succession, and the growing family moved into a large house in an upscale neighborhood, complete with a wide lawn, an in-ground swimming pool, and most important—to Mira, anyway—several expansive walk-in closets.

Theirs was, for the most part, a happy existence. Charlie spent long hours at his construction sites, but he was a natural craftsman, and he enjoyed his job. Meanwhile, Mira seemed content with the semi-affluent lifestyle that Charlie's business income provided. She treated herself to weekly pedicures, bi-monthly salon visits, and frequent shopping trips to high-end boutiques in Minneapolis and St. Paul.

As the marriage reached its five-year mark, however, Charlie became increasingly aware of his wife's spending habits, which seemed to grow more extravagant by the day. He tried several times to bring up the subject of budgetary constraints, to no avail. Whenever he attempted to steer the conversation toward the issue of financial limitations, Mira would flash him a sweet smile, swish her long honey-brown hair, and kiss him softly on the cheek. Somehow, the topic never reached a proper discussion.

As the bills continued to mount, Charlie grew less and less enamored with his beautiful wife, but he was helpless to defend against her winning charms. Resigning himself to the situation, he simply took on more work to make up for the monetary shortfall.

He and Mira might have gone on like that for years, a dysfunctional, economically ruinous union, gradually sliding toward the inevitable breakdown and divorce.

Who knows? They might have found a way to amicably coexist until their children were grown and sent off to college. Perhaps, they might even have made it to their golden years, aging into a peaceful détente before gently drifting off, one after the other, into the great unknown.

But that didn't happen.

One gray frostbitten winter, Charlie fell prey to temptation.

THAT JANUARY, NORTHERN Minnesota's public broadcasting station ran a sweepstakes fund-raiser. The contest featured several Midwestern-themed items and events, including a pair of football tickets to a Vikings home game, a dinner theater performance for two in the Twin Cities, and a family pass for a daylong moose safari. But the grand prize of the affair—and the main topic of conversation at truck stops and coffee shops across the broadcasting area—was a tropical vacation featuring a week on St. Croix.

Charlie tried his best to avoid the nonstop chatter about the island giveaway. He was a practical man, he told himself. Everything a person might need or want could be found right there in northern Minnesota. He had no desire to visit exotic Caribbean locations. There was no reason to mar his often wet and chilly reality with the fanciful distractions of sun and sand.

That resolution lasted right up until the final day of the fund drive.

AFTER A PARTICULARLY arduous roofing job that had required Charlie to harness himself to a steep incline through several hours of frigid wind and sleet, he climbed into the cab of his truck, cranked the engine, and turned the heater's dial to its highest setting.

The radio came on with the engine. Charlie had been listening to the news when he parked the vehicle earlier that morning, and in his haste, he had forgotten to punch the off button before he pulled the key from the ignition.

Despite the fund-raising jabber that immediately filled the truck's cab, he couldn't bear to take his hands away from the heater long enough to hit the volume knob.

As Charlie pressed his frozen digits against the heater vents, the voice of a well-known travel personality boomed out of the truck's speakers.

"The lucky winner will be treated to six days and five nights at a beachside resort on the gorgeous island of St. Croix . . ."

The sound of crashing waves swept through the transmission background while the voice described the prize details: resort lodging in a luxury villa on a golf course overlooking the Caribbean Sea, meals provided by a five-star restaurant with a reputation for tropical delicacies, and endless activities for families with children of all ages.

"You're killing me," Charlie moaned, his frostbitten fingers burning from the blast of the heater's hot air.

More waves swept through the truck's interior as the

singsong sales pitch continued. Outside, the sleet turned to hail, peppering the truck's metal hood with popcorn-sized pellets. It was more than he could take.

Charlie reached for his cell phone and made a call—not to the radio station to sign up for the sweepstakes—but to a travel agent.

"PACK YOUR BAGS, honey," he told his wife when he got home from the work site. He threw his hands in the air, as if capitulating. "We're going to the Virgin Islands!"

~ 4 ~

The Air-Conditioner Salesman

THE OTHER PASSENGERS began filtering out of the seaplane hangar as Charlie stood on the pier staring forlornly at the Christiansted shoreline.

The salesman who had occupied the adjoining seat approached the pile of luggage that had been removed from the plane's underside storage compartment and removed his two items, a roll-around suitcase and a leather satchel. After extending the suitcase's retractable handle, the salesman swung the satchel's strap over his shoulder and nodded to Charlie.

"Later, pal," he said before heading toward the hangar exit.

Charlie issued a cordial grunt and waved an absent-minded good-bye.

IN THE FIRST spot of shade, midway across the secured loading zone, the salesman paused to loosen his tie and unbutton his shirt collar. He brushed his hands over his slacks, trying to smooth out the wrinkles, but the creases he'd ironed that morning had already collapsed in the humid island heat. He held up his suit jacket, which he'd neatly folded and placed on his lap when he'd boarded the seaplane in St. Thomas. Despite the care, that garment hadn't fared any better than the slacks.

Grumbling good-naturedly, the salesman stuffed the jacket into his leather satchel. He pulled a handkerchief from his pants pocket; then he wiped the cloth over his wide forehead and flushed cheeks, which were already shiny with sweat.

The Caribbean was a fantastic sales territory, both in terms of commission and scenery, and none of his colleagues would be sympathetic to his complaints about the weather. Nevertheless, in heat like this, the salesman preferred to stay within range of a finely tuned air conditioner.

It had been several years since his last visit to St. Croix, but, in his experience, that particular amenity tended to be somewhat lacking on the island.

I suppose that's why I'm here, he thought, wryly cracking his knuckles.

The salesman worked for a company that manufactured an array of top-of-the-line air-conditioner units. The firm's global enterprise had captured over a third of the world's artificial cooling market and was poised for increased growth in the Caribbean.

"If ever a place was in need of my services," he concluded, once more wiping his brow, "this is it."

Then he paused, mentally clarifying his assessment. He had other matters to attend to on this visit, issues unrelated to air-conditioning. There was a gleam in his eyes as he amended, "I think it's fair to say St. Croix is ready for *all* my services."

OUTSIDE THE HANGAR, the salesman paused to get his bearings before veering left onto a sidewalk that fed onto the boardwalk. If he remembered correctly, his hotel was located somewhere off the main concourse.

The bright sun shone on his round, rugged face, glinting against its end-of-day, gray-flecked stubble. He was a large man, soft around the edges, but not grossly overweight. His bulky, once-athletic build had begun to succumb to the slow droop of middle age. A gameness in his left leg caused him to walk with a slight limp—an old sports injury, he told anyone who asked.

The salesman reached the sidewalk's merge with the boardwalk, and he stopped to flex a sore spot on his ankle. Then, resuming his pace, he lifted his suitcase rollers over the bump and set off toward the main tourist area.

The wheels on the luggage case bumped across the rough wooden surface, the uneven rhythm a match to the lurch in his gait.

A SHORT WHILE later, the salesman parked his luggage in the shade of a covered bench located near the boardwalk's midpoint. Unzipping his leather satchel, he pulled out a half-drunk bottle of water. As he guzzled down the remaining liquid, he gazed out at the harbor and the collection of boats moored inside its protective reef.

A sprawling cay lay about a hundred yards offshore, a pretty little stretch of sand and palm trees. The cay's curving beach was open to the public, serviced by a tin-roof bar and a kiosk that rented out chairs and umbrella stands. The rest of the tiny island was occupied by a private hotel, most of whose structures were nestled behind a natural blind of blooming vegetation. The hotel's guests were treated to a unique view of downtown Christiansted, one that helped offset the dated furnishings. The accommodations, like many in and around the boardwalk, appeared to have been built or last renovated in the 1970s.

The cay's quaint resort was long overdue for an air-conditioning overhaul, the salesman thought, taking a mental note as he watched a dinghy motor toward the boardwalk with a load of the cay's visitors. He might just have to work a little of his persuasive magic and convince the proprietor that it was time for an upgrade.

He squeezed the empty water bottle in his hand, causing the plastic container to crinkle loudly. Convincing new clients to make a purchase was rarely a problem. Finding money in their accounts to pay for the expenditure, however, was another thing entirely.

He counted the number of hotel guests on the dinghy and smiled optimistically. It was certainly worth a trip out to the cay.

Humming to himself, the salesman dug around inside his leather satchel and removed a packet of papers containing a printout of his itinerary.

After checking the name of the hotel listed on his travel documents, he turned his back to the water and scanned the signs of the businesses fronting the shoreline.

"There it is," he said, locating a coral-pink block-shaped hotel that was, thankfully, less than a stone's throw away from the shade of his covered bench.

He shifted the satchel's strap to the opposite shoulder and grabbed his suitcase handle.

"Boy, am I ready to kick off these shoes."

SWEATING PROFUSELY, THE salesman stepped inside an open-air diner built into the hotel's first floor. He'd been unable to find a boardwalk entrance to the hotel, but after craning his neck around the side of the building, he'd decided to check for access through the restaurant.

The place had wood framing painted indigo blue and decorative accents in a rainbow of bright colors—the style was comfortably worn, classic Caribbean chic. A parrot-shaped lawn ornament perched on the diner's outer railing, but it was a poor day for catching a breeze. The bird's wide nylon wings stood immobile in the late-afternoon heat.

At this short segment of the boardwalk, the sea passed beneath the wooden walkway, forming a small lagoon that lapped at a row of boulders built up around the diner's edge.

An arched footbridge skirted the pool of water, providing access to the main thoroughfare.

For those seated at the plastic tables positioned along the restaurant's open wall, the sailboats floating in the harbor appeared almost within arm's reach. The thriving crustacean community that lived among the rocks was far closer than that.

A speckled brown crab scuttled across the diner's wet concrete floor. Huddling beneath one of the boulder-side tables, the crab watched as the air-conditioning salesman rolled his luggage around the hostess stand and past the bar to a wide hallway leading into the hotel's inner courtyard.

HAVING FINALLY FOUND his way inside the hotel, the salesman proceeded directly to the reception desk. With relief, he leaned over the counter toward the receptionist.

"Good afternoon," he said, his voice a deep charming pitch. "I believe I have a reservation for tonight. The name's Rock. Adam Rock."

The West Indian woman behind the counter smiled placidly in return.

"Welcome, Mr. Rock," she said as she began clicking keys on a bulky computer console.

The salesman laid a heavy hand on the counter, trying to wait patiently for his room. A gold ring on his left hand clinked as he rolled his palm against the surface. He tilted his head to look at the courtyard's covered ceiling, grateful for the shade.

"Ah," the woman murmured after a few minutes typing. "There you are." She glanced up from the screen. "Have you been to St. Croix before, Mr. Rock?"

"Not for a long while," he replied, stroking his chin. "It's been about ten years, I believe." He nodded toward the courtyard's far wall. "I stayed at the Comanche back then."

"We're happy you chose us this time," the woman said politely, once more preoccupied with the computer.

At long last, she selected a room key and handed it over

the counter to the salesman. "Well, Mr. Rock, I hope you enjoy your stay."

The salesman grinned slyly as if contemplating a joke that had just played out inside his head.

"Yes," he said, twirling the metal rod in his fingers. "I'm sure I will."

~ *5* ~

Blame It on Rick

CHARLIE BAKER SCOOPED up his backpack from the pier, the last piece of luggage remaining beside the now-empty seaplane, and slid the straps over his shoulders. Setting off toward the hangar exit, he pulled down the rim of his frayed baseball cap to shield his eyes from the sun's bright glare.

The grimy construction contractor plodded halfway across the loading zone and then paused. His thoughts were still trapped in the memories of that first holiday week on the island—a glossy blur of happy images whose recollection had soon turned bittersweet.

SQUINTING IN THE distance, Charlie found the easy marker of the windmill tower near the boardwalk's midpoint. His gaze then shifted a short distance to the right, stopping on a large hotel painted a distinctive coral pink and the open-air diner built into its lower waterfront level.

His kids, he remembered, had loved the frozen key lime pie at that rainbow-decorated diner. He and his family had eaten there so many times during their vacation that the waitstaff had begun to recognize them on sight.

"Another round of key lime pie!" the hostess would holler back to the kitchen as soon as they stepped up to her stand.

The kids had enjoyed the dish's presentation almost as much as the actual treat. The cook would drizzle a sweet raspberry sauce over each of their plates, creating a happy-face design around the rim of the piecrust.

Sighing in remembrance, Charlie removed his wallet from the rear pocket of his cutoff camo pants. Reaching into the billfold, he pulled out a faded photograph of two youngsters grinning over their empty plates, both mouths smeared with bright-red raspberry sauce.

Still staring at the photo, his thoughts turned to the kids' other favorite boardwalk pastime. After wolfing down large helpings of key lime pie, the family would often walk down to the brewpub to watch the afternoon crab races.

Charlie smiled to himself. He could still hear the children's shrieking voices, squealing with delight as they rooted for their chosen crab to cross the circled chalk line ahead of the pack.

Of course, the family had also enjoyed the island's other tourist activities. They'd taken the obligatory sailboat snorkeling cruise to Buck Island, a nature preserve about a mile offshore. On another day, they'd driven to Point Udall on the island's east end, just so they could say that they'd been to the United States' easternmost edge. Each excursion had been memorable, but, hands down, Charlie's favorite outing had been a jeep tour through the rain forest to visit a farm with beer-drinking pigs.

When they weren't otherwise occupied, they'd gone to the beach at Cane Bay, a sandy stretch on the island's north shore with excellent snorkeling. A tree house–styled restaurant just across the road had served the best conch fritters he'd ever eaten.

It was the beach time that had doomed him, Charlie reflected ruefully.

With every minute of sun-drenched bliss, his dread of

Minnesota's cold, wet winters had grown. As the day of their departure neared, the thought of all those frozen rooftops waiting for him back home had been more than he could bear.

Sometime during that vacation week on the island, his Midwesterner's instinctive practicality had deserted him. Intoxicated by the sunshine and the warm, clear Caribbean waters, he'd begun to consider the once unthinkable.

The morning of their return flight, Charlie had posed the fateful question to his wife.

"Mira, hon, what d'you say—why don't we move to St. Croix?"

ONCE DECIDED, THE move quickly built its own momentum.

The house in Minnesota sold within weeks, leaving little room for second thoughts or reconsideration. A yard sale and a lengthy ad in the local newspaper's classifieds section took care of the minivan and several pieces of furniture that were too large to ship. The family packed what remained into Charlie's pickup and drove south to Miami.

At Florida's southern port, the truck was loaded onto a transport vessel. From there, the family hopped a flight to their new island home: a flat piece of arid land on St. Croix's northeast shore.

The plot was a fantastic bargain—or so they'd been told by their real estate agent.

The land featured thirteen rolling acres complete with a stunning sea view, an overgrown vegetable garden, and a bare-bones lean-to with a leaky roof and inoperable plumbing.

A COMPLETE RENOVATION and expansion of the new residence was at the top of Charlie's to-do list, its priority lying just beneath the successful transfer of his construction business to St. Croix.

He and Mira envisioned a lavish estate, complete with a wide veranda off the master bedroom and a terraced swimming pool for the kids. Together, they'd drawn up a variety of potential house plans and excitedly discussed furnishings and decor.

But as aspirations for the new house ballooned out of control, the family's financial prospects began to rapidly diminish.

Charlie was experiencing, firsthand, the difficulties of island commerce.

ON THE SURFACE, there appeared to be no reason why Charlie's construction business wouldn't succeed on St. Croix. There was no shortage of projects in need of his skills and expertise, and, with his stellar Minnesota references, he quickly accumulated a long list of clients, many of them expats or vacation homeowners, eager to engage his services.

There was a reason, however, for the island's backlog of long-hoped-for and uncompleted projects.

No matter if the property was in downtown Christiansted, north along the picturesque coast, or out in the residential wilds of the East End—each undertaking inevitably became mired in a monumental struggle with local bureaucracy, the idiosyncrasies of Crucian culture, and, last but not least, the black hole of "island time," meaning that any stated time was never the actual time that anything ever occurred.

FOR BETTER OR worse, the Caribbean has always been an inherently laid-back place. Throughout the centuries, numerous colonial empires and countless sugar-trading enterprises have struggled against this immutable trait, to no avail. It is an unavoidable consequence of the environment. Regardless of the might of the opposing force, nature has her way in the tropics.

Where a bitter cold might spur a body to action, if for no

other reason than to generate much-needed warmth, the Caribbean's sweltering heat caused the exact opposite response. Human self-preservation dictated the necessities of dark sunglasses, loose-fitting clothes, and slow measured movements.

On any given day, one could generally expect transport delays of twenty minutes to an hour. A dinner reservation might wander several ticks of the clock. Afternoon excursions often drifted into sunset tours.

In construction-related matters, the time differentials were far greater. Projects were frequently pushed back weeks, months, or even years. Many were never completed at all; they were simply left, exposed and decaying, in the wearing humidity. The rubble of these half-finished structures stood as a warning to newcomers with oversized ambitions.

It was a caution that Charlie had failed to heed.

FOR CHARLIE, THOSE first few months on the island were a maddening period of wrenching adjustment. As his deadlines lagged further and further behind and his cash flow trickled to a halt, the meager nest egg the family had brought with them to the island started to run out.

With bills piling up and his business foundering, Charlie began scrupulously evaluating every purchase, weighing the merits of even the tiniest of expenditures.

He spent hours each night studying his financial spreadsheets, calculating and re-calculating the family's monthly budget. The price of groceries, gas, electricity, and water—everything, it seemed, save the oxygen in the air—cost so much more than he had anticipated. Each line item weighed on his conscience, tormented his sleep, and pushed him deeper into a desperation-driven depression.

And so, as Charlie's stress intensified and the family's financial predicament grew more and more tenuous, the promised renovation to the leaky lean-to and its rustic plumbing suffered its own "island time" deferral.

CHARLIE STARED ACROSS the shoreline at the Christiansted boardwalk, thinking back to that cold winter day in Minnesota and the sound of the waves emanating from the truck's radio as he'd warmed his hands by the heater.

"Rick Steves," he muttered, recalling the name of the celebrity travel show host who had emceed the public broadcast station's sweepstakes.

Charlie lifted his baseball cap an inch off his head and smoothed the sweaty hair beneath. Ramming the hat back down over his forehead, he concluded bitterly.

"I blame it all on Rick Steves."

IF HE'D KNOWN how it all would end, would he still have made the leap?

It was a question he didn't want to answer; guilt prevented an honest response. Ten years later, the truth was still too painful to admit, but Charlie blamed only himself for the events that happened next.

~ 6 ~

The Shoes

A BAGGAGE ATTENDANT pushed a cart full of checked luggage toward the loading zone for the next outbound flight.

"You going to stand there all day?" he hollered at Charlie.

With a startled grunt, Charlie tucked the faded photo back into his wallet. Cramming the wallet into his pocket, he stepped toward the gate. "I was just leaving."

The attendant mashed his foot down on the cart's metal brake, as if he had suddenly remembered something.

"Hey, weren't you here the other week?" he demanded and then nodded his own response. "Yeah, I remember. You were the guy asking about that nice-looking lady with the long brown hair . . . the one in the green dress."

Charlie paused near the hangar exit and shrugged.

The attendant leaned over the top of the luggage cart.

"So—did you find her? Or are you still on the hunt?"

Charlie shifted his weight, visibly uncomfortable. His cheeks flushed with embarrassment. "Both, I suppose," he muttered grimly.

The attendant let loose a loud guffaw as Charlie quickly turned and stepped through the gate.

"Well then, sir," the man said, smirking as if he knew the reason for Charlie's embarrassment. *"Wel-cum back to San-ta Cruz."*

Still chuckling to himself, he released the brake and shoved the luggage cart forward.

"Wel-cum back to San-ta Cruz."

SANTA CRUZ.

The island's original Spanish designation was commonly tossed about in the local lingo. It was a nuanced way for Crucians to distinguish themselves from the tourists, the island's large number of transient refinery workers, and the "Statesiders" (anyone newly arrived from the continental United States). The amusing confusion that the term generated among the uninitiated was seen as an added bonus.

Crucians were nothing if not proud of their heritage, which they saw as distinctly different from that of the Thomasians—residents of St. Thomas, aka "the Rock." (The tiny island of St. John was too small to merit comparison or even a nickname.)

The Santa Cruz title evoked the essence of the island's colorful history. The name was officially bestowed by explorer Christopher Columbus—right before a member of his crew was abducted by the local Carib Indians, fricasseed, and served for lunch.

At least, that's how the story was commonly recounted on modern-day St. Croix.

While warm and welcoming to the majority of its visitors, the island had a long history of disposing of unwanted guests.

"SANTA CRUZ," CHARLIE repeated miserably as he left the hangar. "That's what did me in." He shook his head and sighed wearily. "I bet that poor Spanish fellow never saw it coming."

After a moment of reflective silence, he added bitterly, "I know I didn't."

FOR THE FIRST couple of months after their move to St. Croix, Mira was surprisingly understanding of the family's financial predicament. She seemed to comprehend the gravity of their situation, and she claimed to be fully committed to their new casual, beach-oriented, low-maintenance lifestyle.

Mira told Charlie not to worry about his business struggles. This was nothing but a minor bump in the road, she assured him. They would make do until things turned around. She vowed to live a life of shopping austerity— temporarily, at least.

For a few short weeks, Charlie unclenched, a wee tiny bit, and he let go of some of his stress. After a concerted combination of strong-armed politicking and dogged determination, he began to make progress on a few of his construction projects. He even dared to think he might muddle through after all.

But just as that faint glimmer of hope appeared on the horizon, the dark shadow of the past returned to snuff it out.

WHILE FULL-SCALE RENOVATIONS to the lean-to were on hold, Charlie had installed a few minor improvements to make the living space more habitable. Using a series of free-standing partitions, he sectioned off an enclosed area to use as the master bedroom.

In one corner, he fashioned a makeshift closet, complete with hanger bars and shelving. This allowed Mira to unpack some of her things and to arrange her clothing in the way to which she was accustomed. It brought a small sense of normalcy to the otherwise dysfunctional household, and Mira joyfully set about decorating the new room.

Unfortunately, as Mira started to reassemble her extensive wardrobe, a number of new items began to appear.

A flowery print dress sneaked its way onto a closet clothes hanger. A seashell-themed charm bracelet crept into the jewelry box on the dresser. A colorful scarf slithered into a cabinet drawer. A perfume bottle with an ocean-icon label mysteriously infiltrated the medicine cabinet.

Charlie, for whom one handbag or pair of shoes looked exactly the same as the next, was at first unaware of Mira's relapse into shopping addiction. He was so caught up in his own problems, he was oblivious to the toll the family's dire financial straits had taken on his wife.

It wasn't until he received his credit card statement at the end of the month that he finally caught on.

That night, Charlie calmly confronted her. He was a stoic man, not prone to outbursts or emotional displays, so he broached the subject as dispassionately as possible.

"Mira," he said, carefully placing the bill on the kitchen table, "is there something you'd like to tell me?"

Tears immediately welled up in her eyes. "Oh, Charlie. It's not what you think." Gulping, she glanced down at the bill. Then, slowly, she returned her gaze to his.

"Don't worry," she said, brushing her hair away from her face. "I'll take care of it." She averted her eyes, this time staring at the floor, and let out a dry sob.

"I just couldn't bear to step foot in that stinking Porta Potty one more time," she said plaintively. "I had to go shopping."

Charlie nearly choked on the lump that swelled up in his throat. This was all his fault. He was the one who had brought them to the island. They should have never moved down to the Caribbean. They should have never left Minnesota.

But even then, in that moment of guilt and despair, he knew his sentiment of regret lacked sincerity. The lure of the tropics was already far stronger than the draw of the north's stability.

"Let's just give it a few more weeks," he said, swallowing at the assurance he knew was a lie. "If we can't make it work, we'll pack it in and head back to the States."

"Okay." Mira sighed pitifully as he put his arms around her. Charlie winced at the earnestness in her voice.

"I promise. It won't happen again," she pledged vehemently. Then she flashed her simple smile. "Not until you're back on your feet."

IN THE FRAGILE balance of human emotions, insecurity and doubt are far more lasting emotions than that of remorse.

For the first few days after his heart-to-heart with Mira, Charlie fought a mighty struggle with his conscience. He cursed himself for being a suspicious man. He desperately wanted to believe his wife—and yet, some inner demon deep within his tortured mind persistently conspired against her.

Every moment they spent together became a test of trust.

Was that a new dress or one from her existing wardrobe? That wraparound skirt she wore on their outing to the beach . . . it looked familiar—or was it? Had he seen that necklace before? Those earrings? He couldn't be sure. He nearly drove himself mad with questioning.

One thing he knew for certain: he wouldn't be fooled a second time.

CHARLIE SOON FOUND himself making regular trips into Christiansted's shopping district. He paid several lengthy visits to the area, intent on becoming an expert in women's fashion.

Armed with a notepad and pencil, he conducted a thorough and methodical survey of all the clothing boutiques in the island's main town, creating a list of their available inventory. He studied each dress, handbag, and pair of ladies' shoes, writing down a description along with the item's corresponding price tag.

Then, every night after his wife had gone to sleep, he sneaked into her closet with a penlight to check for any new purchases.

For weeks, nothing pinged his radar. His tiny light failed to illuminate any out-of-place items. He began to feel foolish, but he continued his vigilance. He couldn't stop himself; he was obsessed.

Because Charlie was so avidly searching, he eventually found something that verified his suspicions—critical, damning evidence that confirmed his worst fears.

IT WAS LATE one evening, near midnight, when the discovery occurred. After several hours of tossing, turning, and lying awake worrying over a construction-related matter, Charlie had at last crawled out of bed and removed his trusty penlight from his work tool belt.

Taking care not to wake Mira, he crept across the bedroom's concrete floor to the closet. After stepping inside, he flicked on the light and began his nightly surveillance.

There, in a dark corner, behind the long tail of a trench coat, he spied something that made his blood run cold with fear and loathing.

It was a pair of three-inch-high emerald green heels.

He instantly recognized the open-toed shoes. He'd been fretting over the fate of this particular set of footwear ever since it had gone missing from the storefront of a prominent King Street shop the previous afternoon.

"It's the s-s-seven hundred dollar pair of shoes!" he gasped out loud, nearly apoplectic with shock.

The volcano, slow to erupt, blew its stack in spectacular fashion. Forgetting that his wife was fast asleep in the next room, Charlie repeated the phrase he'd shouted when he first realized someone on the island had purchased the pricey item. His indignant voice rumbled through the lean-to.

"Who would pay seven hundred dollars for a pair of shoes?!"

THE NEXT MORNING'S breakfast was a silent affair. Mira refused to look at her husband, much less speak to him.

After Charlie left for work, she packed her bags. She took the children with her to the airport, and the group boarded the first available flight to Miami.

It would be ten long years before Charlie would see them again.

~ 7 ~

Wisdom

NOT FAR FROM the seaplane hangar, near an empty lot where chickens scavenged among the trash and weeds, Gedda stood slumped over the handles of her rusted shopping cart. To the casual observer, she appeared to be half-drunk, half-asleep, or perhaps a little of both—regardless, no one was particularly interested in assessing her condition.

In reality, her senses were keenly attuned. Her body, conditioned from years of rum consumption, had already burned off the earlier shot from the sugar mill bar. Her yellowed eyes cracked open the tiniest of slivers as she watched the hangar doorway, where the most recent seaplane arrivals were exiting the secured loading zone.

She waited, her gaze sifting through the passengers until the last one finally walked through the opening: a scruffy little man in cargo boots, T-shirt, and cutoff camo shorts.

"*Char-lee Bak-ah,*" Gedda said with a seedy stare. "*Ah, dere you are.*"

GEDDA HUNCHED HER thick neck down into her shoulders as Charlie strode purposefully out of the hangar and turned left toward the boardwalk. Her dry lips rolled inward, gumming what little remained of her whittled-down teeth.

Charlie seemed confident in the day's mission; his expression was firm and resolute. He glanced at the hag's crippled form as he walked past, tapping the brim of his cap in greeting.

But ten steps farther, he paused, appearing to hesitate. His face began to soften, as if he were reconsidering his game plan. He reached down to the return ticket stuffed inside his pants pocket, his fingers fiddling nervously with the top edge.

Muttering to himself, Charlie stopped and stared out at the harbor, his emotions now clearly conflicted.

After a long pause, he checked the time on his watch. Then he took in a deep breath and continued, this time far more tentatively, down the boardwalk toward the Comanche Hotel.

Gedda shuffled after him, pushing her cart out of the empty lot and onto the walkway's wooden boards.

"Oh, Char-lee," she whispered softly. *"You shudda nevah complain'd about dem shoes."*

~ 8 ~

The Comanche

HASSAN RODE ON his mother's hip, one hand wrapped around the folds of her cloak, the other clutching the edge of her headscarf, as she crossed the gravel courtyard to the rear entrance of the Comanche Hotel.

His free-spirited sister had already slipped free from their mother's grasp. Elena ran ahead, skipping down the crumbling path that circled beneath the hotel's elevated pool and second-floor pavilion.

"'*Ey*, Elena, come on," the mother called out in frustration, struggling to keep up. It was difficult to maneuver over the rough ground in her high-heeled shoes. "Hassan, you're going to have to walk," she said briskly. Disentangling the boy's fingers from the cloak's dark fabric, she set him down and secured her hand firmly around his.

The woman glanced up in time to see her daughter disappear into a covered walkway that ran beneath the side of the pavilion.

"Elena, wait!"

The woman sucked in on her teeth, shaking her head with disapproval. Hassan gasped as his arm jerked forward, but his protesting cry went unheeded.

"She'll be the death of me, that girl."

THE MOTHER TEETERED down the path, vigorously tugging Hassan along behind her.

The surface soon transitioned from a composite of coral and concrete to a layout of uneven paving stones, further impeding the woman's progress. Ducking beneath a low-hanging branch, she pushed aside an overgrown fern and peered anxiously down the narrow walkway. She pushed the folds of the scarf away from her face as she searched for signs of her wayward daughter, but the passage was empty.

The belligerent *honk* of a delivery truck sounded from the next street over, and the woman rushed forward, her heart in her throat.

Hassan winced as one of the fern fronds whipped back and slapped him in the face.

A MOMENT LATER, the mother rounded the corner at the end of the covered passage and entered an alley that serviced, on one side, the hotel's main entrance, and, on the other, a small convenience store. Hassan in tow, she chugged up to the store's open doorway.

Just inside, she found her daughter's curly pigtails bouncing in front of a rack of candy bars.

"Elena," the woman panted, her anger tempered with relief.

Smiling cheekily, the girl turned toward her mother and pointed at the rack.

"Momma, I'm hungry."

AFTER A LENGTHY negotiation over the selection of two candy bars, one for each child, the mother finally managed to herd her charges across the alley toward the hotel.

Heavy wooden hurricane doors surrounded the front entrance. The hinges had been loosened so that the flat boards could be propped against the building's stone-wall exterior. Just above, a balcony ran along the outside of the second floor, casting shade onto the porch and providing much-needed cooling for the reception area inside.

Ushering the children over the threshold, the mother stepped briskly into the reception area and crossed to the front desk.

"Hello, how are you?" she asked the man seated on the desk's opposite side, trying to effect a courteous tone as she quickly addressed the required pleasantries.

Crucian culture demanded the conversation begin with a respectful greeting. She was in a hurry, but the momentary delay would be well worth the desk clerk's willing cooperation.

With effort, the woman stifled her impatience as she waited for the man's measured reply.

"Fine," he said stiffly. There was a long pause. "Thank you."

She smiled politely and then launched into her request.

"I made arrangements for your child-care service this afternoon . . ."

BUILT IN THE mid-1700s, the Comanche Hotel was one of the oldest buildings on St. Croix. The ground floor of the four-story estate house was comprised of brick and rock; the upper levels transitioned to a covering of wood siding. The roofline followed a typical Danish-colonial design, with the shingles wrapping over the eaves and extending down around the top floor's cornered windows.

There had been numerous add-ons and renovations over the years, a tug-of-war between the growing town and the hotel's need for waterfront access. As Christiansted grew up around the original estate house, the hotel complex expanded toward the boardwalk. The balcony attached to the exterior of the main building's second level connected to a footbridge that stretched over the alley and led to the pool and pavilion. These newer structures featured views of the harbor and easy access to the boardwalk.

In its guest brochures, the hotel claimed to have served as the childhood home of Alexander Hamilton. Details, however, of exactly when that occupancy occurred and for how long were difficult to nail down. Much like the island of his youth, the founding father's early history was shrouded in myths and half truths.

THE HOTEL'S FRONT desk was located in a front sitting room of the original estate house, perhaps explaining the reception area's improvised arrangement and furnishings. The front desk, a massive mahogany piece, sat in the corner farthest from the door. It was flanked by a decoratively wound rattan chair, a sturdy wooden side table, and a pineapple-shaped lamp.

Off to the side, in front of a shuttered window, stood a tall wooden statue, presumably the hotel's namesake Comanche—although the figure bore little resemblance to the Plains Indians of the American Southwest.

Instead, the carving appeared to be a caricatured cross between an aborigine Carib and a Spanish conquistador.

THE MOTHER WAITED while the desk clerk called the maid who would be providing the requested sitting service. He wiped his brow as he waited for the phone line to be answered, glancing apologetically across the desk for the stifling heat.

Screens covered the room's open windows, but no breeze filtered in from the alley outside. A slow-churning ceiling fan offered little respite, while a freestanding fan rotating in the corner of the room served only to flutter the papers stacked on the desk. Modular air-conditioning units were available in the individual guest suites, but such cooling mechanisms were expensive to run—and not a luxury afforded the front-desk staff.

ENERGIZED BY THEIR candy-bar sugar rush and seemingly unaffected by the heat, Elena and Hassan stood in the middle of the reception area, finger-poking each other behind their mother's back as she leaned over the front desk, anxiously awaiting word on the sitter.

A large fly droned, buzzing between the children. Elena swatted at the bug; then she turned toward her brother.

"Hassan," she said, officiously wagging her finger. "When she comes for you, when she hauls you off to her lair, you've got only one chance to escape being eaten."

"Eaten? Who's going to eat me?" he demanded, bristling at the suggestion. He crossed his arms in front of his tiny chest and then added, somewhat meekly. "And what's a *lair*?"

Elena issued a haughty, matter-of-fact response. "Don't be silly. I told you before. The Goat Foot Woman is out there looking for little children to eat, and you're just her type." Her expression softened as she noticed his confused face. "The lair is where she locks up the children she's kidnapped. It's a top-secret location. Nobody knows where it is."

With a sympathetic smile, she patted him on the shoulder. "Sorry, Hassan. It's only a matter of time. You have to be prepared."

The boy resisted, giving his sister a suspicious sideways glance. "How do you know all this stuff?"

Elena tossed her pigtails indignantly. "I learnt it in school, of course."

Hassan hesitated. He didn't like to give his sister any more leverage over him than she already possessed. And he certainly didn't want her thinking she knew things he didn't.

But, as Elena had explained to him numerous times, the preschool he attended each morning wasn't the same as the "real" school where she was enrolled.

What if his sister was right? He didn't want to miss out on any valuable information, especially if he *did* happen to find himself captured by the Goat Foot Woman. That was a frightening and downright disturbing proposition.

Finally he assented. "Okay, go ahead," he said, sighing wearily. "Tell me."

Elena's green eyes sparkled with mischief. "Once she's trapped you in her lair, and she's about to slice you up and eat you, there's only one way you'll make it out alive." She held up her index finger, pointing it at her brother's nose. "Just one."

Hassan sucked in his breath, and his lower lip began to tremble. His earlier disbelief had fallen away. He was now fully engaged in the story.

Elena paused, watching Hassan's face turn blue from lack of oxygen. She waited until he looked as if he were about to pass out; then she swung her finger toward the wooden statue standing against the wall by the front desk.

"You have to call on the Comanche. He's the only one the Goat Foot Woman is afraid of. He's the only one who can save you."

Hassan released his pent-up breath. With a raspy gasp, his chest heaved as he refilled his lungs.

"He's been hunting her for years," Elena said, wrapping her arm around Hassan's shoulders and turning him to face the statue. "Each night, the Indian comes to life. The wood becomes flesh, and real blood pumps through his veins. He jumps off that perch and walks right out the front door. They say he roams the streets of Christiansted, searching for the Goat Foot Woman. If she catches you, he's the only one who can rescue you."

Hassan's eyes stretched wide, and his mouth gaped open. He stared up at the statue, taking in every detail of its peculiar, rigid figure.

The red-stained wood and broad facial features were those of a native Carib, but the clothing carved onto the body was that of a Spanish conquistador. A draping tunic layered with armor covered the statue's torso; shiny epaulets capped its shoulders, and a domed helmet rested on its head.

On the statue's lower half, puffy, pleated pants fed into pointed boots that featured swooping, upturned toes.

Elena watched with a big sister's conspiring zeal as Hassan apprehensively surveyed the Comanche statue. The little boy swayed back and forth, leaning in for a closer look and then recoiling away, his curiosity overwhelmed by surges of repulsion.

The statue's menacing expression was far from reassuring. Eyeballs the size of eggs bulged out from the skull. Stringy black facial hair extended from swollen cheekbones and loose-hanging jowls.

Midway down the torso, the figure's muscular hands gripped a long staff, holding it in the air like a club that might be swung at the next guest who dared to check in to the hotel.

With a shudder, Hassan turned and whispered to his sister. "Are you *sure* he's the one who's supposed to save me?"

BEFORE ELENA COULD answer, a plump West Indian woman with shiny brown skin entered through a side door. The mother turned from the front desk.

"Okay, you two," she said, bending toward her children. "You're going to stay with this lady while I go to my meeting." She gave her daughter a stern stare. "Don't give her any trouble."

The maid smiled and nodded toward the wooden ceiling. "Come with me, little ones. We have some toys in the office for you to play with."

Elena charged up the stairs, eager to check out the stash of playthings. The heavyset maid hurried after her, panting as she tried to keep up. Hassan dutifully followed the pair, but as he neared the second-floor landing, he stopped and turned to look back.

Squatting at the top of the steps, the boy peered down through the side railing's wooden slats to the reception area below. He wanted to get one last glimpse of the Comanche, just in case he needed to call on the statue's rescue services at some point in the future.

After a long moment of squinting at the statue, Hassan nearly fell off the step in surprise. Anchoring his feet to the ledge, he returned his gaze to the first floor, rubbing his eyes in disbelief.

He could have sworn the Comanche's square head had rotated, ever so slightly, so that its bulging eyeballs were staring right at his mother.

~ 9 ~

Paradise Lost

CHARLIE BAKER TRUDGED down the boardwalk, his worn combat boots thumping across the wooden pathway as he headed toward the sugar mill tower and the turnoff for the Comanche Hotel.

He'd been back to St. Croix twice in the last few months, but he was still struck by the changes.

This was a different island than the one that had enchanted him on that first visit ten years earlier, he thought, glancing at the row of businesses—and empty lots—along the Christiansted shoreline. The decaying downtown district bore little resemblance to the amusement park fun-land he thought he remembered. This wasn't the location that had inspired his impulsive move to the Caribbean. Or had he been that deluded?

The Danish fort still glowed from its outcropping at the far end of the harbor, but the downtown area seemed to have lost much of its luster. The boardwalk's wooden planks had splintered from the sun's blistering wear; the surrounding shops had suffered from a decade's worth of persistent economic downturn.

Across from the seaplane hangar's exit, he'd seen a

homeless woman standing in the middle of a junk-strewn field. The old hag had stared at him as she gripped the handle of a rusted shopping cart that was, itself, loaded with rubbish.

A few steps later, Charlie had walked by an abandoned nightclub that had once blasted its music across the harbor into the wee hours of the morning. The establishment had changed hands several times, falling into greater disrepair with each new owner. The empty shell was now occupied by a pair of vagrant coconut vendors, whose entreaties Charlie had casually waved off.

What's happened to this island, he wondered, sadly shaking his head.

To be fair, Charlie conceded with a sigh, his perspective had shifted. These days, everything felt different to him, regardless of location. His time in the Caribbean had made him harsher, wiser, and far more cynical.

It now took more than warm weather to impress him.

A DECADE HAD passed since Mira had packed up the kids and left him on that lonely thirteen-acre plot on St. Croix's east end. Charlie had spent most of the intervening years on St. John, a much smaller island about forty miles to the north.

The least populated of the three main holdings within the US Virgin Islands (the territory also included a small handful of tiny islands and cays), St. John boasted dozens of pristine beaches and a national park that encompassed over half of the island's landmass. An isolated location with relatively little crime or commercial development, St. John had become a favorite holiday retreat for many Americans.

High-end villas now dotted the hillsides above the main town of Cruz Bay, creating a collage of dramatic coral stone archways, sun-soaked balconies, and infinity-edge swimming pools that overlooked the Pillsbury Sound.

Charlie knew the intricate details of almost every one of those buildings, their foundations, floor plans, lot slopes, and rooflines—because the majority of the structures had been built by his construction company.

CHARLIE LANDED HIS first St. John contract a few days after Mira's departure.

His client was an expat landowner who had already hired and fired three previous contractors before offering the job to Charlie. The project would require him to abandon several half-finished (i.e., stalled out) construction sites on St. Croix. It was a gamble, but he'd decided to take the risk. In his view, he had nothing left to lose.

Using every last trick he'd learned during those first frustrating months in the Caribbean, Charlie threw himself into the new project. He moved his base of operations to St. John and rented a cabin at the national park's Cinnamon Bay campgrounds. He spent every waking hour either walking the job site or on the phone to inspectors and regulatory agents. If a telephone call didn't work, he took the ferry over to St. Thomas and planted himself in the obstructing bureaucrat's office until they had reached a compromised solution. Money, he found in the more difficult instances, was almost always the compromise that led to the solution.

After paying out bribes—or, depending on your perspective, additional fees—to over half of the government agencies in the territory, Charlie managed to bring that first St. John project to completion. A flood of new contracts followed, and before long, he was managing a large crew of both permanent and day laborers who were fully occupied year-round, six days a week.

Cut off from his family, immersed in his business, and thrown into the distinct culture of a much smaller island, he slowly pulled himself back from the financial—and emotional—brink.

WHILE CHARLIE REMAINED busy on St. John, he sent a few of his workers back to St. Croix to tear down the lean-to. In its place, they built a basic but functional villa that he began renting out by the week, mostly to the local oil refinery's visiting executives and traveling upper management.

Using that rental income, Charlie eventually transitioned out of the Cinnamon Bay cabin and into a cinderblock house on an inland hill not far from Cruz Bay. The house had a leaky roof, faulty plumbing, and at times, it seemed there were more insects living inside the place than out. But the selling feature was a functional wraparound porch with northern views of Jost Van Dyke and the western edge of Tortola. Each night, he retired to the porch, curled up in a hammock, and watched the sunset.

Charlie was kicked back in that swing one evening, sipping a cold beer, when he discovered a packet of divorce papers, which had arrived in that day's mail. Hands shaking, he pulled open the envelope's flap and removed several stiff sheets of paper stamped with legal letterhead. Scanning the communication, he sucked in his breath, as if reeling from a blow to the gut.

The request for the marriage's formal dissolution had arrived a year to the day from Mira's sudden flight to Miami.

CHARLIE SPENT A long night in the hammock, staring out across the top of the dense forest that surrounded the porch. Beyond the jungled hillside stretched a black sea and, in the distant horizon, the twinkling lights of Tortola. Above it all hung an impossibly distant moon, a glowing all-knowing orb.

He pulled out his wallet and removed the key lime pie photograph of his kids. The picture was already crumpled and worn from constant reference. Too much time had passed since he'd seen his children and held them in his arms.

Over the course of the last twelve months, his previous life had slipped away, ebbing like the tide into a gray oblivion.

The dedicated family man who'd traveled to St. Croix for that fateful vacation had slowly disappeared. He'd spent one too many nights sitting outside the local dive bar drinking with St. John's resident crop of expats. He'd lost a part of himself in the tropical haze and rum-induced stupor.

More significantly, he'd lost access to his children.

CHARLIE STAYED OUT on the porch until early morning, rocking back and forth in the hammock. With the sun's rise, he finally returned inside. Red-eyed and exhausted, he reluctantly signed the agreement, accepting the stated alimony and giving Mira full custody of the kids.

Every thirty days, he dutifully sent a check north to Minnesota, but for nine long years, he had no substantive contact with his family.

Over time, Charlie carved out a niche for himself in St. John's luxury villa market. He became the go-to guy for high-end properties with potentially tricky approval features. Despite the global recession, there was a constant flow of newcomers willing to shell out big bucks for their own private island paradise.

Charlie was happy to take their money, but he took little joy in the prospering of his business.

He'd long since given up on his idea of paradise.

~ *10* ~

The Coconut Trade

THE TWO COCONUT vendors stood in the entrance to the abandoned nightclub, watching as the last passenger from the afternoon seaplane passed their station without stopping. It had been a long hot day, and they had little to show for their efforts.

"Well, Mic," the shorter of the duo said with a weary nod at the lone dollar the Dane had given them earlier, "looks like we're eatin' out of the Dumpster again tonight." He put his hands on his hips and tapped his bare foot against the concrete. "I really thought this idea was a winner. It should have worked out much better than this."

His lanky partner leaned against a concrete column. "Aw, don't beat yourself up 'bout it, Currie. Nobody appreciates fresh produce anymore. They're lettin' these kids grow up eatin' way too much junk food." He patted his lean stomach. "Speaking of which—I would kill for a basket of French fries right about now."

Currie chuckled. Mic had a voracious appetite. He'd eat anything he could get his hands on, but generally speaking, the greasier the better.

"Hey, Mic. What's the special on the board at the brew-pub tonight?"

Mic lifted his head and sniffed the air. The bridge of his nose wrinkled; his nostrils flared. After a moment of intense concentration, he announced his findings.

"Grilled pork chops," he said, smacking his lips with anticipation. "Hey, Currie. We'd better get our order in to Gedda so she saves us some good cuts."

Currie grinned up at his friend. Mic's dinner-menu predictions were almost never wrong, but he didn't rely entirely on his olfactory skills. Currie knew Mic sneaked into the brewpub's kitchen each morning to see what would be on the evening special.

Mic stepped away from the post, stretching his long legs. "I think I'll take a side of garlic mashed potatoes with my chops," he said as he bent over to pick up his ragged T-shirt. After shaking the dust from the garment, he tugged it on over his head. "And a fried pickle."

Currie threw up his hands in protest. "Stop! You're making me hungry!"

A BEAT-UP TRUCK pulled into the alley behind the abandoned nightclub. Mic and Currie turned as the driver, the vehicle's lone occupant, flashed his lights and tapped the horn.

The man who stepped from behind the wheel had a sturdy muscular build, the physique of someone who ate three square meals a day—and none of them out of the refuse pile.

The coconut vendors nodded a wary welcome. The newcomer was a regular on the boardwalk, although he rarely traveled solo. He was usually accompanied by a few thuggish friends and several scantily clad women with bright garish makeup. No one knew his real name, but everybody called him Nova, short for Casanova. He was a beautiful, brawny man—and his reputation with the ladies was known throughout the island.

"Mic, Currie," he called out, motioning for the men to join him at the truck.

The pair looked quizzically at each other, surprised that Nova knew their names and even more shocked that he wanted to speak with them.

After a mutual shrug, Mic and Currie walked over to the parking area.

The trio leaned against the pickup's dented hood for a few minutes of casual conversation before Nova got down to business.

"So, you fellas wanna make some real money?"

Currie cleared his throat and cracked his knuckles. He tilted his head, yawning as if he were weighing the proposal against his other (nonexistent) options. It was a carefully performed act, one in which Currie took great pride. He was the designated negotiator for his team.

"What kinda money?" he asked, slowly scratching his round chin with a stubby finger, trying to mask his keen interest.

Nova chuckled at the poorly veiled posturing. "More than you're making selling stolen coconuts," he replied with a cynical grin.

"Hey, hey," Mic cut in, strutting back and forth like an offended rooster. He wagged his finger in Nova's face. "These aren't stolen, my friend. Oh, no. They're *liberated*. This here's freedom fruit, I tell you." He strung out the next phrase, emphasizing each syllable. *"Re-vol-ution-ary co-co-nuts."*

Rolling his eyes, Currie pushed Mic out of the way. All the earlier talk about pork chops had woken the hunger in his belly. It was time to cut to the chase.

"What'ch you want us to do?"

Nova's handsome face broke into a shining smile. His dark skin gleamed in the late afternoon sunlight, the near-perfect complexion hiding the shadows beneath.

"I've got a job for you two over in Fred'sted." He gestured to the truck's rear cargo bed. "Hop in."

Mic and Currie looked at each other, communicating with their eyes. The decision took only seconds to reach.

"We'll do it," Currie said eagerly. The two men ran back

to the club entrance to scoop up their supply of coconuts. One by one, they fed the green balls into a mesh bag they'd lifted from the dive shop at the opposite end of the boardwalk.

"Mic, don't forget that one over there," Currie cautioned, pointing to a dusky corner of the nightclub where the last coconut had rolled.

As Mic scrambled after the rogue fruit, Currie called out sarcastically.

"It's your fault it's run off like that. *Ya've given it cra-zee notions about its in-de-pen-dence.*"

~ 11 ~

Self-Sufficient

TEN MINUTES LATER, Mic and Currie sat beside each other in the bed of the pickup truck, their backs leaning against the rear of the cab as it bounced over the pothole stricken pavement.

After winding out of Christiansted's thicket of one-way streets, the truck merged onto Centerline Road, the slower of two east-west arteries that ran across the length of the island.

The alternative route, Highway 66, provided the primary access to the airport, circumnavigating the island's main commercial center, and boasted the highest posted speed limit within the US Virgin Islands. While traffic had to slow for intermittent stoplights, stretches of the road were marked up to fifty-five miles per hour.

Currie preferred Centerline's more leisurely option. He rested an elbow on the truck's left side railing, taking in the sights. Without transportation of his own, it had been over a year since he'd been to the other side of the island—or, for that matter, outside of Christiansted. He and Mic had been sleeping on benches in the park beside the Danish fort for the last month and a half.

The truck passed a spattering of grocery stores, gas stations, and fast food restaurants offering burgers and fried chicken; then the road transitioned to a more rural, residential mix.

Mahogany trees at least two hundred years old lined the thoroughfare, cooling the ground below. The spreading limbs reached high over the pavement. In places, the branches on either side almost met in the middle.

Currie gazed up at the greenery, taking comfort in nature's protective canopy. He sighed, enjoying the scene. For all its problems, this island was his home, the only one he had ever known.

LIKE MOST CRUCIANS, Currie was a fiercely independent, self-reliant individual. It was a trait that had been passed down through the generations, one that was firmly imprinted on the modern day mind-set.

The temperament had its roots in the colonial era, when St. Croix was the workhorse of the Danish West Indies, producing the bulk of the territory's sugar export. The barrels had been traded for a range of commodities, from mercantile to foodstuffs, providing everything the island's residents needed to survive the Caribbean's harsh, humid climate.

Over the years, St. Croix gradually transitioned away from that agricultural foundation. Sugar distillation and oil refinery facilities moved in, providing steady jobs, a reliable source of power, and, most important, a free flow of rum. Crucians took great pride in their island's economic diversity, particularly the development of its non-tourism-related industries.

Of all the Virgins, Santa Cruz was the least reliant on the ever-fickle vacation business. At least a third of its residents were employed, either directly or indirectly, by the mammoth refinery on the island's south shore. Another third found work in the wide-ranging government sector. Tourism swept up the remainder.

This much-touted diversity and perceived self-sufficiency,

however, belied an economic base that was far more fragile than the numbers let on.

Currie gazed out at the island as the pickup bumped along. They passed numerous landmarks from his life, familiar sights that were in equal parts pleasing and painful to behold.

In the hard luck of his twenty-seven years, he had worked on the bottom rungs of all three of the island's economic sectors. He had failed miserably in each one, multiple times over.

CURRIE TILTED HIS head back, letting the hot breeze hit his face. His thoughts shifted to the nebulous work assignment waiting at the end of the pickup ride.

As a rule, he generally preferred self-employment. After many aborted attempts to fit into the regular workforce, he found he got into a lot less trouble if he rowed his own boat. He hoped he and Mic hadn't made a mistake throwing in their lot with Nova.

As the truck braked for a stoplight, Currie peeked through the cracked glass in the pass-through window at the back of the cab.

He watched as Nova drummed his hands against the steering wheel, impatiently waiting for the signal to change. The radio was tuned to a local reggae station, the volume turned to its highest bass-thumping setting.

Nova didn't seem to notice Currie's head looking through the back window—or the coconut vendor's eyes sliding toward the black canvas bag that lay on the passenger seat.

With the release of the light, Nova pounded the gas pedal, and the truck surged forward. The sudden momentum combined with the jolting *bump* of yet another pothole caused the mouth of the bag to slide open—revealing the heavy metal handle of a gun.

Currie quickly returned his gaze to the truck's back bed. Weaponry was not an uncommon sight on the island; the populace of Santa Cruz was heavily armed.

But still, it gave him pause.

From the right side of the truck bed, Mic rubbed his stomach and hollered over the roar of the engine. "Hope we make it back to Chri'sted in time for the pork chops."

Currie smiled his response, hoping Mic didn't pick up on his anxiety.

He was beginning to think they might have bigger problems to worry about than missing dinner.

~ *12* ~

An Eerie Intuition

ABOUT A HUNDRED yards off the Christiansted boardwalk, a woman in a black cloak and headscarf walked down the narrow hallway on the top attic level of the Comanche Hotel. The green high-heeled shoes on her feet tapped lightly against the wooden floor as she entered room seventeen, turned, and locked the door behind her.

With her two youngest children secured in the hotel's second-floor office, playing under the watchful eye of their babysitter, the woman had plenty of time to take care of the afternoon's business, collect her kids, and get back home before her husband returned from work. If everything went according to plan, he need never know that she'd been to Christiansted that day—much less with whom she'd been meeting.

After flicking the wall switch for the ceiling fan, the woman circled the room's perimeter, opening the windows on the two exterior walls. The meager cross breeze added little ventilation to the stuffy room, but she didn't mind the heat. She had specifically requested this unit knowing it was likely to be warm.

She'd chosen this location for its quiet isolation from the

rest of the hotel, which was, in any event, only partly occupied. Despite the Comanche's unique historical niche, it had a tough time competing with the other boardwalk-area hotels for the island's dwindling numbers of tourists.

Dusting her hands together, the woman approached a wooden wardrobe pushed against the tallest interior wall. She pulled open the swinging doors of the wardrobe's upper compartment, unhooked her cloak, and hung it inside. Untying her scarf, she looped it over the bar of another hanger. Then she closed the doors, pressing the slats to hook the inner latch.

Smoothing out the length of her tailored green dress, the woman turned to check her reflection in a decorative wall-mounted mirror. Pivoting, she tugged at the tight-fitting silk fabric to pull the seams into alignment.

Satisfied with the dress adjustments, she shifted her attention to her makeup. Stepping into the bathroom, she removed several small containers from her purse and set them on the edge of the sink. After dotting her nose and cheeks with powder, she used an eyeliner pen to expertly trace the contours of her lids. Next came the lipstick, which she rolled slowly around the edge of her mouth, coating the surface with a deep-red paste. As a final touch, she picked up a small glass vial shaped in a seashell design and spritzed a fine mist of perfume against her neck and wrists.

The woman gazed at her reflection and nodded with approval before reflexively arching her eyebrows. She'd forgotten one important item.

Reaching back into her purse, she fished out a foil-wrapped pack of breath mints. She popped a disc onto her tongue and swirled it around, waiting for the sharp wintergreen flavor to mask the residual nicotine from her earlier smoke in the courtyard.

Charlie, she remembered, had always hated the smell of cigarettes on her breath.

STROLLING INTO THE bedroom, the woman reached behind her head and unclasped a pin that had been holding her hair up in a bun. She shook her head, sending a honey-brown mane cascading down past her shoulders. After a few smoothing strokes with her brush, she gathered her hair into a looser knot and reattached the clip. She gave the hairdo a quick check in the mirror, pulling out a few wispy strands around her forehead for seductive effect.

There, she thought, pleased with her appearance. I'm ready.

WITH A SIGH, the woman moved to take a seat on the bed. But as she crossed the room, she felt a slight breeze whisper against the back of her neck.

She froze in place, struck by an unexpected shudder.

Goose bumps prickled her skin as an odd sensation swept over her psyche, a sudden inkling that something in her world had just been knocked off kilter. Somehow, her life's neat, rigid order had been thrown into disarray.

Perplexed, she paced a slow circle through the room, her green heels clicking on the floor's wooden planks.

"It's nothing," she said, trying to calm her nerves.

There were dozens of routine explanations for the errant breeze: the ceiling fan, the open windows, perhaps there was a hidden vent in the ceiling—anything could have caused the airflow disturbance.

But even as she tried to rationalize away her unease, she knew her apprehension was about more than a vagrant puff of wind.

She couldn't shake the eerie intuition that a figure from her past had just arrived on the island.

Someone other than her troublesome ex-husband.

~ 13 ~

Adam Rock

A SHORT DISTANCE away, on the second floor of the coral-pink hotel, Adam Rock rolled his suitcase along a humid corridor, searching the numbered doors for his assigned room.

Rock dabbed a handkerchief across his sweating brow. The air in the hallway was not much cooler than that outside the building. As he weaved from left to right, peering at the marked doorways, he carried on a one-sided conversation with the hotel's manager.

"Let me install just one of my machines," he muttered wearily. "You'll see. You won't be able to pry your guests away from it. You can charge extra for the room. We'll call it the Refrigerator Suite."

Breathing heavily, he paused outside a corner unit and checked the number hanging from the entrance.

"This is it," he said gratefully. Heat exhaustion had drained all his energy. He felt as if he couldn't have walked another step.

Rock slid his key into the slot and turned the knob, eagerly anticipating a refreshing chill on his sweat-soaked cheeks. He pushed open the door and leaned into the room, hoping for a blast of cool air.

He was sorely disappointed. The room was hotter than the hallway.

Pulling his suitcase inside, Rock glared despondently at the silent air-conditioning unit mounted on the wall beneath the room's corner window. After a quick scan of the machine's exterior, he flipped open the control panel and began fiddling with the dials and switches, to no avail.

"Come on, please," he begged. "Give a guy a break."

Rock knelt to the floor. Twisting his neck, he tried to see through a gap in the machine's underside framing, but even from that angle, it was impossible for him to determine what had disabled the interior components.

As a last resort, he pulled the electrical plug from the wall, counted to ten, and then reinserted the plug into its socket.

There was no response. It seemed nothing could wake the machine.

Frustrated, Rock slammed his hand against the metal facing.

"Worthless piece of junk."

Just then, a slight hum began to rattle from deep inside the cooling unit.

WITH THE TEMPERATURE in the room slowly beginning to drop, Adam Rock set his roll-around luggage on a chair, unzipped the main compartment, and propped open the lid. He removed a pair of neatly pressed chinos, a mint-green golf shirt, and a clean pair of socks. Carefully, he laid the clean clothing on the edge of the bed.

Unhooking a few more notches on his shirt collar, he wandered into the bathroom. He grinned at his reflection in the mirror, his face boyish despite the fringe of gray, before turning on the sink faucet and ducking his head beneath a stream of cold water.

Feeling semi-refreshed, Rock returned to the bedroom. He took a seat on the corner of the bed and gently untied the laces of his dress shoes. Swinging his right foot up onto his left knee, he pulled off the shoe and then the sweaty sock.

"Ahh." He sighed with relief, wiggling his toes.

The air conditioner was finally starting to kick in. The system generated far more noise than air, but at this point, even the faint whisper of a cooling breeze received a joyful welcome.

Dropping his bare foot to the carpet, Rock lifted his left leg and began to remove its lower coverings. After a few jerks and wiggles, the shoe popped off and dropped to the floor. With his fingers, he pushed the sock's upper hem down toward his ankle, exposing the top of a stiff skin-colored prosthetic. A few more tugs revealed the full shape of a plastic foot.

Rock slid the cuff of his slacks up toward his knee in order to better access his leg's junction with the artificial limb. Grunting and groaning, he unhooked the straps and buckles of a large brace. Once the fittings began to loosen, he firmly gripped the false foot and rotated it sideways until, with a sucking *pop*, it released from his body.

Rock let out a second sigh of relief as he held the stump of his left leg up to the air vent.

"That's much better," he said, collapsing backward onto the bedspread.

Closing his eyes, he positioned his lower appendages to receive the full force of the anemic air vent: the regular human foot and the stump, which terminated in a hard circular structure that had been hidden by the prosthetic—a cloven two-toed piece of keratin in the shape of a goat's hoof.

~ *14* ~

The Thanksgiving Surprise

CHARLIE BAKER CONTINUED his slow, increasingly anxious pace down the boardwalk toward the sugar mill bar. A few feet from the bar's round coral stone tower, he stepped off the boardwalk and onto the path that led to the Comanche Hotel.

Staring across the gravel courtyard, he straightened his cap and thunked his thumb against the brim.

If she stayed true to her word—a big if, in Charlie's view—Mira would be waiting for him in a room on the hotel's top floor. He could only hope that, this time, she had brought the children with her.

After ten years of minimal interaction, he was about to have his third meeting with Mira in under six months. The first had taken place the previous Thanksgiving, the second earlier that spring. Both instances had ended disastrously—for Charlie anyway.

He had dim hopes for today's rendezvous. If this encounter didn't go well, he was not inclined to make himself available for a fourth.

Charlie walked over to a nearby picnic table and pulled out his return plane ticket. The paper's top edge was crumpled from his constant fiddling. He had a seat reserved on the first flight back to St. Thomas the following morning. From there, he would take the ferry over to St. John and be home by early afternoon.

Soon, this would all be over. He would finally be able to put this sad chapter of his life behind him.

He gave the front end of his baseball cap another reassuring *thwack*.

At least, that was his plan. Where Mira was concerned, he'd learned to expect the unexpected.

IT HAD STARTED out so promising, the recent thaw in their relations.

The first contact had come in the form of a phone call. After all their time apart, it had taken Charlie several seconds to process the identity of the woman on the other end of the line. The number was blocked, and her voice hadn't immediately registered—the stranger had sounded only distantly familiar.

Would he like to meet up with her and the kids on St. Croix for the Thanksgiving holiday week, she'd asked pleasantly.

"Mira?" he'd replied incredulously. "Is that you?"

"Yes, Charlie, of course it's me."

He was completely thrown by the request. She'd spoken as if they had the type of healthy relationship common to many divorced couples, the kind in which the parental exchange of children happened routinely and without much hassle or difficulty.

He let out a short cough, trying to clear his head. There was something odd about Mira's voice. He couldn't quite put his finger on it. The pitch seemed a little off. But as she repeated the question, he quickly dismissed his concerns.

"Ab . . . absolutely," he'd stuttered in disbelief. "That . . . that would be wonderful."

The kids, he'd thought with elation. I'm finally going to see the kids.

MIRA COULD NOT have thrown out a more tempting lure. The severed relationship with his children was Charlie's greatest regret, his life's unending shame.

In the ten years since Mira's departure, his only exchanges with his ex-wife had been through tersely written letters and, more recently, the occasional e-mail. In that correspondence, the child-custody arrangement was the only matter they had discussed.

Charlie had soon regretted his quick signing of the divorce settlement. The terms severely limited his ability to negotiate for access to the children, and Mira had made it clear he was not allowed to communicate with them by phone. It was a detached, sparing relationship, one that held him apart, firmly at a distance.

Up until her recent Thanksgiving offer, Mira had stead-fastly refused to bring the kids back to the Caribbean. The onus was on Charlie to travel up to the States to see them.

And therein lay his complicity in the deplorable matter.

Perhaps it was an inherent reluctance to return to his hometown or the fear of the difficulties he might encounter once he got there, but despite purchasing several airline tickets to Minnesota over the course of the past decade, Charlie had never managed to board a departing plane.

Some excuse, it seemed, always got in the way. Construction emergencies cropped up at the last minute; inclement weather generated a string of flight cancelations; or a perfect day at the beach won out over twelve hours in a cramped airplane seat.

Eventually, the slew of missed opportunities piled up, higher and higher, until the time lapse itself became an additional, overwhelming impediment.

CHARLIE WAS A failure as a father, and he knew it.

He had heard his friends and neighbors on St. John whisper about his parental shortcomings. It happened in bars, busy restaurants, the grocery store—places where the speakers probably thought the surrounding ambient noise would drown out their voices.

"He's a nice guy," the line would go, always followed by the same damning commentary. "But it's a shame about his kids. He just abandoned them . . ."

In Charlie's opinion, the situation was far more complicated than that summation implied. To his credit, he had never missed a child support payment. Even when he experienced occasional cash-flow problems, he made sure the check went out, registered mail, in plenty of time to reach Minnesota by the first of each month. Financially speaking, he had checked all the boxes for fatherly responsibility.

But the physical separation was a crime all the same, an unintended and yet wholly foreseeable consequence of his actions—or lack thereof.

For that, he bore the burden of his full share of the guilt.

SO, WHILE MIRA'S invitation to meet up for Thanksgiving had caught Charlie completely off guard, he had immediately jumped at the offer.

After all this time, he'd thought, he would have a chance to make amends.

Of course, he had known the visit might go badly, and that his children, now teenagers, might hate him or, worse, refuse to come at all. In the weeks leading up to that Thanksgiving trip, he had worried nonstop about the holiday get-together: where they would stay, what restaurants he would take them to, what activities would be best suited for the group.

Most of all, he was terrified of how the kids would react in their initial meeting.

Charlie had no idea what he was in for.

He'd been totally unprepared for the ambush that took place.

"SANTA CRUZ," CHARLIE muttered bitterly as he stood in the gravel courtyard, remembering his fateful Thanksgiving adventure on St. Croix.

He glanced down at his cutoff camo shorts, hairy shins, and beat-up combat boots. He was dressed far differently for this journey than the debacle last November.

Gone were the pressed khaki shorts, the crisp white T-shirt, and the new leather sandals he'd purchased in the hopes of making a good impression. He'd ditched those tourist-mimicking clothes in the back of his closet when he'd returned home from the first errant trip to St. Croix.

Today, he'd gone for the familiar comfort of his working-man's armor. This was not meant to be a cordial visit. He was prepared to do battle.

He gripped the shoulder straps of his backpack, feeling the reassuring weight of the contents he'd packed inside. Gripping the brim of his cap, he shoved it firmly down onto his head. He was focused, alert, and resolute.

This time he was ready for whatever Santa Cruz—or Mira—had to throw at him.

~ 15 ~

The Room at
the Top of the Stairs

GLOWERING WITH DETERMINATION, Charlie set off on the
path to the hotel. Looking up over the pavilion's roofline,
he could see the row of windows on the fourth floor of the
hotel's main building and the corner room where he and
Mira had met the previous Thanksgiving.

The event was still burned in his memory. Details from
the November encounter flooded his head, even as he tried
to focus on the rendezvous ahead.

THE SEAPLANE HAD made a relatively uneventful landing in
the Christiansted harbor that day. The spear-fishing snorkeler had just begun his battle for control of the runway, and
the arriving aircraft had avoided the errant swimmer with
only a minor swerve.

Charlie had stepped out onto the seaplane's concrete pier,
full of hope and optimism. He could hardly believe that after
ten long years, he was at last going to see his children.

He had invited Mira and the kids to stay at the rental
villa, which he'd cleared of tenants for the week. There
would be plenty of space for each of them to have their own

room, and, he'd reasoned, it would provide a nice private location for the reunion.

When he'd landed in Christiansted, however, Charlie had found a message on his phone from his ex-wife asking him to instead meet her at the Comanche Hotel.

It was an odd choice, he'd thought. If she'd changed her mind about the villa, there were several full-service resorts on the island that would have been a better fit in terms of room size and amenities for the kids.

Nevertheless, he had dutifully trotted down the boardwalk to the sugar mill bar and taken the right turn along the concrete path that circled the gravel courtyard.

Trusting Mira, Charlie now realized, had been his first mistake.

As he continued down the same path, each step bringing him closer to yet another confrontation, he vowed not to repeat that error.

AFTER SKIRTING THE lower side of the raised swimming pool, Charlie traversed the line of paving stones that led to the covered walkway beneath the second-floor pavilion. Passing through to the opposite side of the short tunnel, he turned onto the narrow alley that ran in front of the entrance to the Comanche Hotel.

Seconds later, he paused outside the reception area. Reaching for the glass door's brass handle, he steeled himself for entry. He glanced at the wood paneling of the storm covers propped against the building's stone walls, sucked in his breath, and pulled back on the handle.

The man sitting behind the reception desk looked up as Charlie marched sternly inside.

"Mister Baker," he said with rigid formality. "Welcome back. We've been expecting you." He slid a pair of keys across the dark surface of the mahogany desk. "In case you don't remember, the green one is for the second-floor access to the guest area. The brass one is for the room."

The clerk nodded at the ceiling. "She's waiting for you

upstairs in number seventeen." With a curious smile that Charlie tried to ignore, he added, "It's the one all the way at the top of the stairs."

"I remember. I remember," Charlie replied warily as he snatched up the keys. It was the same room as before, he thought nervously. Shifting his backpack on his shoulders, he asked, "Did she have any kids with her?"

The man's dark face was frustratingly oblique.

"I'm sure I couldn't say, sir."

Grumbling, Charlie turned and began the long climb to the top floor. Halfway up the first flight of steps, he stopped and looked down over his shoulder—not at the desk clerk, but at the statue standing on the far side of the room.

Charlie stared for a long moment at the Comanche's wooden figure and shuddered.

"I always feel like that crazy bugger is watching me."

CHARLIE CLOMPED THE rest of the way up the stairs to the second floor and took a left down the exterior balcony. Using the green access key, he navigated through a locked door into the secured guest area.

The hotel's upper floors were decorated in a nautical theme. Oil paintings depicting ocean landscapes hung from wainscoted walls painted in light yellow and cream. Refurnished side tables with intricately carved legs displayed glass light fixtures fashioned out of inverted hurricane lamps.

It was a pleasant, comforting scene, if a bit rough around the edges. Here and there, nicks marred the wooden furniture; the occasional crack or chip could be seen in the glass mirrors mounted onto the walls. A small seating area overlooked a tropical garden that was overgrown and in need of a good pruning. The hotel, like many businesses in downtown Christiansted, was struggling for its economic survival.

Charlie rounded a corner and continued up a wide staircase to a similarly furnished third floor. Midway down yet another hallway, he approached the last flight of stairs, this one so steep and narrow that the steps resembled those of a ladder.

"All the way to the top," Charlie said with a grimace as he gripped the railing and began the final ascent.

A MOMENT LATER, Charlie reached the fourth floor, the attic level. The curving roof above him cut in on either side, creating a tight, claustrophobic space.

The rubber soles of his worn combat boots creaked across the wooden floorboards as he proceeded to the end of the main corridor and a pair of doors, which were positioned diagonal to one another in a triangular-shaped corner.

A square placard affixed to the facing of the door on the left marked it as number seventeen.

Charlie didn't need the signpost. Over the last six months, he had stood in this same spot before—more times than he now cared to count.

Whipping off his backpack, he dug inside its main compartment and pulled out a painter's respirator mask. Stretching the mask's back strap over his baseball cap and around the base of his skull, he positioned the plastic centerpiece over his nose and mouth. Short disc-shaped canisters protruded from either side of the contraption, each one containing a filter designed to capture toxic particulates in the air.

Grimly sucking in his breath, Charlie slid the brass key into the lock.

"Here goes nothing."

CHARLIE PUSHED OPEN the door, poked his masked face inside, and glanced around.

Like the rest of the hotel's attic level, the room had a steeply sloped ceiling that rose at its center to a series of sharp points. Windows cut into the roofline provided a view over downtown Christiansted and, beyond, a small blue slice of the harbor.

There was a double bed, fitted with a cream-colored

spread that had been overlaid with a dainty lace detailing. A flowered rug lay across the open space just beyond the door, and a wardrobe had been positioned against the tallest wall.

Charlie's gaze briefly skimmed over the furnishings. He took only a quick glimpse out at the exterior vistas. His primary focus was trained on the woman standing in the center of the room.

"Hello, Mira."

~ 16 ~

Mira

MIRA STOOD IN the middle of room seventeen on the top attic floor of the Comanche Hotel, watching as her ex-husband edged tentatively through the doorway.

Oh, Charlie, she thought, feeling momentarily sorry for him. Why do you keep coming back here?

She had received confirmation from the seaplane operator that he'd been booked on that afternoon's flight, but she was still surprised that he had actually shown up. Given the outcome of their last two meetings, not many men would have risked making a third appearance.

But there he was, all five foot two inches of him, valiantly pursuing the search for his children—ten years too late.

TILTING HER HEAD, Mira cast her gaze over the man whose stocky figure had once been so familiar. Their last two encounters had been brief, and she hadn't taken the time to study him closely.

He was dressed in his regular construction clothes. The wardrobe was the same as the day she'd first met him at a little truck-stop diner up in northern Minnesota: a plain white T-shirt, ragged around the edges, and cutoff camo pants, fitted loose around the waist.

There on his feet were the beat-up combat boots. She let out a barely audible sigh. How many identical pairs of those boots had he worn through the years?

She turned her attention to the painter's mask that Charlie had strapped over his face. Presumably, he thought this precaution might prevent a repeat of the outcome of their two previous meetings. He had concluded—erroneously—that it was some noxious component of her perfume that had rendered him unconscious.

That won't help you a bit, she thought, trying not to laugh at his stern expression.

Charlie Baker. You always were such a stubborn man.

MIRA TOOK A few steps toward her ex-husband, carefully measuring her stride as she decreased the distance between them. She stared at his masked face, taking in the details. There were little signs, here and there, of the wear ten years of aging had done to his body.

He still wore his hair long and tied back in a ponytail, but touches of gray had started to lighten the strands near his temples. Crow's-feet had begun their inevitable march across his upper cheekbones. His shoulders, while still sturdy, curved ever so slightly inward.

Overall, she thought, sizing him up, he'd held together well. Such a shame things hadn't worked out between them.

It had ended so suddenly, his usefulness to her.

MARRIAGE, MIRA REFLECTED, was a fragile balance, a teeter-totter of give and take, a symbiosis between benefactor and provider. Her relationship with Charlie had grown shaky long before they left Minnesota; the move to the Caribbean had only widened the expanding gulf between them.

Every day on the island, it seemed, her husband had

drifted farther from her grasp. She had worked for weeks to regain his attention, all the while fearing she might never reel him in again.

Just as the marriage reached a tipping point, Mira met someone else—a better-funded suitor, flattering and attentive, who promised a return to the stability and quality of life she had once enjoyed.

The blowup over Charlie's endless snooping through her closet had been the last straw. That was the point where she had shifted her allegiance.

It was a sad affair, but in the end, she'd had to dispose of him.

Like a worn out pair of shoes.

~ *17* ~

Beware the Woman
in the Green Shoes

MIRA CONTINUED HER slow measured approach, sauntering across the room toward her ex-husband. The flowery fog of her perfume swilled the air as she reached up and pulled out her hair clip, releasing her long mane to drop down past her shoulders. With every step, her silk dress creased against the curves of her slender figure. The soles of her green heels tapped seductively against the wooden floor, a hypnotically repeating cadence.

"The shoes," Charlie gurgled beneath the mask. He pointed indignantly at her feet. "You're wearing the shoes."

Mira nodded a silent confirmation, continuing her steady pace until she stood mere inches away from him. With her sizeable height advantage, she towered over her ex-husband. It was a mismatched standoff, the Amazon and the troll.

Charlie glared sternly up at her, his eyes watering from the concentrated scent of her perfume. The stringent smell burned his nasal passages, searing his lungs. His sinuses began to clog, and he choked into the mask.

He staggered sideways, overcome by dizziness. He veered toward the door, a desperate attempt at escape, but his wobbly legs crumpled beneath him, and he slumped to the floor.

Helpless, he watched as Mira's fuzzy form bent over him.

She lifted the brim of Charlie's baseball cap and slipped her hand around the base of his neck to tilt his head upward.

"Where are the kids?" he demanded weakly as she gently lifted the mask from his face.

In the far reaches of his numbing mind, he picked out the scents of breath mints mingling with cigarette smoke as Mira leaned toward him and planted a perfect lipstick imprint on the center of his forehead.

FIFTEEN MINUTES LATER, Mira knelt on the floor next to Charlie's unconscious body. Reaching for his wrist, she held her index finger against his skin and quietly checked his pulse.

Seemingly satisfied with his vitals—or lack thereof—she rose to her feet. Returning to the wardrobe, she removed the cloak from its hanger and wrapped it around her body, covering the green dress. She wound her long locks into a tight bun at the nape of her neck and fastened the clip around it. Then she turned to the scarf, floating the fabric in the air to shake out the folds before spreading it carefully over her head.

The heavy mascara and lipstick she'd applied earlier were already gone, removed with several damp tissues from the bathroom. With her pale face once more framed by the black cloth, she appeared slightly tired and drawn. The only external sign of her previous glamour was the pair of open-toed shoes, which peeked out from beneath the cloak's bottom hem.

After a last glance around the room to check that she'd gathered all of her belongings, Mira slid the strap of her purse over her shoulder and gingerly stepped over the motionless body heaped on the floor by the door.

Glancing at her watch, she walked into the hallway and locked the door behind her.

As she started down the narrow ladder-style stairs, she gathered the folds of the cloak, holding the hem off the ground to avoid tripping on the steps.

On the descent, she gazed down at the strappy green heels—the shoes that had led to the dissolution of her first marriage and the initiation of her second.

Funny how an inanimate object could cause such a dramatic change in lifestyle, she thought as she reached the third-floor landing. Before the cloak swished to the ground, she stretched out her leg to take one last look, angling her foot to admire the stylish detailing sewn into the leather.

Every so often, Mira reflected, it pays to be impulsive.

THIS SAME MANTRA had been enthusiastically adopted by her youngest daughter.

~ 18 ~

An Impulsive Offspring

THE HOUSEMAID WHO had been commandeered for baby-sitting duty sat at a desk in the Comanche's second-floor office suite, reading a gossip magazine from the States that a guest had left in her room when she checked out a few days earlier.

The maid's two charges were sprawled on the floor a few feet away. Hassan worked to assemble a set of LEGOs into a small dump truck, while Elena accessorized a collection of Barbie dolls, switching dresses, purses, hats, and shoes from one plastic figure to the next.

The hotel manager stopped in the hallway outside the office and leaned in through the open doorway. His face bore the harried expression of a man who had already juggled one too many crises that day.

"The people in number eight are asking for a fresh set of towels. Can you run them down there for me?"

"Of course," the woman replied, guiltily blushing as she dropped the magazine on the desk. She reached into a drawer for a set of keys.

Standing from her chair, she turned to look at the children. Both appeared to be thoroughly engrossed in their play.

"You two stay right here," the maid said softly as she tiptoed to the door. "I'll be right back."

THE SECOND THE maid left her post, Elena looked up from her dolls. Raising herself onto her knees, she watched as the woman hurried down the hallway toward the linen closet. The girl's green eyes slanted mischievously.

"Come on, Hassan," she whispered, jumping up from the floor.

"But I'm not done," he replied, holding out his half-finished dump truck.

"You can play with it later," she hissed, grabbing his arm.

"But . . ." Hassan's brown eyes widened as he remembered his mother's parting words. They were under strict orders to stay in this office until she finished with her meeting and came back to get them.

"Hurry," Elena said, urgently yanking on his elbow.

Hassan didn't like to get into trouble. By nature, he was an obedient child. And with a hungry Goat Foot Woman out there looking for children to eat, it seemed like a particularly bad time to be wandering off without adult supervision.

"But what about the Goat Foot Wo . . ." Hassan protested, to no avail.

The truck fell to the ground as Elena tugged him out the door.

~ *19* ~

Counting Chickens

AROUND THE CORNER from the Comanche Hotel, the taxi drivers gathered in their regular afternoon spot, a shaded alley across from the green space surrounding the Danish fort. The drivers' marked vans were stationed nearby, parked along a straight portion of King Street, Christiansted's main vehicular roadway.

From the comfort of their foldout chairs, the drivers had views of the east end of the harbor as well as Government House, the St. Croix annex to the administration facilities on St. Thomas.

The alley's strategic position allowed the drivers to monitor all of the area's important comings and goings. News of any significance was generally brought to the taxi stand alley for rapid conveyance.

From this collection point, information was then relayed around the island via text message or cell-phone call, quickly spreading through a network of family and friends. Often, the reporting carried in St. Croix's printed newspapers was merely a confirmation of the taxi driver rumors that had circulated the day before.

IT HAD BEEN a slow day—on both the passenger and news fronts—leaving the men plenty of time for gossip and debate.

That afternoon's heated topic involved the cruise ship that was scheduled to arrive the following morning and whether it would be worth the drivers' while to cross to the other side of the island to try to pick up fares.

St. Croix saw a fair number of cruise ship layovers, but the coral reef that surrounded much of the island, including the Christiansted harbor, precluded the most advantageous landing points. There were only two places where the mammoth ships could dock: a deepwater port next to the south shore refinery, and a recently renovated pier at the small west-end town of Frederiksted. Given the refinery's industrial vista of barbed-wire fencing and smoke-spewing metal pipes, the Frederisksted pier was the easy winner.

The downside to Frederisksted was its remote location. Christiansted's boutique shops and boardwalk entertainment were a thirty- to forty-minute taxi ride away. Given the numerous amenities available onboard a ship, many potential day-trippers opted to spend their port day on the boat or simply snorkeling off the Frederiksted pier.

As a result, while each arriving cruise ship was met with a great deal of anticipation by St. Croix's tourist-catering community, the occurrences rarely resulted in much tourist traffic or additional revenue.

The taxi drivers were evenly split on the next day's plans.

A tall Crucian man crossed his arms over his thin chest and sighed belligerently.

"Last time, I waited all day over there, and I didn't get a single fare. It's supposed to rain tomorrow afternoon. I'm stayin' put right here."

The driver seated to his right, a man from the island of Nevis, blew out a triumphant snort.

"Hey, Emmitt. That's fine with me. I'll take them all

in my van. You can sit around in this alley and count chickens."

SECOND ONLY TO the pros and cons of the cruise ship schedule, the most frequent discussion point at the taxi stand related to the daily assessment of Christiansted's feral chicken population.

The building that housed the national park's public restrooms lay across the street, on the south side of the King Street curve, kitty-corner to the drivers' alley. Leaky pipes attached to the outside of the building provided a water source for a number of free-roaming chickens, many of whom built their nests in the row of bushes lining the structure's concrete exterior.

For several hours each morning, the hens paraded their hatchlings back and forth across King Street's busy thoroughfare, a lesson in survival skills as well as an unfortunate but necessary process of winnowing down the flock. The average batch of hatchlings resulted in more chicks than one hen could possibly hope to keep track of or feed.

For the taxi drivers, whiling away long hot days with an ever-diminishing pool of riders, the road-crossing exercise had become a gruesome game of chance. They had organized an informal gambling ring, betting on the number of chicks that would survive the day's carnage.

Since joining the group, the driver from Nevis had crushed his fellow chicken-counting competitors, racking up a sizeable stash of prize money. He wasn't about to let the others forget his successful run—particularly Emmitt, who had ended up on the bottom end of the wager pool for the past five days.

"Hey, Emmitt. What'd you do to them chickens to make them hate you so?"

He pulled out a wad of cash from his pocket, the last week's winnings, and waved it in front of the Crucian's nose.

"All right, Nevis. You just wait," Emmitt said, waving him off. "Your luck's bound to run out soon."

GRUMBLING BITTERLY, EMMITT shifted his weight in his chair and turned a cold shoulder toward the driver from Nevis. He'd had more than enough of the fellow's bragging. He certainly hoped the man opted to make the Frederiksted run the next day. His absence would dramatically even the odds in the chicken competition.

A movement on the fort's wide lawn caught Emmitt's attention. Leaning forward in his chair, he craned his neck around the corner of the alley to get a better look. He watched as a man in a cutoff T-shirt, running shorts, and sneakers jogged away from the gazebo.

Emmitt heaved out a relieved sigh as he noted the stack of sheet music the man carried in his arms.

"Thank the Lord, 'Berto's finished with that blasted singing. It's bad enough I have to listen to you lot all day. That opera nonsense gives me a headache."

Nevis stretched and yawned, seemingly oblivious to Emmitt's turned back.

"Oh, I don't know, Emmitt. Today wasn't too terrible." He straightened the collar of his stained shirt and leaned toward Emmitt's chair. "'Course, Bach is more to my taste."

The Crucian rotated in his chair, returning his gaze to the alley. He stared at the Nevisian driver for a long moment, his stony face expressionless.

Then he swatted the air, as if shooing a fly.

"Oh, git on wit' you."

~ 20 ~

A Pleasing Existence

AFTER A VIGOROUS two-hour vocal performance, Umberto reached the last stanza of the afternoon's practice session. He cleared his lungs, letting the final note hang in the salty sea air. Then, with a nodding bow to the taxi drivers across the green space, he scooped up his cutoff T-shirt and slid it over his head, once more hiding the tattoos spread across his chest and shoulders. Neatly restacking the sheet music, he carried the pile down the gazebo's wooden steps and jogged off toward the boardwalk.

A few sleepy hens cooed in the narrow shade of grass by the gazebo, groggily lifting their feathered heads. The chicks that had survived the morning traffic lesson cuddled beneath their mothers' plump bodies, safe for at least one more day.

SETTING OFF DOWN the boardwalk, Umberto waved to an approaching dinghy filled with passengers coming ashore from the cay. The skipper saluted back as he hopped out and secured the vessel to the boardwalk's harbor edge. He then began unloading his guests, firmly gripping each one as they transferred from the bobbing boat to the wooden walkway.

The skipper's night shift was just beginning. It was a job that would grow increasingly difficult as the night wore on. His human cargo was far easier to wrangle at the beginning of the evening than on the return trip at the shift's end.

Several hours' worth of Confusion cocktails tended to make for unsteady footing.

UMBERTO CONTINUED DOWN the walkway, popping in at a sandwich shop for a liter-sized bottle of water and a collection of local newspapers. Loaded up with his purchases, he trotted through a security gate and onto the pier, where his small boat was docked.

As Umberto stepped up to the rigging, two miniature dachshunds bounded out of the ship's galley, eager to greet him. Their tails wagging, they raced wild circles around his feet, nearly knocking him off balance. The vessel had been moored in the Christiansted harbor for several months now, and the dogs were well accustomed to their master's daily routine.

"Senesino, Farinelli—*hup, hup*," the opera singer called out, a firmly issued command that was utterly ignored. If anything, the dogs were more rambunctious, not less.

Sighing, he bent to untie his running shoes. After kicking them off on the deck, he relented and playfully rubbed the dogs' silky heads. Unscrewing the lid from the bottled water, he topped off the liquid in the aluminum bowl of their feeding station.

Humming to himself, Umberto stepped into the boat's kitchen area and removed a kettle from one of the cabinets built into the sidewall. He emptied the rest of the bottled water into the pot and lit the fuse on the stove's mini-burner.

No matter the day's humid heat. It was time for his afternoon tea.

THE DOGS LAPPED at their bowls while Umberto opened a sealed canister and scooped out a serving of dried tea leaves. Using a cutting board built into the counter, he sliced a small lime into wedges—an acceptable substitute for lemon, at least when one lived on a boat.

Across from the kitchen, the boat's center living area featured a foldout table anchored to a long bench, which doubled as a narrow bed. Between the cabinetry and the rows of circular windows that lined the cabin's upper sides, there was little unoccupied wall space, but Umberto had managed to find a spot to hang a few plastic frames.

The plaques featured faded clippings commemorating some of the more acclaimed performances of his singing career. The figure standing on stage at the Boston Opera House in a full-length tuxedo, gloves, and top hat was almost unrecognizable as the sweaty singer from the gazebo.

Off to the boat's starboard side, a slim doorway led to a tiny cubicle-shaped bathroom. After the sun went down, Umberto would use the handheld shower nozzle to take a quick, refreshing rinse. He glanced at the shower door and shrugged. In this humidity, it was pointless to try to clean up until the island had settled into its evening cool.

A BLAST OF steam pulsed through the slatted hole in the kettle's lid, peeping out a perfectly tuned high C note. Umberto slipped an oven mitt over one hand and removed the kettle from the stove, immediately pouring the boiling water into a carafe designed for steeping. He set the carafe, his cup, and a saucer full of lime wedges on a tray and carried the tea service onto the boat's back deck.

The dogs were already settled on the floor beside Umberto's frayed lawn chair. Positioned beneath an awning that stretched out from the cabin's eaves, the spot had plenty of shade.

A three-legged stool had been anchored to the deck, within arm's reach of the chair. Gripping the edges of the tray to keep it level, Umberto set the tea service on the stool and then eased into the comfort of the lawn chair's loose-hanging seat. With a sigh, he stretched his arms out over his head and waited for the tea leaves to brew.

When the liquid had reached a suitable darkness, Umberto poured a few ounces into his cup, drizzled in some lime juice, and took a small sip.

"Ah," he said with contentment. *"Perfetto."*

After thumbing through the stack of local newspapers he'd picked up on his way home from the gazebo, Umberto selected the one with the most colorful headline and unfolded it on his lap. Taking a full drink of the tea, he crossed one tanned leg over the other, and wiggled his toes.

What a civilized life, he thought as he gazed out at the water's shimmering afternoon shadows.

He couldn't have dreamed up a more pleasing existence.

UMBERTO SETTLED INTO the newspaper, yawning as he skimmed through the first couple of articles.

The Italian opera star was well known to almost everyone in and around the Christiansted boardwalk—but as an eccentric, not a confidant. He occasionally exchanged pleasantries with the sugar mill bartender and the crazy old hag with the rusted-out shopping cart. Otherwise, he spent most of his days in peaceful solitude, insulated from the island's rabid gossip chain.

Even if Umberto had been connected to the local social scene, its news source wouldn't have reached him; he steadfastly refused to carry a cell phone during the months he spent in the Caribbean.

So as he scanned the newspaper's front page, he was one of the few readers receiving its information for the first time.

Umberto briefly perused the daily weather update, noting that a storm would be passing through the following afternoon, before moving on to an enthusiastic description of the pending cruise ship's arrival. He continued skimming through the crime blog, the sports listings, and the beach report.

Finally, he turned to the paper's main coverage: the upcoming Transfer Day ceremonies.

MARCH 31 MARKED the ninety-plus-year anniversary of the 1917 sale of the Danish West Indies to the United States— Transfer Day, as it was colloquially known.

The USVI calendar was filled with several notable holidays: the Carnival Festival in the spring, Emancipation Day in the summer, and, in the fall, Liberty Day, celebrating the life of labor leader D. Hamilton Jackson. Transfer Day's end of March marker fell awkwardly in the mix. Among many of its residents, the territory's purchase by the United States was a milestone of dubious distinction.

Nevertheless, tomorrow's date would be commemorated by several public activities, with the main event scheduled to take place at a refurbished Danish plantation in the dense rain forest that covered the island's northwest corner, not far from the cruise ship dock in Frederiksted.

The paper proudly announced that the territory's governor would be flying in from St. Thomas to oversee the plantation festivities. Several Danish dignitaries along with a couple hundred Danish nationals, many of the latter group with family ties to St. Croix, had already arrived.

The article made no mention of the Americans, Umberto reflected as he refilled his cup and squeezed another slice of lime into the tea. Representatives of the island's current owner would be conspicuously absent on the day celebrating its acquisition.

UMBERTO TUCKED THE paper beneath the stool. Contemplating the cultural oddities of his adopted home, he cupped his hands beneath his head and leaned back in the chair.

St. Croix was a lonely, isolated place, surrounded by a

flat horizon that was barely dimpled by the glitzier islands to the north. Far more dominant on the landscape was the glowering power plant that scarred the harbor's west end, a sooty reminder of the belching refinery that swallowed several acres of the island's south shore. This working class outpost, unknown by most of the continental United States and generally ignored by its sister Virgins, had a depth of character that only an artist could appreciate.

Umberto was a keen observer of the fascinating individuals who populated downtown Christiansted. While he was careful to maintain his oddball, outsider status—he preferred quiet solitude to the idle chitchat brought on by neighborly familiarity—he spent far more time watching the Islanders than the other way around.

His favorite pastime involved imagining the colorful life stories of the people he spied on from his boat's rear deck.

There were the American refinery workers, brought in to consult on the local plant, men who were separated from their families in the States for months at a time. To Umberto's eye, the blustering brutes with tattooed muscles and gruff Popeye demeanors were closet softies, secretly nursing the pangs of homesickness. Despite the long evenings they spent in the local bars, their constant cell-phone usage suggested they were in regular contact with their families and loved ones.

Next up were the weatherworn sailors, bowed at the knees, their balance permanently skewed to a boat's bobbing buoyancy. These men had made a far more permanent break with society.

Umberto liked to picture what the old salts had looked like in their youth. He saw them as clean-shaven men with straight postures and unwrinkled faces, trading in their wives and girlfriends for the mistress of the sea.

Perhaps the best shoreline characters were the Crucian women, whose beautiful skin varied in every shade from cream to dark brown. The younger ones were easy to pick out, strutting along the boardwalk, bursting with pent-up adolescent rebellion, desperate to escape the island's claustrophobic confines. They were almost matched in numbers by the returners, a few years older, still beautiful but now bearing a certain dignified reserve, having ventured to the bright lights of Miami only to find themselves put off by its wild flamboyance.

Umberto tilted the cup to drain the last sip of tea. Lightly smacking his lips, he turned his head toward downtown Christiansted, eager to see what the evening's voyeurism might bring.

His vision drifted along the walkway to the crowd gathered outside the brewpub, where the afternoon's crab races were about to begin.

Sitting up in his chair, Umberto watched as a girl of about seven with bouncing pigtails tugged a younger boy, his demeanor clearly reluctant, toward the edge of the spectators.

~ *21* ~

Off to the Races

DRAGGING HASSAN BEHIND her, Elena pushed to the front of the crowd converging on the brewpub's outdoor seating area for the daily crab race. The tables and chairs had been moved to the side to make room for the racing ring, a five-foot circle drawn out in chalk on the concrete.

It was an event for all ages and nationalities. Several sun-flushed Danes stood watching from the boardwalk, while a number of rum-bleary Americans mingled in the middle of the pub's dining space. Up front, closest to the designated racing spot, a growing horde of excited young children ran madly about.

Elena soon forced her way through to the inner group, pulling Hassan along with her.

A cheer rose up from the crowd as a waitress brought out a large plastic bucket. About fifty hermit crabs squirmed inside, each one with a colorful number painted on its shell. The youthful spectators tightened around the container, eager to get a look at the crawling heap of contestants.

For a dollar ante each, the waitress dutifully wrote the sponsoring individual's name on a clipboard and matched it with the corresponding crab number. Alongside the number, she took down the crab's newly assigned racing name. Some of the monikers were chosen to highlight the crustacean's speed, athleticism, or perceived personality, while others were more a reflection of the sponsor's personality. Flash, Big Bopper, and Crab Cakes were all quickly selected.

Elena hopped up and down, worried that the best crabs would be taken before she got a chance to pick. When it was finally her turn, she peered anxiously inside the bucket.

"That one," she squealed, thrusting her finger at the bulkiest crab in the pile. "Fat Louie for me!"

As the waitress scribbled the name and number, Hassan edged in beside his sister. Caught up in the excitement of the event, his hesitance at disobeying his mother had now diminished.

"I like that guy on the edge of the bucket," Hassan said, nodding toward a tiny crab whose number was almost bigger than its shell. "Number thirteen."

"Don't be silly. It's way too small," Elena replied dismissively. "And besides, thirteen is an unlucky number."

Hassan crossed his arms in front of his chest. "That's my crab," he insisted. "His name is Ferdinand."

With a sigh, Elena looked up at the waitress. "Make it two crabs for us."

The woman smiled. "Do you have your dollars, kids?" She looked out at the surrounding adults, searching for one associated with the two youngsters.

"I got it," Elena said, yanking on the woman's sleeve before she had time to realize that they were there without parental supervision.

Brow furrowed, the girl dug inside the pocket of her sundress. She pulled out a dollar and seventy-five cents, the change from the earlier candy bar purchase, and held it out hopefully.

"I'm a little short, but my brother's pick is only half a crab," she said, rolling her eyes at Hassan.

The woman laughed and took the money.

"Close enough," she responded with a wink.

AFTER EVERYONE'S ANTE had been collected, the waitress handed the clipboard to the brewpub's owner, who served as the race announcer. Flicking on his microphone, the man stepped toward the center of the chalk-drawn circle and addressed the crowd.

"*Welll*-come to the world-famous Christiansted board-walk crab race!"

The amplified voice boomed out across the busy shore-line, drawing still more gawkers to the fringes of the racing area. Those on the outer edges began climbing on top of chairs and tabletops to see into the racing circle.

"We have some fabulous prizes for today's winners. A selection of colorful T-shirts, shot glasses"—he glanced down at the number of children near his feet—"and an assortment of water toys. Something appropriate for all ages."

Taking in a deep breath, he continued. "Now, if every-one's ready, let's get this thing started."

The announcer stepped aside as the waitress moved into the chalk-drawn circle with her bucket. The contents had been pared down to include just the participating hermit crabs. With a clattering *whoosh*, she dumped the shell-carrying crustaceans onto the marked center starting point.

"*Aaaaaaand* they're off. *Andale. Andale.* We've got quite a race going for you tonight, folks. Neck and neck, right out of the starting gate."

The announcer's call didn't in any way reflect the slow-moving crawl of the crabs dragging their shells across the concrete, but you wouldn't know it from the wild cheers of the packed crowd.

"Fat Louie's jumped out to an early lead. He looks like a ringer, that one. A good pick by the little lady here on the front row . . . But wait! Who's this small guy coming up on his left flank?" The announcer paused to squint at the numbers on his clipboard. "It's number thirteen, *Ferd-i-nand* the Great!"

"Hey, that's my crab!" Hassan piped out as the tiny crab scrambled nimbly over its competitor, who was loaded down with a much larger shell. "Come on, Ferdy!"

AFTER FIVE MINUTES of heart-stopping drama (for the audience) and uneventful ambling (for the crustaceans), Ferdinand was announced the winner. There was a generous offering of prizes, and all of the child participants were given the opportunity to select an item from a water-toy grab bag.

With the crowd quickly dispersing, the waitstaff scurried about, reassembling the tables for the night's dinner service.

As the winner, Hassan had first pick of the toy prizes. He held up his selection, a three-foot-long super-soaker, and aimed its plastic tube toward the boardwalk.

Testing the plunger, Hassan pumped the handle, imagining a solid stream of water pulsing out the end piece, across the dining area, over the heads of a pair of waitresses, and straight onto . . .

"Elena," he whispered tensely. "Elena, she's here."

The super-soaker was pointed at the homeless West Indian woman, who stood about fifteen feet away in the shadows just off the boardwalk.

The hag wrapped her gnarled hands around the handle of her rusted shopping cart and shifted her weight so that she could lift up her lame foot. She propped the floppy left shoe on the cart's lower back rim and rocked it back and forth.

Then, with a sudden lurch that caused Hassan to nearly drop his water toy, she shoved the cart forward, on a direct line toward the brewpub.

"Elena," Hassan pleaded, tugging on his sister's arm. She was still bent over the toy sack, trying to make her decision. "Elena, she's coming this way."

The girl's head jerked up from the bag.

"Mamma?" she asked, whipping her head around. She wasn't quite ready to be caught. "Where?"

"No," Hassan hissed. "It's the woman . . . the—the Goat Foot Woman." His little face paled with terror. "Elena, she's going to take me to her lair and . . ."

But his sister had already returned her attention to the collection of toys.

"You'll be fine," she replied, reaching for a plastic water pistol.

"Elena!" Hassan squealed urgently as the old woman drew closer, her cart bumping rapidly over the boardwalk's rough surface. Within seconds, she would be inside the brewpub's dining area.

"Elena," Hassan mouthed, his small body paralyzed with fear. He couldn't move, couldn't speak, couldn't breathe. His cheeks flushed as beads of sweat broke out across his face.

Gedda left her cart at the edge of the brewpub and limped toward the boy. Soon, she was but a few feet away.

She stopped and leered down at him, her yellow eyes glowing against her dark graying skin. Her mouth gaped open, exposing the rotting interior.

Suddenly regaining his mobility, Hassan dove around the hag, hurdled over an upturned chair, and ran screeching down the boardwalk toward the old Danish fort.

~ 22 ~

The Feeding

REFRESHED FROM A shower and a change of clothes, Adam Rock left the moderate comfort of his thinly air-conditioned room in search of a cold drink and something to eat.

A piece of plump, tender meat ought to do the trick, he thought hungrily to himself.

He strode stiffly down the humid hallway, turned at the end of the corridor, and entered a stairwell leading to the first floor. Clunking down the steps, he tugged at the front of his golf shirt, lifting the cotton fabric away from his skin, which had already begun to moisten with sweat. There was a growing dampness in his socks, even the one encasing his prosthetic. His brown walking shoes usually provided his most stable footing, but as he marched down the stairs, it became more and more difficult to maintain his balance.

At last, he reached the bottom. Grumbling again about the hotel's need for a more robust cooling system, Rock lumbered out of the stairwell and into the interior courtyard.

As he yanked a handkerchief from his pocket and wiped it across his brow, a cheerful splashing sound drew his attention. He glanced over at a small fountain, where a pair of young children were playing, cooling their bare feet in the pool of water while they waited for their parents to complete the check-in process at the reception desk.

Rock's sour expression began to soften, and his mood noticeably lightened. As he stared at the chubby toddler legs and plump, tender toes, the corners of his lips twitched with craving. He pushed down on his left foot, causing the hoof to grind against the prosthetic.

Shrieking with delight, one of the youngsters ran past the salesman, his bare feet slapping against the courtyard's concrete floor.

Rock eyed the wet footprints. His mouth salivating, he murmured out loud.

"Now, I'm really hungry."

WITH DIFFICULTY, ROCK pulled himself away from the children and headed out the waterfront side of the hotel to the open-air restaurant.

The evening crowd had started to filter in, a mix of tourists looking for some grub to go with their sunset cocktails and locals stopping in for refreshment after a day's work.

Rock took a seat at the bar. With a casual wave at the bartender, he pointed to a Red Stripe bottle from a lineup on the back wall.

The server nodded a confirmation and reached into the cooler. There was a slight *hiss* of air as he flicked off the lid. With a minimal flourish, he plunked the squatty bottle on the counter.

Rock wrapped a hand around the glass, savoring the chill. Then he brought the bottle to his lips and took a long sip.

"Ahhh," he sighed, swiveling in his chair to gaze across the diner's open harbor-facing wall.

The sun sank into the western horizon, throwing pink and purple hues across the sky. Pointed shadows stretched out from the unfurled masts of the myriad sailboats floating in the harbor. Even the most run-down locations could be transformed into a tropical mirage by the colors of a Caribbean sunset.

Rock took another sizeable drink of the beer and smacked his lips. He tapped his ring finger against the bottle, listening to the comforting *tink* of metal on glass. While it was still warm and muggy, a light breeze had begun to flow out of the east, bringing with it a temperature decrease of at least four or five degrees.

He could almost forget his earlier discomfort when he was enjoying scenery like this.

ROCK QUICKLY DRAINED the first lager and ordered a second. Carrying the bottle, he walked across the restaurant to the railings overlooking the small lagoon of water that ran beneath the boardwalk.

The sleepy harbor saw its busiest bustle of the day as the dive-shop boats puttered in from their afternoon outings. Boatloads of sunburned snorkelers stumbled onto the piers that branched out from the main wooden walkway while tired crewmembers hurried through their end-of-shift cleanup and rigging checks.

Closer in to the diner's railing, Rock watched as torpedo-shaped shadows circled the lagoon's shallow waters. A bullish snout broke the surface, snapping testily at the air.

At the next table, a local peered over the railing. Tapping his fork against the side of his plate, he gestured to his dinner companion.

"The tarpon are out."

EVERY NIGHT, GANGS of tarpon converged on the lagoon for a free meal, courtesy of the diner's chef, who would dump into the water the meaty scraps left over from the dinner prep. The fish had grown accustomed to the routine of this free meal, and the water beneath the boardwalk was soon brimming with their taut, muscular bodies. The tarpon seemed to sense that, with the increased foot traffic on the walkway, the moment of the food drop was drawing near.

Tourists crowded in with their cameras as the chef

brought out a plastic bucket filled with a dark smelly soup. Flies buzzed around the bloody brew of pork trimmings, chicken carcass, and fish guts. As the chef stepped onto the short footbridge that connected the restaurant to the boardwalk, the water below erupted into a violent frenzy.

A swarm of snapping beasts wrestled in savage one-armed combat for a chance to tear at the loose strips of flesh. It was a gruesome cannibalistic orgy, one that drew murmurs of both surprise and disgust from the surrounding crowd.

For Adam Rock, the tarpon feeding only intensified his appetite.

Pushing back from the railing, he began a methodical search of the boardwalk pedestrians. His round eyes sank into his pouchy skin, his pupils glittering like tiny black marbles.

As his practiced gaze skimmed over the gathered crowd, he murmured softly to himself.

"Time to eat."

~ 23 ~

The Search

MIRA GLIDED DOWN the last steps to the Comanche Hotel's
second floor. As she reached the hallway's flat surface, she
paused to adjust her headscarf, smoothing the folds of cloth
over the back of her head.

Everything was going to plan. She should be home in
time to prepare dinner, with a half hour to spare. Her current husband would have no reason to know about her inter-
lude here at the hotel. She would pick up the children from
the office around the corner and be on her way in no time.

But as she stepped through the security door and onto
the second-floor balcony, she realized she might have been
overconfident in her assessment.

The maid who had been assigned the babysitting task as
well as several members of the hotel staff were scurrying
madly along the outer hallway, peering into closets and
underneath furniture. A quick glance across the short footbridge that stretched over the alley revealed more searchers
scouring the pool and pavilion areas.

"What happened?" Mira demanded as the tearful maid
rushed up to her.

"I turned my back for . . . for no more than a second,"

the woman said, fretfully wringing her hands. "I just . . . I don't know where they could have gone."

With difficulty, Mira swallowed her irate response. She knew from firsthand experience how fast Elena could get into trouble. The girl's escape skills were legendary—her capers even more so. This time, she had apparently co-opted Hassan into her getaway scheme.

Mira clenched her fists, digging her fingernails into her palms, and then released. Better to channel her energy toward finding her children. She would dole out punishments once she had the duo safely back in her charge.

"When did you last see them?" Mira asked tensely.

The maid looked up at a clock mounted over the office door.

"It was ten . . . no, twenty minutes ago now."

Mira gauged the time. She had better find the children quickly, or she was going to have a lot of explaining to do.

Sucking in a deep breath, she tried to imagine what would have drawn her daughter's interest. Elena had several preferred downtown play spots. All of them were located along the shoreline.

After a moment's concentration, Mira addressed the maid.

"Keep looking in the hotel," she instructed briskly. "I'll go check for them out on the boardwalk."

BLACK CLOAK BILLOWING, Mira clicked rapidly down the steps to the ground floor.

Her feet began to pinch inside the fancy green shoes. The designer footwear was not made for such a hurried pursuit. No matter, she would have to make do.

Rushing out the hotel's front door, Mira dashed into the alley and quickly turned off on the path skirting beneath the pool.

Eyes peeled for Elena's bouncing pigtails, she hurried toward the boardwalk as fast as her high heels would take her.

~ 24 ~

Distinctive Feet

STILL ON THE hunt for his dinner, Adam Rock returned to the bar inside the rainbow diner. Swiveling on his stool, he rotated his round body to survey the guests seated at the diner's rows of tables.

His beady vision quickly honed in on a single female, seated alone at a table near the boulders on the lagoon edge of the restaurant.

Rising from the stool, Rock strolled a few steps across the room to get a better look. He leaned over the railing on the restaurant's open wall and pretended to gaze out across the water.

He estimated the woman was in her late thirties. She was American, he judged, but not a tourist—she wore eyeglasses instead of sunshades. Nor was she a local. Her skin was far too pale.

A half-eaten plate of fish tacos had been pushed to one side while the woman scribbled in a small notepad. A professional-grade 35mm camera sat on the table beside the plate. She was a journalist, perhaps, or maybe a freelance writer.

Either way, he thought with elation, he had stumbled

upon a rare finding in Caribbean travel circles: a sheep separated from the herd.

HAVING SELECTED HIS target, Rock set his beer on the railing and shifted his posture to turn his back to the seated woman. Wetting his fingers on the side of the bottle, he worked the gold wedding band over his swollen knuckle and slipped it off his finger. Surreptitiously, he tucked it into the flap of his wallet.

He held up his hand, spreading his fingers wide. The skin was evenly tanned. No whitening demarcated the ring's earlier position. During his frequent trips to the Caribbean, the ring spent far more time in his wallet than on his finger.

Reaching for the beer, he took another steadying sip as he prepared to make his approach. It was important to come off as confident, but not overly so. Casual, but attentive. He was a pro, he told himself. After all, he'd done this maneuver countless times before.

Red Stripe in hand, he closed the gap on the remaining ten feet to his unsuspecting prey.

With his appetite now surging in voracity, he made his way, slowly but surely, toward the unsuspecting writer.

THE WOMAN FINISHED taking her notes and set down her pen. She gazed thoughtfully at the sailboats in the harbor, before a movement at her feet captured her attention. Grabbing her camera, she aimed her lens at a crab that had cautiously emerged from the boulders near her chair.

"Hey there, little fellow," the woman said as she zoomed in on the speckled brown creature. The beady eyes ogled up at her curiously.

At about four inches across, the crab was one of the larger specimens living in the diner's rocks and, consequently, well accustomed to being photographed. As the woman clicked away, it skated across the concrete floor beneath the table, maneuvering in a sideways crawl via the eight gangly legs attached to either side of its flat body.

The crab had two shorter front legs, designed to facilitate eating. The modified legs were equipped with pincers, which scooped up potential nourishment from the ground and fed it into the crab's mouth. Constantly in motion, the whirring mandibles filtered through the ingested items, spitting out anything that didn't suit the crab's taste.

The writer watched, fascinated, as the crab circled to within a foot and a half of the camera.

Then, suddenly, the creature darted back into the protection of the rocks.

The woman looked up to see a man in khakis and a mint-green golf shirt walking toward her table.

"Hello there, fellow traveler," he said smoothly as he reached for an open chair. "You look like you could use some company. Do you mind if I join you?"

"No, not at all," she replied, bemused. She flipped the notepad shut and slid her pen into her pocket. "Go right ahead."

"I'm Adam. Adam Rock. Pleased to meet you."

ROCK SLID INTO the unoccupied seat, expertly making non-threatening eye contact.

You're on a roll, he told himself as the woman looked over at him inquiringly. Just take it nice and easy.

"So, Mr. Rock, what brings you to St. Croix?" she asked conversationally.

"I'm an air-conditioning salesman." He puffed out his chest, preening in spite of himself. Pausing, he coughed for effect. "Regional sales director for the Caribbean."

She suppressed a laugh. "You don't say."

"There's nothing funny about refrigeration and cooling, ma'am," Rock replied with mock sternness. "Especially in this heat." He took a sip from his beer and added offhandedly, "I have a meeting with the governor tomorrow morning."

"Oh," she replied, playing along. "That is impressive."

Leaning back in his chair, Rock angled his head for a quick glance down at the woman's feet. She wore thong-style sandals, exposing bare ankles and, he nearly drooled at the sight, all ten of her toes.

He cleared his throat, trying to regain his composure.

"Do you mind if I ask your name . . ."

But his voice suddenly broke off as he caught sight of a woman in a black cloak and headscarf scurrying down the boardwalk outside the restaurant.

"I'm sorry," he said brusquely, jumping up from his seat. "Please excuse me."

The woman watched, baffled, as the salesman trotted to the bar, paid his tab, and then rushed for the exit.

OUTSIDE THE DINER, Rock glanced back and forth along the boardwalk, searching for the female figure who had disrupted his promising conversation with the writer.

Late afternoon had begun the transition to early evening. Dusky shadows spread across the downtown shoreline. Dinner crowds gathered in groups, choking the walkway, inhibiting his line of sight.

He quickly grew desperate, dodging around a pair of tall Danish tourists. A pack of screeching kids ran in front of him, further hindering his progress.

But then, he saw her, a hundred yards in the distance, walking across the green space outside the old Danish fort.

It had been ten years since their last meeting, but he'd recognized her in an instant.

Even with most of her body hidden by the dark cloak, he couldn't mistake the delicate step, the emerald green shoes, and . . . those dainty feet.

His fleshy face pillowed into a triumphant grin as he mouthed her name.

"Mira."

~ 25 ~

Just an Appetizer

THE TARPON MADE quick work of the chum and other left-overs from the diner's kitchen, and the fish soon retreated to the cooler water beneath the boardwalk, which had been shaded throughout the day.

As the lagoon returned to its previously calm mirror, the crowds moved away, leaving only a haggard West Indian woman standing next to her rusted shopping cart. She had arrived late to the feeding, having stopped at the brewpub's crab races a few doors down.

Gedda hobbled to the side of her cart and reached inside for a heavy plastic bag. While not quite as slushy as the bucket that had been brought out from the diner's kitchen, it had a similarly rank odor. The contents were a mishmash of skin and bones, likely the remains of something she'd culled from the Dumpster—or trapped and hunted down herself.

Whistling through the gaps in her teeth, Gedda carried the bag onto the footbridge. The tarpon instantly reappeared, as if the fish recognized her bent, rag-covered silhouette. Holding the bag out at arm's length, she leaned over the water and spilled the contents into the lagoon.

Gedda watched the tarpon engulf the meaty offering, a loving expression on her wrinkled face. She felt a primal connection with the beasts; she understood their ruthless, cannibalistic nature.

They shared a fearful symmetry.

WADDING UP THE plastic bag, Gedda limped over to a public trash can. With a last glance back at the tarpon, which were once more receding beneath the boardwalk, she dropped the empty bag through the bin's opening and wiped her hands on the lower folds of her skirt.

Gripping an ache in her hip, she straightened her crippled back and returned to her cart. As she wrapped her stiff hands around the cart's rusted handle, she glanced down the shoreline toward the old Danish fort.

Eyes narrowing, she focused on the solid figure of the air-conditioner salesman striding quickly along the boardwalk. There was a brisk purpose to his pace—as if he were hot on the trail of something . . . or someone.

Leaning toward the lagoon, Gedda whispered hoarsely to the tarpon.

"Done' go far, my friends. Tha wuddn't nuttin but an appetizah."

~ 26 ~

The Scale House

ELENA SPRINTED DOWN the boardwalk, chasing after her fleeing brother.

Night was falling quickly now. In the tropics, the setting sun dropped like an anvil, rapidly picking up speed as it neared the horizon. A mere wink could separate the sky's transition from flaming gold to charcoal gray.

"Hassan!" she called out, but it was difficult to make her voice heard over the noise from the evening crowds.

Despite the waning light, Elena could still make out Hassan's little shadow, chugging away in the dusky distance toward the Danish fort, running as if his life depended on it. If he heard her cry, he showed no signs of slowing.

"Serves me right," she panted as Hassan turned in to the national park's green space and disappeared from her line of sight. "I should have never told him about the Goat Foot Woman."

She stopped to grab a stitch in her side.

"Should have just let her eat him."

AFTER CATCHING HER breath, Elena set off again, this time at a more reasonable trot. A few minutes later, she reached the boardwalk's eastern terminus. She paused at the edge of the park, scanning the grounds for signs of her brother.

About fifty yards away, the gazebo stood in the center of the green space, the area empty save for a scattering of chickens pecking in the surrounding grass.

Just beyond, the fort's massive yellow walls glowed in the darkness, lit by a network of rectangular accent lights mounted at varying levels across the sprawling complex.

The fort was connected to the main road by a long concrete walkway. A pair of streetlamps had been positioned on either side of the path, but the spreading branches of the mahogany trees lining the pavement smothered most of that illumination.

Surveying the scene, Elena shook her head. It was impossible to be certain, but she didn't think Hassan had chosen any of these areas to hide. They were all far too exposed. She and her brother had played hide-and-seek in the park on numerous occasions, and she knew his tendencies.

A flash of movement to her right confirmed her hunch.

Raising the water pistol she'd picked out of the crab race toy bucket, Elena pointed the plastic barrel toward the arched entrance of the colonial-era Scale House, a box-shaped building located a short distance away on the park's southwest corner.

"I've got you now, little brother."

STEALTHILY, ELENA CREPT toward the squatty two-story Scale House.

The lower level's concrete walls were coated with the same yellow ochre as the Danish fort, but the paint on this smaller structure was stained with rot and wear. The Scale House was third in line among the park's colonial-era buildings for the recent wave of refurbishments, but its much-needed makeover would be months, if not years, away.

An exterior flight of brick stairs led to the Scale House's second floor, a wood-siding addition that had once served as an army barracks. Elena disregarded the building's upper half. She knew from her previous explorations that that portion was locked up tight. If Hassan was hiding inside the building, he had to be on the first level.

Elena glanced back toward the harbor. The sunset was starting to fade. Within minutes, the Scale House interior would be pitch-black. By now, she imagined, Hassan had likely scared himself silly.

Her little brother was notoriously afraid of the dark. In the bedroom the two of them shared, he kept three separate night-lights plugged into the wall by his bed, just in case one burned out while he was asleep. She had been woken on numerous occasions by his panicked screams.

Raising the water pistol to her chest, Elena smiled triumphantly, the signature expression of one sibling about to spring an unpleasant surprise on another. As she eased her head around the corner of the stone-rimmed entranceway, her eyes scanned the first floor's dimly lit room, searching for her brother's huddled form.

After the long run down the boardwalk, she was ready to give him a much-deserved fright.

INCHING HER WAY through the doorway, Elena blinked her eyes, trying to adjust her vision.

Despite the darkness, it was a familiar scene. During her mother's frequent trips to Christiansted, she and her brother had spent countless hours inside this room.

A massive scale had been built into the recessed center of the yellow brick floor. The apparatus had seen heavy use back in the colonial days, when all official shipments in or out of St. Croix, including the barrels of sugar, rum, and molasses that were produced on the island, passed through this building to be weighed. Officials in the Customs House next door had used those measurements to assess taxes and duties.

The weighing portion of the scale was a flat, tongue-shaped platform forged out of two-inch iron. The platform was hinged to a narrower counterweight fashioned into a shelf to which discrete numerical weights could be added until the seesaw swung into balance.

The scale was now cordoned off with an aluminum-pipe barrier, but it was easy to observe the mechanics of the device, either by leaning over the railing, or, in Elena's case, slipping beneath it.

After a momentary stop on the scale, Elena crawled back under the railing and slowly circled the room. Waving her water pistol in the air, she stopped at a display case mounted on the west wall.

This item was dedicated to another important feature of St. Croix's colonial past, one less tangible than the bulky scale. The display commemorated the island's connection to Alexander Hamilton, who spent much of his boyhood in downtown Christiansted. Most of the display space was taken up by a chart detailing Hamilton's complicated family tree—or rather, the complicated love life of his mother, Rachel.

According to the official story, Rachel wed her first husband at a young age, perhaps as part of an arranged marriage or under orders from her family. The couple did not get along very well, and their ongoing marital strife culminated in the husband having Rachel confined for several months inside the Danish fort. When she was finally released, she fled to Nevis, a couple hundred miles to the east.

It was there that Rachel met Hamilton's father, James. After a few years, Rachel returned to St. Croix with James and their two young sons. Details on the next aspect of the tale were fuzzy, but not long after their arrival, the second husband disappeared. Rachel remained in Christiansted with her children until she died of yellow fever three years later, leaving Alexander Hamilton and his older brother effectively orphaned. They were eventually taken in by a kindly shopkeeper. In 1773, Alexander departed St. Croix for the British colonies in New England and never returned.

ELENA STARED AT the shadowed display case, tapping the tip of the water pistol against the palm of her hand.

The Hamilton history was taught in all the local schools; it was a staple of the curriculum, meant to help cement the island's ties to one of America's esteemed founding fathers.

It had been an easy lesson for the young girl. Her mother had repeated the story to her countless times, and she knew the narrative by heart.

Her mother, however, told a slightly different account than the version she'd learned in school, Elena remembered, her brow furrowing.

In Mira's rendition, instead of the Danish fort, Rachel's first husband had confined her to a rustic lean-to with a leaky roof and an inoperable toilet.

~ 27 ~

The Ambush

THE LIGHT CRUNCH of footsteps sounded near the Scale House entrance. Elena spun away from the Hamilton display. Dropping to her knees, she crouched on the yellow-brick floor and listened intently.

She was surprised she hadn't found Hassan inside the Scale House—she had been so certain that this was where he would hide. The person shuffling outside the building had to be him.

Eyes narrowing, she tapped the tip end of the pistol against her chin. She was finally closing in on him. She was about to give him the scare of his life.

Bent over at the waist, Elena tiptoed around the scale's aluminum-piping barrier and headed toward the building's front entrance. A faint glimmer of light still glowed across the park outside. She could barely make out the unsuspecting shadow of a person standing beside the exterior wall.

She treaded silently toward the arched doorway, grinning as she imagined Hassan's shocked reaction. He might just pass out from the fright. Another couple of inches, she estimated, and she would whip around the corner for the big surprise.

As she closed the remaining gap, she aimed the pistol at the opening and puckered her lips, preparing to make a series of ammunition-mimicking *pops*.

Chuckling to herself, she eased forward, taking one last step—and screamed as a blast of water hit her square across the middle.

Hassan stepped through the Scale House entrance, proudly holding his super-soaker, which he had filled from the water tap in the men's restroom across the street.

"LOOK WHAT YOU'VE done, Hassan," Elena scolded, wringing out the front of her sundress. "I'm drenched. You've *soaked* me."

Hassan was unapologetic.

"The Goat Foot Woman is out to get me," he replied, waving his super-soaker in the air. "I couldn't wait for that Comanche guy." He leveled his weapon at his sister's torso and pulled back the plunger. "I had to defend myself."

Rolling her eyes, Elena deflected the soaker's nozzle away from her body.

"We should be getting back to the hotel," she said with a reluctant sigh. "They're going to be looking for us." She shuddered with apprehension. "You're going to wish you'd been eaten by the Goat Foot Woman after Mamma gets done with us."

THE TWO CHILDREN hurried out of the Scale House. Hassan stepped toward the open green space and the boardwalk's terminus on the park's north end, but Elena tugged him back, grabbing his sleeve.

She gestured toward the King Street curve on the opposite side of the building. "It'll be quicker if we cut through the alley. The hotel's right around the corner."

Just as the pair was about to turn for the street, however, a woman in a black cloak and headscarf bustled across the field toward the gazebo.

"Mamma," Hassan tried to cry out, but Elena reached across his chest and clamped a hand over his mouth, muffling the sound.

"Wait," she whispered. "There's someone else."

"Is it the Comanche?" Hassan asked, pulling himself free.

"No," his sister replied softly. She stared at the second figure, perplexed. "No, it's definitely not the Comanche."

~ *28* ~

An Unexpected Reunion

MIRA RACED INTO the green space outside the old Danish fort, her panic for her missing children now far exceeding her concern about whether her current husband might find out about her clandestine trip to Christiansted. Pushing back her headscarf, she frantically scanned the park.

"Elena! Hassan!" she called out hoarsely, but only a few chickens in the grass near the gazebo looked up at the muted sound. She'd spent the last twenty minutes searching the boardwalk, most of that time hollering the children's names, and her voice was almost gone.

She'd picked up a lead at the brewpub. A waitress had remembered seeing the children at that afternoon's crab race—Hassan had championed the winning crab. Unfortunately, the pair had left the pub as soon as they selected their prizes from the toy bucket.

The race announcer thought he'd seen the kids running toward the park, so Mira had rushed down the shoreline to the east end of the boardwalk, desperately hoping to catch sight of her wayward offspring.

Now, standing in the middle of the wide lawn beside the fort, she tried once more to shout their names.

A dry *croak* was all that came out.

She was going to have to rely on a visual search.

MIRA SLIPPED OFF her shoes and tucked them into the folds of her black cloak, the blisters on her toes, heels, and ankles the price for having worn them while navigating the boardwalk's rough splinters. The grass was more amenable to bare feet—the chicken-pecked dirt surrounding the gazebo's exterior far less so, she thought as she limped up to its front entrance.

The gazebo was the easiest place to check and quickly eliminate, she reasoned. The white gabled structure appeared to be empty, but she proceeded inside just to be sure. Her eyes swept over the floorboards, looking for any sign her children had been there, but she found nothing, no clue to their whereabouts.

Exiting the gazebo, she turned toward the Danish fort. With darkness falling, the spotlights were beginning to glow against the building's ochre walls. The fort was closed for the night; the iron bars on the front gate had been securely fastened shut.

Surely, Mira thought with despair, the children hadn't managed to get themselves locked inside.

She set off across the short span of connecting grass, intending to peek through the bars into the interior courtyard, but halfway to the gate, she stopped in her tracks.

She sensed a heavy presence moving in behind her. Her fists clenched tightly around the soles of the shoes, preparing to use them as a weapon.

A man's deep-throated whisper sounded in her left ear.

"Mira," he said softly. "What a pleasure to see you again."

~ *29* ~

On the Boardwalk

A BANK OF clouds slid over the moon as downtown Christiansted drifted through its typical evening routine. The dinner crowds swept in and then slowly retreated, leaving behind a residue of casual drinkers at the brewpub and on the stools surrounding the sugar mill bar.

Sweaty sailors mingled with tall Danes, while broody refinery workers swilled shots and kept to themselves. The crew from the dive shop guzzled down their day's tips, merrily recounting tales of hapless tourists and their escapades on the water. Off to one side, a mystery writer researching her next book quizzed a gathering of local Crucians about a local legend involving an old woman with a cleft foot who stole children off the street and ate them for dinner.

As the night wore on, bottled beer and Confusion cocktails were consumed in voluminous quantities. A competitive game of darts started in a cordoned-off section of the pub's open-walled second floor. The lines dividing the various groups began to blur as strangers became acquaintances and then fast friends.

The mood on the boardwalk cycled back and forth from quiet relaxation to boisterous energy. Occasional bouts of impassioned opinion-making punctuated the air. Discussions of docking cruise ships, abandoned dance clubs, and the ethics of the sitting governor could be heard, along with occasional random references to the infamous Goat Foot Woman.

"They had a picture of her hanging in the principal's office when I was in school," one man told the writer. "If you got into trouble, they'd haul you in there and make you sit on a chair in front of her. She had these buggy yellow eyes that stared out of the wall, straight through to your soul. Totally creeped me out." With a shudder, he took a long gulp from his beer. "I'm not kidding. That woman scarred my childhood."

Despite all this activity in and around the boardwalk, none of the night's revelers appeared to have noticed the earlier interaction between the woman in the black cloak and the man who approached her outside the gazebo—nor did anyone see what became of the cloaked woman afterward.

~ *30* ~

The Reception Desk

MIDNIGHT EVENTUALLY AGED to half past, and the bartenders announced their weary last calls. The dinghy captain made his final run from the boardwalk to the cay, and a lone taxi driver packed up the stragglers for the last shuttle to the resorts outside town. The few remaining inebriated stalwarts retreated without protest, disappearing into hotel rooms, apartments, or floating homes in the harbor.

As the hours slipped by, the streets of Christiansted gradually fell silent and still, save for a few chickens roaming the alleys and a haggard old woman rummaging through the garbage bins behind the boardwalk restaurants.

But inside the Comanche Hotel's dimly lit reception area, a dormant wooden figure began a slow awakening.

Dry bulging eyelids blinked. Thick knuckles cracked, causing the stiff joints to send out a series of creaking *pops*. Two boot-covered feet broke free from their rigid post and dropped to the ground.

Thunk. Thunk.

Reaching sleepily for a tray of breath mints that had been left out on the mahogany desk, the man's shadowed figure plodded heavily across the concrete floor to a small closet on the side of the room.

Thunk. Thunk. Thunk.

The closet door swung open, revealing a five-foot-long, tarp-covered package that had been crammed inside. The man bent to his knees and, with effort, lifted the load up onto his wide shoulders. Turning, he carried it toward the front entrance.

Thunk. Pause. *Thunk.* Pause. *Thunk.*

After navigating through the doorway, the man stepped into the alley outside the hotel. The moonlight glanced across his chiseled features, casting a menacing reflection in the door's glass panes. Apparently concerned that he might be recognized, he shifted the bundle's weight so that he could tug a hood over his head, masking his identity.

Grunting, the man centered the package across his left shoulder, balancing it lengthwise. Then he proceeded down the alley toward the harbor, a soldier setting off on a night-time mission.

Thunk. Pause. *Thunk.* Pause. *Thunk.* Deep breath.

With each labored step, the weight of the package moved farther down the man's back. Half a block later, a hole emerged at the bottom end of the tarp. The opening grew wider until a portion of the package's interior contents began to slide out and drag along the ground.

Thunk. Slide. Thunk.

It was a foot encased in a woman's green high-heeled shoe.

~ *31* ~

The Monster in
the Room

HASSAN HUDDLED IN a pile of blankets, pushing himself against a wall in a dark shadowed room, desperately trying to see into its blackened corners.

He gripped his plastic super-soaker as his brown eyes blinked, fighting back tears. Never in his short life had he been so horribly afraid.

"Comanche?" his voice squeaked into the night. "Mr. Comanche? Are you out there?"

He cupped his hands around his ears, bat-like, in an effort to amplify his hearing. Straining his senses, he listened for the slightest indication of movement. Every sound, no matter how soft or minute, required his intense analysis.

An easing sigh of wood floated down the hallway outside the room. Was that a routine shift in the floor's foundation— or the footstep of the Goat Foot Woman?

A cracking *snap* echoed down from the ceiling. Was that the regular nighttime contraction of a piece of wood—or the old hag hanging from the rafters, preparing to drop down on him from above?

Hassan cringed as a more familiar sound emanated from a few feet away. With a crunching of bedsprings and a fluttering of sheets, a belligerent beast grumbled groggily into the night.

The little boy trembled, his heart pounding in his chest as Elena lifted her head from her pillow and propped herself up on her elbows. Her curly hair, released from its pigtail ties, poked wildly into the air—giving her the look of a miniature medusa.

She scrunched her face into a tortured pout and whispered an exasperated plea.

"Hassan, go back to sleep already."

HASSAN HUNCHED DOWN in his sheets and covered his head with his pillow. He squeezed his eyes shut, trying to block out the terrifying images that instantly flooded his brain.

Where, he thought desperately, was the Comanche when he needed him?

Suddenly a shadow appeared against the blank wall on the far side of the room.

On the center stage the Comanche now occupied in Hassan's imagination, the wooden carving had grown in size and stature. The red-skinned warrior had morphed into a comic book–style action figure, equipped with overwhelming strength and an impressive athletic physique.

As Hassan now envisioned him, the statue possessed a far kinder, much more benevolent expression. The bulging eyeballs had shrunk to a less intimidating size, and his thick lips had bent into an iron smile.

One of the muscular hands waved out from the wall as the Comanche gave a steady nod of reassurance, as if guaranteeing his protection.

With this comforting image firmly fixed in his head, the little boy finally drifted off to sleep.

~~

IN TIMES OF great distress, the human mind often distorts reality, seeking solace in the realm of fantasy. The creation of a fictional world containing everything needed to secure a person's safety is a natural coping mechanism, more pronounced in those with vivid imaginations.

But sometimes, a statue is just a statue, an old woman is nothing more than a crippled hag with a creepy stare, and a man with a prosthetic leg is just a salesman . . .

Wait a minute. Strike that last item.

Adam Rock was always more than just a salesman.

~ *32* ~

The Gazebo

THE WEE HOURS of Thursday morning were just taking hold when a tiny alarm clock with a pitch-perfect ringer sang out its wake-up call into the Christiansted harbor. The jarring noise reached a few annoyed chickens roosting on the pier, a steely-eyed tarpon floating in the depths beneath, and its intended recipient, an Italian opera singer snoring on a fold-out bunk inside his tiny boat.

With darkness still blanketing the island, Umberto crawled sleepily out of bed. Stretching his arms over his head, he slipped on his cropped T-shirt and then quickly added running shorts and sneakers. Traversing the few feet to the kitchen, he poured himself a tall glass of bottled water and guzzled it down.

From a cushion on the floor, Senesino raised his head and yawned, releasing a soft trilling yowl suggestive of his operatic namesake. His canine partner, Farinelli, snuggled his snout deeper into the pillow, refusing to budge.

Petting both dogs on the head, Umberto stumbled grog-gily onto the back deck. Straddling the short gap from the boat to the pier, he proceeded down the wooden path to the boardwalk.

WAKING WITH EACH step, Umberto jogged along the quiet shoreline toward the national park's green space. By the time he reached the gazebo and trotted up its front steps, his heart was pumping, and he was fully alert.

He stood in the entranceway, gazing appreciatively at the fort's glowing ochre walls, the placid harbor, and the gentle water lapping at its edge.

It was a quiet, serene—secret—time of the day, one perfectly suited for centering thought and self-reflection. Not a soul was stirring; he was all alone.

He kicked off his tennis shoes and took a seat, cross-legged, in the middle of the gazebo floor. Unfolding his arms so that his palms faced upward, he pressed the tips of his fingers together, sucked in a deep, cleansing breath, and let the oxygen permeate his brain. He lifted his chin and sent a buzzing hum through his lips.

What a perfect way to start the day, he thought, thoroughly satisfied with life, the cosmos, and his own existence.

AS UMBERTO SETTLED into his moonlight meditation, a small rumbling began to gurgle in the pit of his stomach, the after-effects of the meal he'd eaten the night before.

The Rastafarian deli around the corner from the Comanche Hotel was one of his favorite dining spots. All of the deli's dishes were prepared from raw, uncooked vegetables that were artfully sliced, diced, and shaved into tiny slivers.

While Umberto wasn't a strict adherent to the Rasta culture's *Ital* principles, he admired the movement's dedication to food purity, and he ate at the deli a couple of times a week. Last night's special had been a red-beet salad, with the round roots cut into thin slices and configured with a nut paste into tiny vegetable sandwiches.

There was one small drawback to his Rasta dinners, Umberto thought as a hiccup disrupted his fond remembrance of the meal.

They were often followed by a series of aggressive burps, particularly when beets were at the center of the plate.

Just another part of the purifying process, he concluded with an extra-long belch.

A HALF HOUR later, his meditations complete and the gazebo's interior fogged with a distinct gaseous odor, Umberto began limbering up for his regular predawn yoga session.

Tossing his cropped T-shirt onto the floor, he assumed an upright stance in the center of the gazebo. Swooping his arms up over his head, he reached toward the rafters and breathed in a chest-swelling volume of early morning mist. He held the breath for as long as he could, before whooshing it out, dropping his hands to the floor as he expelled.

Crumpling into a crouched position, Umberto allowed his body a short minute of recuperation. Then he began again, his bony rear end slowly rising into the air. Arching his back, he lifted his chin upward and assumed a standard downward-facing dog position.

Focused on his straining muscles and the contortions of his spine, he transitioned into a state of extreme awareness. His senses were tuned in to every facet of his surroundings: the air, the sky, the sea, and . . .

Wait a minute. What was that?

UMBERTO COCKED HIS head to one side, the rest of his body remaining frozen in the awkward yoga pose. He stared up at the gazebo's ceiling, trying to confirm the source of the odd shuffling sound that had disrupted his concentration.

Releasing his downward dog, he crawled across the floor to the gazebo's south side and poked his nose over the railing. The sound continued as he peered through the darkness toward the wide sidewalk leading from the street to the fort's main gate.

The mahogany trees growing along the cement walkway blocked his view, but Umberto was able to identify three distinct noises: a human's labored breathing, the *thump* of plodding feet, and a long sliding *grate*.

He leaned farther out over the railing, trying to see into a clearing at the near end of the sidewalk where the streetlamp's beam was unimpeded.

Suddenly, a hooded figure emerged from beneath the trees—a dark-skinned man carrying a log-shaped bundle over his shoulders.

Umberto ducked behind the gazebo wall. Heart racing, he listened as the man drew nearer. After a few steadying seconds, he summoned his courage and once more peeked over the railing.

Whatever was in the bundle, it must have been heavy. It seemed to take all of the man's strength to move it forward.

Near the fort's front gate, the path curved, and the man turned his back to the gazebo, giving Umberto a better look at his load.

The package was wrapped in a black tarp, obscuring the bulky contents trapped inside, but a hole had opened up near the bottom end. Something had fallen out and was dragging along the ground.

This was the source of the grating sound.

Umberto gasped as he identified the object.

It was a pale foot encased in a woman's emerald-green high-heeled shoe.

~ *33* ~

The Captive

UMBERTO STARED OVER the gazebo railing, struggling to process what he had just seen.

As the hooded man lumbered up the concrete walkway leading to the Danish fort, the opera singer shook his head in confusion. He had to be mistaken. Surely the object poking out of the man's pack *wasn't* a human foot.

But as the shrouded figure hauled the lifeless human bundle up to the fort's front gates, Umberto had a perfect view of the back side of the tarp.

The item dragging along the ground couldn't be anything other than a leg attached to a woman's green high-heeled shoe.

QUICKLY, UMBERTO TUGGED his T-shirt over his head and slipped on his tennis shoes. Hunching over, he sneaked down the gazebo steps and moved stealthily across the grass toward the fort.

A red-painted guard tower positioned outside the front gates provided convenient cover. Tucking himself behind the tower's narrow cylinder, Umberto watched as the suspicious character shifted the human-sized bundle from his shoulders and dropped it onto the ground. After fishing a key from his pocket, the man unlocked the gates and heaved the package inside.

His concern mounting, Umberto glanced down the tree-lined walkway toward the King Street curve and the taxi stand at the far edge of the park. No one manned the station at this early hour. The drivers' alley would be vacant until at least seven thirty.

He scanned the surrounding downtown area, his eyes passing over a darkened Lutheran church, rows of unlit commercial buildings, and a span of empty streets. The entire space was devoid of activity. Nothing stirred but the chickens, and they were unlikely to provide any meaningful assistance.

The eccentric opera singer, of slender build and slight physique, seemed an unlikely hero.

Umberto pressed his hands across his shoulder blades, taking courage from the fearsome images tattooed on the skin beneath his shirt. Then he stepped nervously from behind the guard tower and up to the front gates—intent on following the hooded man, his tarp-covered cargo, and the trailing woman's shoe.

FLOODLIGHTS MOUNTED THROUGHOUT the fort lit up the recently renovated property, highlighting the yellow ochre walls, the dark green framing around the windows, and the white trim that detailed the numerous edges and railings.

The refurbishments were intended to restore the structure to its colonial-era condition, when St. Croix was at the heart of the Danish West Indies' sugar enterprise.

The fort's original construction began soon after the Danish government purchased the island from France. Built in the aftermath of St. John's 1733 slave revolt on the ruins of an earlier French bunker, the Danish fort was designed to present a facade of overwhelming military strength and to provide the infrastructure to mete out discipline to the agricultural island's growing slave population.

In order to dissuade aspiring rebel leaders from attempting to organize insurrections on St. Croix, punishments for even the slightest insubordination were swift and uncompromising. Anyone suspected of plotting rebellion was immediately brought to the fort for interrogation. The subsequent proceedings almost always resulted in the death of the accused.

The whipping post that had once stood outside the fort's front gates was one of the few features that had been omitted by the renovation committee; its display had been deemed too gruesome for historical recreation.

Even without the pole's grisly reminder, the place still evoked an eerie atmosphere, particularly when engulfed in predawn darkness.

As Umberto peeked timidly through the front gates, he couldn't help but think that the scene was playing out like one of his operas: a location tainted by tragedy of epic proportions, a scoundrel intent on adding his misdeed to the blood-soiled ground, and a conflicted protagonist battling both the dastardly villain as well as his own cowardly demons.

He could almost hear the opening stanzas of a full-piece orchestra, musically narrating the story. His vocal cords pulsed, as if preparing to enter the full-throated chorus—only this time, he didn't yet know how the song would end.

FROM THE GATED entrance, Umberto tracked the hooded man as he carried his load across the interior courtyard, which sloped upward to the fort's main building.

Concrete walls rose fifteen feet from the courtyard's yellow-brick floor; pointed iron stakes planted into the wall's upper edge added an additional six inches to its height. The villain and his captive were completely concealed within the fort's confines.

Umberto dithered at the gates, fearful of being discovered, but anxious to see more. He peered inside as the man lugged his bundle past a supply shed and a low-ceilinged bunker to a pyramid of concrete steps. With effort, the dark-skinned figure heaved his human cargo up the flight of stairs to a white-painted archway leading into the main building. Dragging the bundle across the stone floor, he soon disappeared down a center hallway.

Umberto remained at the courtyard's gated entrance, weighing his options. Much as he wanted to return to the safety of his boat, he couldn't bear to leave. Intrigue had begun to outweigh caution. This was, far and away, the most fascinating sequence of events he had ever observed on the Christiansted shoreline.

Slowly Umberto sneaked across the courtyard. Should the man up ahead turn and look back, the opera singer was fully exposed; the floodlights illuminating the area left him nowhere to hide.

But with every step, the musical background playing in his head grew in complexity and volume. As Umberto reached the main building and mounted the stairs to the central arched hallway, he was now firmly committed to his role.

Adrenaline coursing through his veins, he stepped from the audience and into the play itself.

MOMENTS LATER, UMBERTO stood in the arched foyer, peering down the unlit central corridor. The shadowed walkway was empty; the hooded man had already taken his human bundle farther inside the fort.

Beyond the foyer, the hallway opened up to a second, much larger courtyard, this one flat and rectangular in shape. The area was covered in a thick layer of grass, cut short and closely groomed to mimic the fort's once-military precision.

Cannonballs were stacked into two cone-shaped piles against the far wall in front of an ammunitions storage unit. Ten feet above, a colonnade held a row of colonial-era cannons. The machines' stubby metal cylinders were pointed out into the harbor, aimed toward the reef. Historically, the reef's natural barrier had proven to be a far more formidable threat to incoming vessels than the line of artillery, which over the course of the last three centuries had never once been fired.

AFTER A QUICK glance through the corridor to the enclosed yard, Umberto shifted his attention to the building's tunneled interior. Hallways branched off on either side, following the line of the fort's main walls.

Minimal lighting had been wired inside the structure, and the spotlights on the roof cast only angled shadows across the brick flooring. As Umberto ventured down the left-hand hallway, he waved his hands in front of his body, seeking to guide his way forward.

He took a few steps before his fingers brushed against the wooden door to a holding cell. Similar cramped compartments were scattered throughout the fort and honeycombed down into the basement. Any available space that might have been used to store provisions or prisoners had been configured into the layout.

The fort provided countless places to dump a body—or, Umberto realized, pulling his arms toward his chest—to lie in wait for a second attack.

It was as he stood there, nervously gripping his waist, that a sliding *bump* broke through the darkness.

THE HERO NEARLY abandoned his quest right then and there. His courage departed, leaving him weak-kneed and shaking. It took every ounce of Dante-inspired bravado to keep him from fleeing the building.

But after a steadying gulp and a renewed commitment to the opera music playing in his head, Umberto plastered his back to the wall and slowly inched down the hallway toward the source of the sound.

Carefully lifting one sneakered foot over the other, he gradually made his way to the corner of the building. He paused in a dark recess, waiting for another clue to the perpetrator's location.

Suddenly, the hooded figure moved into a patch of light, lugging his bundle toward an opening in the floor.

Umberto hardly dared to breathe; his face paled with anxiety. Wincing, he waited for an inevitable confrontation, but the villain appeared not to notice his presence.

The hooded man dropped his bundle to the ground and loosened the top portion of the tarp. Reaching inside the newly created hole, he pulled out the victim's limp hand and slung it and the attached arm over his shoulder. With a loud grunt, the man eased the dead weight down a narrow flight of stairs. Accompanied by several loud *bumps* and shoves, he moved into the lower basement level.

Straining his neck, Umberto looked down over the top of the steps to a small landing in the basement below. He watched as the man wrenched open an iron door and pushed his prisoner inside.

After a short pause, the hooded man returned to the stairwell, this time carrying an empty tarp loosely folded over his right arm. As he began climbing the steps to the fort's main level, Umberto dove into the nearest holding cell.

Yawning sleepily and moving with far greater ease now that he had been relieved of his human cargo, the man rapidly traversed the hallway to the main entrance.

Seconds later, he slipped out the front gates and vanished into the night.

UMBERTO LAY ON the dusty floor of the holding cell until he was sure the man had gone. Slowly picking himself up, he cautiously stepped back into the hallway.

He stood there for several minutes, horrified both at what he had just witnessed and his own fear-driven inability to intervene. Even now, he was struggling to work up the nerve to see the corpse that had been left in the basement below.

Draining his last reserves of musical inspiration, Umberto crept toward the opening in the floor that led down to the lower level. No more than a foot and a half wide, the stairwell was a tight fit, even for his slender build. The concrete steps had seen hundreds of years of use; the edges had been worn down to slick, dipping curves.

The small square of space at the bottom of the stairs was pitch-black, but the metal door that the hooded man had passed through creaked open under Umberto's touch. Ducking his head, he climbed over a rimmed threshold and into the basement's main prison chamber.

The ceiling was low, only half a man's height, so Umberto had to stoop as he entered. A rectangular-shaped window fitted with bars had been built into the upper portion of the near wall, providing a foot-level view of the front courtyard. A harsh beam from one of the fort's floodlights cut through the window, illuminating a human form slumped on the ground in the middle of the room.

The figure was turned on its side, facing away from the door. Freed from the tarp covering, the rest of the body's clothing was now visible. In addition to the high-heeled shoes, Umberto could make out a sleeveless green dress that ran from the shoulders to the knees. A mass of curly brown hair spilled out from the back of the head and spread across the concrete.

Umberto knelt to the floor, his internal opera transitioning to a sad, poetic refrain. The closing stanza took up a moving funeral dirge, with string instruments striking a somber mood.

His fingers trembling, he reached for the figure's stiff shoulder and rolled it onto its back—revealing an image that caused the music to terminate in the violent screech of a violin that had snapped a string.

"Oh," Umberto uttered with surprise, his face registering confusion. Stroking his chin, he leaned in for a closer look. "Hmm."

GEDDA STOOD ON the fort's upper colonnade, above the inner courtyard, as the dawn's early half light broke over the harbor. The sun's first rays glanced across the water, casting her crippled profile in a stark shadow against the glowing sky.

She'd held this position throughout the early morning epic. The elevated colonnade had given her a perfect view of the fort's front walkway, while the windows lining the inner hallway had provided enough glimpses to allow her to follow the action taking place in the fort's interior.

She now watched, her yellow eyes gleaming with delight, as the slender opera singer hefted a short unconscious man in a green dress and matching high heels out of the basement dungeon. The curious duo stumbled along the hallway to the main corridor, down the front steps, across the courtyard, and out the front gates.

Tilting her head back, Gedda let loose a hoarse cackle.

"Char-lee Bak-er," she whispered with a shake of her head. *"San-ta Cruz got you again."*

~ *34* ~

The Knockoff

CHARLIE BAKER BLINKED as the white fog of the last sixteen hours began to lift, and he returned to the blurry edge of consciousness.

He felt a slight swaying beneath his back and shoulders. Above him, morning light soaked through a row of oval-shaped windows. As the soft rays warmed his cheeks, a gentle lapping caressed the wooden sides of the boat where he lay. In the distance, a rooster *cadoodle*d out a wakeup call.

Yawning himself awake, he opened his eyes to a painful, yet familiar, throbbing on the back of his head.

Massaging his aching skull, he raised himself up onto his elbows and groggily surveyed his surroundings.

He was sprawled on a bench that had been built into one of the boat's inner walls. It was a small vessel, but functional. There was more than enough room for a man to sustain himself while at sea.

Charlie let out a queasy groan. He desperately hoped this boat was not afloat somewhere out in the Caribbean. Please let me be docked in the Christiansted harbor, he silently pleaded.

A framed newspaper clipping hung on the wall above his bed. The story featured a Boston opera performance by an Italian man in a tuxedo with a top hat and tails. Although Charlie had never once set foot inside an opera house nor listened to classical music, the man's face looked vaguely familiar.

A ceramic coffee cup clinked in its saucer, drawing his attention to the boat's kitchen area a few feet away.

Charlie rotated his head to look at a skinny man in running shorts and cutoff T-shirt sitting on a chair by the sink. A pair of wiener dogs with short stubby legs lay on the floor nearby.

"Café?" Umberto asked cordially, raising his cup.

"Yep. That should help," Charlie grunted as he dragged himself into a fully upright position.

Standing from his chair, Umberto reached for a carafe and poured out a steaming cup of coffee.

"Sorry, I'm fresh out of sugar," he said as he stepped across the boat and handed over the drink.

Charlie slurped down a sip of the hot liquid and skewed his face into a rough grin. His head was still pounding, but the coffee did wonders to deaden the pain.

He nodded at the clipping on the wall. "You're the guy in the newspaper story?"

Umberto nodded confirmation, bending his torso in a small bow.

"Well, then we're both out of costume," Charlie mused bitterly, looking down at the green dress still wrapped around his sturdy frame. The matching high-heeled shoes were laid out neatly on the floor beside his bunk. "Let me guess," he said crassly. "You found me in the old Danish fort."

"Mm-hmm," his host replied, arching his eyebrows inquisitively.

Charlie bent to pick up the nearest shoe and held it up to the light streaming through the row of portals.

There were few things that could add to the humiliation of being knocked out, dressed in women's clothes, and dropped off in the basement of the Danish fort, but his face soured as he studied the adhesive used to bind the heel to the shoe's sole.

"Hmph," he muttered, drawing on the fashion expertise he'd gleaned ten years earlier. "Just like the others."

Umberto took a puzzled sip of coffee as Charlie offered a cryptic explanation.

"It's a knockoff."

~ *35* ~

A Blended Family

ABOUT TWELVE MILES away from the Christiansted board-walk, inside a gated community located near the center of the island, the occupants of a secluded villa started their day.

Four children crawled out of their beds and stumbled sleepily down the hallway to the kitchen. The mother looked up from the stove as the pajama-clad figures slid into their seats at the table.

The two oldest siblings slumped in their chairs, their faces drowsily drooping toward their place settings. Their growing teenage bodies had reached the stage where sleep was a treasured commodity, one not easily shaken loose by an alarm clock. A knowing smile on her face, the mother set a basket of hot pita bread on the table between them. The reviving scent worked its magic, and eager arms reached in from either side to pull out steaming pieces of the folded flatbread.

The younger set was much quicker with the transition from dream world to reality. The pair chattered back and forth with each other as they reached for a turn style loaded with honey and a selection of jams.

"Hassan," Elena said with a head-tossing flip of her wild curls. "You kept me up all night with your carrying-on."

Her brother's mumbled response was lost in a mouthful of honey-drizzled cheese.

Elena leaned forward in her chair, testily tapping her fork against her plate.

"That's the last time I tell you anything about the Goat Foot Woman . . ."

The comment was cut short by the mother, who set down a glass of cold milk, diverting her daughter's attention.

"Oh, thanks, Mamma," Elena said between gulps of the drink.

ON THE SURFACE, the household was a typical example of many within the island's growing Middle Eastern community.

While Muslim groups had been present throughout the Caribbean for centuries, their influx into St. Croix's middle inland hills was a relatively recent immigration trend.

The members kept mostly to themselves, rarely venturing outside the confines of their close-knit society, and they generally went unseen by the island's non-Muslim residents. The families took their prayers at the local community mosque; the women shopped in community-owned grocery stores; and the children attended private community-run schools, often with the help of scholarships from the community-supported bank. Most group gatherings were held on restricted private land, well out of the sight of casual passersby.

St. Croix's landmass spanned over eighty-two square miles. It was a big enough island to afford even a sizeable sect the cherished privilege of privacy.

DESPITE THE APPARENT normalcy of that morning's breakfast scene, there were a few subtle indications that this particular blended family deviated somewhat from the rest of the quiet Muslim community's norm.

The regular Middle Eastern breakfast spread had been

supplemented by a few distinctly American dishes, including Elena's favorite, blueberry pancakes. Numerous decorating and design touches throughout the house conveyed a Western flair, and the children's rooms, particularly the teenagers', were indistinguishable from those of youngsters up in the States.

In addition, the predominant language spoken around the table that morning—despite years of tutoring in Arabic—and the only language ever used by the mother and her two older children, was English.

THE MOTHER WAS the one responsible for the family's Western influences. A delicate woman with pale skin and long honey-brown hair, she was an American, originally from the upper Midwest.

She had entered the Muslim community almost ten years earlier, upon her engagement to her current husband, Kareem. She'd brought with her two children, now teenagers, from her previous marriage.

While shielded inside the family's luxurious villa, the woman typically wore casual slacks and a short-sleeved blouse. Her hair, she kept tied in a loose ponytail, the end of which dropped to the small of her back. For special occasions, an extensive collection of high-end clothes filled the home's numerous walk-in closets.

She looked for all the world like the Minnesota housewife she had once been—until she prepared to leave the cloistered protection of her home.

Hanging from a hook on a coatrack by the front door was the black cloak she would put on over her clothes when she left to take the children to school or, in the case of her youngest, the kindergarten at the nearby mosque. A matching headscarf was carefully folded in a nearby drawer. She would secure that cloth over her head before exiting the villa.

Both garments were made of a lightweight Caribbean-optimized fabric, expertly tailored to flow when she walked, providing an unexpected venting of air.

Of course, even the most technologically advanced *abaya* could feel oppressive in the island's humid heat, but Mira had found the liberation provided by the clothing's concealment often far outweighed the downside of its physical confinement.

MIRA GLANCED ACROSS the table to her husband, whose head was buried behind the morning newspaper.

Kareem was a taciturn man, reserved in both speech and emotion. Even so, he had been unusually quiet after her late return home the previous evening. She had apologized for her absence, telling him that she had been delayed while visiting a female friend from the mosque. She'd been relieved when he'd accepted her excuse without further questioning.

If he had concerns about her whereabouts, he hadn't voiced them out loud. Still, there was a noticeable tension between them.

Placidly fulfilling her domestic role, Mira placed a bowl of boiled eggs next to his plate. Returning to the kitchen, she fetched the canister from the coffeemaker and topped off his mug.

Her husband would be heading to work in less than an hour's time. She just had to get him on his way without incident.

She smiled to herself, contemplating the future. After today, she would no longer have to worry about placating him.

His usefulness had run its course. Her second marriage was rapidly nearing its end.

~ 36 ~

The Second Husband

KAREEM CHUCKLED AS his daughter ran through the house, a wild tempest of swinging pigtails.

"I'm not going to school," Elena sang out, her ritual morning rebellion. "I'm going to play *all* day long."

Far more serious and subdued, Hassan climbed onto his father's knee to help him review the newspaper. The boy was precocious for his age, and, with a little assistance, he could read most of the headlines.

Everyone remarked on the striking similarities between Kareem and his son. They were mirror human images reflecting different ages, the same physical features at four and forty-five.

It was a point in which Kareem took great pride. Despite the trials and tribulations of his marriage and the Muslim community's frequently expressed disapproval of his wife, he regretted none of the choices that had led to his blended family and the gift of Hassan.

THE SEVENTH SON of a wealthy Riyadh merchant, Kareem immigrated to St. Croix from his native Saudi Arabia just over ten years earlier. With the hefty financial support of his father, he quickly built up a thriving grocery business on the far-flung Caribbean outpost. A network of five established shops now spread across the island, and a new venture had just opened in downtown Frederiksted. Bimonthly transport of duty-free goods on commercial airline crates from the Middle East had, in large part, facilitated his success.

Educated in English boarding schools and universities, Kareem was in many ways as Western-leaning as his wife. Proficient in several languages, he was equally comfortable in both religious and secular settings—which didn't mean he wasn't still intimidated by Mira's winsome beauty.

Unlike a number of the men within St. Croix's Muslim community, Kareem rarely wore the traditional garb of his homeland. He typically went to work in a starched cotton shirt and a sharp double-breasted suit.

Even in those instances when he took up a robe and headdress, he managed to convey a sense of affluent panache. The casual but overt sparkle of his jeweled watch and the hand-stitched shine of his leather shoes were intentionally designed to draw attention. He drove a fleet of expensive cars, and his family lived in one of St. Croix's most elegant villas.

Kareem's brash, flashy manner was off-putting to many in the community, and the showy way in which he flaunted his wealth caused much consternation among his brethren, although no one would dare voice such negative opinions out loud. Kareem was one of the principal benefactors to the community's school and mosque, and his financial support propped up the community bank.

Regardless, whatever discomfort might have been caused by Kareem's flamboyant personality paled in comparison to the ire generated by another aspect of his life.

Particularly among the staunchly conservative members of the community, no topic caused more rancor and suspicion than that of Kareem's spouse.

THE CONTROVERSIAL PAIR met not long after they both moved to St. Croix.

Kareem had been staying in a guesthouse connected to a villa owned by a family friend. The temporary lodging was serving as his home office while he perused the real estate listings and worked through the myriad details and regulatory hurdles surrounding the opening of his first grocery store. It had taken far longer than anticipated to get his business up and running, and the tedious process was sorely testing his patience.

He was inside the guesthouse, halfway through his fourth meeting of the day, this time with a potential vendor for the industrial-sized air-conditioning units that would be needed to cool the grocery's commercial space, when the fateful moment occurred.

Somewhere within the numbing discussion of BTUs and circuit loading, Kareem's eyes glazed over. Just as he tried to suppress a wide yawn, the sound of footsteps drew his attention to the front window. He looked out to see a woman walking up to the main house carrying several large packages in her arms.

The sight immediately wakened his senses.

During the weeks Kareem had spent holed up within the community's gated enclosure, he'd seen only cloaked female figures. This newcomer was distinctly different.

Her graceful figure was dressed in Western clothing, a tasteful but tight-fitting dress that put her slender curves on full display. Even as she struggled with the load of packages, her balanced stride conveyed a certain classic elegance.

The air-conditioning salesman noticed his client's distraction.

"What are you waiting for?" the man asked with a grin. He nodded toward the window. "Get out there and introduce yourself."

KAREEM JOGGED ACROSS the connecting lawn to the side-walk, knowing that the women inside the main house were likely watching his approach.

Self-consciously aware of the audience and awed by the unaccustomed physicality of the female form, he found himself completely tongue-tied. It was an awkward, unfamiliar sensation for the typically confident Kareem. To make matters worse, he tripped on the edge of the concrete path, and it took him several seconds to regain his footing. Even after he'd righted himself, he could think of nothing suitable to say.

Bashfully smiling, he motioned his offer of assistance. By the time they reached the front stoop, he had managed, through mime, to relieve Mira of all but one of her packages. Dutifully, he set them on the front porch, where he could hear the raucous giggles of the women on the other side of the door.

He retreated, red-faced and embarrassed, to the guest-house.

Back inside the office, he confided in the salesman.

"I don't know what came over me," he said apologetically. He pointed to his left hand and shrugged his disappointment. "She's wearing a wedding ring. She's a married woman."

The salesman let out a loud guffaw. Then he patted Kareem on the shoulder and winked encouragingly.

"I wouldn't let that dissuade you, my friend."

KAREEM WAITED UNTIL later that evening before venturing to the main house to inquire about the woman he'd escorted down the sidewalk. After a few discreetly placed questions that fooled no one, he learned that she had visited the main house in her capacity as a personal shopper.

While many of the community's female members preferred nice clothes and accessories to wear beneath their traditional garb, they often felt uncomfortable browsing in

Christiansted's boutique shopping district. The inventory was limited, and the dressing rooms quite small. Moreover, the West Indian shop staff tended to treat the cloaked women with suspicion.

Mira had stepped in to fill the void. Newly arrived on St. Croix herself, she had started a personal shopping service to help out with her family's finances. The women in the Muslim community had been a perfect target group. The first initial meetings had only had two or three participants, but the clothing club had rapidly expanded. On average, twenty or more shoppers were now showing up to peruse and discuss the merchandise Mira had collected.

Once or twice a week, Mira would meet with the women inside one of the community's private homes. After taking note of their sizes and style preferences, she would obtain a variety of items on credit and bring them to the next meeting.

The operation had quickly become a wild success. Mira had doubled the number of items she'd sold at the last meeting, and she'd left with a long wish list for the next get-together.

KAREEM WAS BESOTTED. He was intrigued by Mira's entrepreneurial spirit and enamored by her beauty. He tried desperately to dismiss her from his thoughts, but he couldn't get her out of his mind. Even as he tried to concentrate on the pending opening of his first grocery store, the obsession consumed his thoughts.

The morning of the women's next get-together, Kareem was once again meeting with the air-conditioner salesman. They had reached the last step of the negotiation process. The units needed for the store had been selected, and the contract terms had been agreed upon. Kareem's signature was the only piece missing.

The two men were seated at the office table sipping on cups of coffee, working through the obligatory chitchat before finalizing their business arrangement. The conversation inevitably turned to Kareem's romantic quandary.

"If only I could buy her a present," he said dreamily. "Something to let her know how I feel."

The salesman tapped the side of his cup as he considered Kareem's options. After several seconds, he snapped his fingers. "Get her a pair of shoes," he suggested with a wise pump of his eyebrows. "All women like shoes."

Kareem's face lit up, as if pleased by the idea. Then he frowned.

"But how would I know which ones to get?" Kareem asked worriedly. "How would I choose the right size?"

"Leave it to me," the salesman replied, a gleam in his eyes. "I was taking a stroll through the Christiansted shops the other day, and I saw just the pair." He cleared his throat. "Now about that contract . . ."

THAT AFTERNOON, KAREEM waited nervously for the women's shopping session to wind down. He paced back and forth inside the guesthouse, rehearsing the lines he'd devised to go with the gift.

When Mira finally emerged from the main residence with the day's unsold goods, he rushed out to the sidewalk to greet her.

Once more, words failed him.

He held out the ribbon-tied shoe box and mouthed silently, "For you."

The shoes, it seemed, spoke for themselves.

"Oh no, I couldn't," she said, but her hands had already wrapped around the corners of the box.

Kareem at last found his voice.

"I insist," he managed to croak hoarsely.

With a serene smile, she graciously accepted the present. Giddily, she sat down on the front porch, pulled off her old shoes, and eagerly slid on the new ones.

KAREEM RETURNED TO the guesthouse, his triumphant glee soon deflating to despair. He had no chance with the beautiful brunette, he thought ruefully, and he chided himself for making such an impertinent gesture to a married woman.

But a few days later, he received a tearful phone call. After a marriage-ending argument with her husband, Mira had packed her bags and fled to Miami with her two children.

Kareem caught the next flight out. He found Mira in the airport's departure lounge, her lovely face wan and tearstained. She'd been unable to get seats on the connecting flight to Minneapolis, so she and the kids were stranded in the waiting area until a row for the three of them opened up.

He still remembered every detail of that crucial moment. It was the middle of the airport's early evening rush. Hundreds of people hurried past as he took Mira's hands in his. The two children stood in the near background, a girl and a boy, neither of them old enough to understand what was happening.

Kareem took one look into those bewitching green eyes and proposed on the spot.

It took another nine months of wooing, but Mira finally accepted. As soon as her divorce with Charlie was finalized, she converted to Islam and married Kareem.

On the day of the wedding, Mira wore a traditional Middle Eastern dress and headscarf for the ceremony, but in the private celebration afterward, she danced in the banquet hall in her favorite new pair of green high-heeled shoes.

~ 37 ~

The Rumors

AFTER SUCH A scandalous beginning, Mira and Kareem's relationship was bound to be the target of gossip and rumor. Among the members of the otherwise quiet and secluded Muslim community, the topic was too tempting to resist. While Kareem received his fair share of criticism, the bulk of the speculation revolved around Mira.

Had she married Kareem for his money? Was her religious conversion sincere? What had happened to her first husband? And why did he never visit his children?

Adding fuel to the fire, in recent years, Mira had begun to venture farther and farther afield from the community's safe confines.

She made frequent outings to Christiansted, where she was reportedly sighted wandering through the clothing boutiques, trying on jewelry and otherwise perusing the merchandise. While her kids were at school or the community child-care center, she flew day trips to St. Thomas and San Juan, usually returning with shopping bags stuffed full of new purchases. She was always properly covered in a veil and a flowing black cloak, but the solo excursions still drew interest and, in some quarters, vigorous disapproval.

Of course, the most intense scrutiny came from Mira's former clients, the community women who now envied her voluminous—and apparently ever-growing—wardrobe. Despite the women's endless angling for an invitation to Mira and Kareem's luxurious villa and a tour of its countless walk-in closets, few had ever been inside. The secrecy only deepened the intrigue surrounding Kareem's mysterious wife.

At any social gathering, the most pressing behind-the-scenes question was posed by the female guests.

What was Mira wearing beneath that *abaya*?

FOR THE MOST part, Kareem took all this in stride. He enjoyed the attention that focused on his beautiful wife; it fed into his already healthy ego. He soaked up the adoration and disregarded the negative, writing it off as petty jealousy. He took confidence in knowing that, upon entry into any given room, his presence and that of his wife were immediately noted.

Kareem dismissed without worry the fact of his wife's previous marriage—or at least, he valiantly tried to do so. He had welcomed Mira's two older children into his home and gladly paid their tuition at the private community school.

While there was no doubt that Elena and Hassan received preferential treatment, Kareem tried his best to be a good father to his stepchildren, particularly since their biological father had apparently fallen out of the picture.

But the stepchildren, now teenagers, had never warmed to Kareem. They were emotionally distant and stiffly polite, wordlessly unaccepting of his role in their lives.

MIRA NEVER SPOKE of Charlie, and Kareem preferred not to ask. As far as Kareem knew, the ex-spouses had no contact—and that was just fine with him.

In the nearly ten years of their marriage, the topic had

been inadvertently broached only once. Kareem had suggested taking the family to St. John for a short weekend vacation. He had never been to the tiny island, but he'd heard its national park beaches were well worth the trip.

He'd read the look on Mira's face the instant he made the proposal. Silently, she shook her head. It was the tiniest of movements, but the communication conveyed volumes.

"Then again"—Kareem had shrugged, quickly backtracking—"they say it gets awfully buggy over there. Why don't we just go to Cane Bay instead? That'll be much more convenient."

Mira smiled her relief, and Kareem internally vowed never again to mention St. John.

The next time he had a private moment in his office, he pulled out a local map. He sized up the distance between his island and that of the ex-husband, taking comfort in the forty-mile buffer of sea between them.

⌒

KAREEM SET DOWN his morning coffee and gently helped Hassan off his lap. He smoothed out his slacks and straightened the tie over his collared shirt. He was dressed to precision, despite the island heat.

"Well, Mira, I'm off," he said, reaching for his keys. "I'll be at the Frederiksted store again today. I'm going to have to stay onsite for another week or so. I want to make sure everything's running smoothly before I hand things over to the new manager."

Mira smiled serenely as he kissed her on the cheek.

Kareem had tried to dismiss his concerns about where she'd been the previous evening. He had vowed long ago not to let the community's gossip and innuendo affect him.

But beneath that outer shell of confidence a seed of doubt was growing.

The excuse she'd given him had been blatantly false. He knew she hadn't been with another female friend from the mosque.

He had smelled the whiff of cigarette smoke on her

breath when she finally came home. He'd seen the aversion in her eyes when she complained of a headache and retired to the bedroom.

Much as he steadfastly ignored the swarm of whispers that constantly surrounded his wife, he couldn't help but hear the latest rumors that she'd been sighted on the Christiansted boardwalk several times over the last couple of months, going in and out of the Comanche Hotel.

Some had even speculated that Mira had been secretly rendezvousing with her first husband and that he had flown down from St. John on the seaplane to meet her.

It was more than Kareem could bear to contemplate, but he couldn't tamp down his niggling suspicions.

Ten years was a long time for jealousy to fester.

KAREEM SLIPPED ON his coat and walked toward the foyer.

"I'll be home after six," he said, stopping for a last look back at the kitchen.

She nodded and then turned to clear the breakfast table.

Pulling open the front door, Kareem stepped out into the damp morning heat. As he crossed the driveway to his car, his handsome face pinched with worry.

He desperately hoped she would be there when he returned.

~ 38 ~

The Morning's Entertainment

CHARLIE BAKER CRAWLED out of Umberto's boat, carrying the green shoes but still wearing the dress.

He'd politely declined the opera singer's offer of his spare pair of running shorts and cutoff T-shirt. One whiff of the other man's clothing had convinced Charlie he was better off in the green dress.

Besides, he didn't have much time left before the early morning seaplane departed. He suspected he would find his wallet, ticket, and, most important, his regular clothes in the room on the top floor of the Comanche Hotel. That's where Mira had left his personal items after their last two meetings, when she'd pulled the same stunt on him.

Obviously, the gas mask hadn't provided any deterrent to whatever mechanism she'd used to render him unconscious.

He glanced down at the dress and groaned. He'd been a fool to get caught up in her tricks—*again*.

"What in the heck is that woman up to?" he muttered bitterly.

And where, he wondered with renewed frustration, were his kids?

AFTER SCAMPERING DOWN the pier and across the board-walk, Charlie ducked behind the sugar mill bar. With a quick glance at the empty serving station, he set off across the rough concrete and coral path that skirted the courtyard, hoping to avoid the bartender's notice.

A trilling whistle told him he'd been unsuccessful.

Grimacing, Charlie looked back to see the bartender holding a crate of supplies at the mill's rear entrance. The man had a whimsical expression on his face as he stared at Charlie's outfit.

Charlie shrugged and offered a glib explanation, one perfected by his two previous experiences with wearing a dress in downtown Christiansted.

"I had a wild night."

The bartender nodded his approval. As he carried the crate inside the mill, he called out over his shoulder.

"Next time, send me an invite!"

GRUMBLING UNDER HIS breath, Charlie resumed his deter-mined march to the Comanche Hotel.

Halfway down the path, he spied the old hag, gripping the handle of her shopping cart like a walker. She was in a narrow alley on the opposite side of the courtyard, easy to miss where she stood motionless in the shadows.

He paused, self-consciously smoothing the wrinkled folds of the dress, as the woman tilted her head to look at him. Her yellow eyes glinted mischievously; her thin lips curled into a shrewd smile.

Charlie had the impression that she knew exactly why he was dressed in this manner.

SHRUGGING OFF THE old woman, Charlie continued along the paving stones leading to the tunnel beneath the pavilion. The rough surface caused even Charlie's toughened soles to send out tender shoots of pain, but he refused to consider putting on the high heels. He would have walked on bloody stumps before resorting to that contingency.

With relief, he rounded the corner into the alley that ran in front of the hotel. He was just fifty feet of smooth pavement away from the entrance. Maybe he could sneak inside without running into anyone else.

But as he approached the hotel's front doors, a couple of taxi drivers peeked around the alley's far corner. Word of the curiously dressed man in the green dress had apparently reached the taxi stand on the next street over. The men's eyes widened at the spectacle as Charlie trotted down the alley.

"Got to make sure everyone's thoroughly entertained," he said with a wry wave to the onlookers.

AT LAST, CHARLIE pulled open the hotel's glass door and stepped into the reception area. Panting, he approached the front desk.

The woman seated behind it yawned as she looked up. Her expression instantly transitioned from one of boredom to startled concern.

"What happened to you?" she demanded warily.

Before Charlie could answer, she shook her head and held up a hand, palm facing outward. "No, no. That's okay. I don't want to know."

"I seem to have lost my room key," Charlie said, a touch of sarcasm in his voice. "It's number seventeen."

Raising her eyebrows, the woman reached into a drawer and pulled out a spare.

"Do you have ID?" she asked sternly.

Charlie stepped back from the desk and motioned down to the dress.

"I seem to have misplaced my purse."

"Hmph," she said, grimly looking him up and down. Reluctantly, she slid the key across the desk toward him.

"There'll be a charge for that." She paused and rolled in her upper lip before adding, "Just like last time."

Charlie grunted wearily. On top of everything else, Mira had the nerve to book the room under his name.

"Put it on my bill."

~ 39 ~

The Governor

THE SEAPLANE FLOATED at its dock in the Charlotte Amalie harbor, bobbing in the water as it waited for the first passengers of the day to board the early morning flight from St. Thomas to St. Croix.

Adjusting his dark aviator sunglasses, the pilot climbed into the narrow cockpit and began his preflight ritual. He quickly scanned the dashboard's numerous dials and gauges. Then, he opened his regulatory notebook and began checking off the required list of instrument readings.

A moment later, he looked up from the console as a group of heavyset men in suits and ties marched down the pier toward the plane. They presented their boarding passes to the steward monitoring the loading process and began tromping over the gangplank. The craft sank several inches as the men climbed into the passenger cabin.

Muttering, the pilot reached for a dial positioned beneath the fuel gauge, adjusting the craft's weight settings.

The Governor and his entourage packed a full load.

AFTER COMPLETING HIS preflight check and assuring himself that the plane was ready for operation, the pilot picked up a handheld radio receiver and adjusted the channel to the frequency for the hangar operator at the Christiansted harbor.

"Hey, Chuck," the pilot said, pressing on the receiver's transmission button. "This is Charlotte Amalie."

He cleared his throat, preparing to pose the same dreaded question he asked every morning.

"What's the status on the lobster hunter?"

⌒⌒

THE GOVERNOR EASED his substantial rear end into the seaplane's tiny passenger seat. Sucking in his breath, he wrapped the seat belt across his bulging middle and secured the buckle. With a grunt, he shifted his weight, trying to find a more comfortable position. The seaplane was a convenient, if painfully compact, form of transport.

Settling in for the short flight, the Governor leaned his head against the seatback and mentally reviewed the day's itinerary.

He had several business meetings scheduled for his visit to St. Croix, most of them obligatory glad-handing sessions with various economic interests. He'd done thousands of similar meetings during his four-and-a-half-year tenure in office—and he'd found each and every one of them tedious.

The Governor let out an involuntary yawn. He depended on his aide to take notes during these predominantly one-sided conversations and to prompt him when he needed to speak up or pay attention. He generally occupied himself with eating (these get-togethers almost always involved some type of food) or sleeping (he'd mastered the technique of dozing with his eyes half-open).

He felt a semi-conscious snooze coming on already. The mere thought of all that endless chitchat made him both drowsy and hungry.

But as the seaplane began to motor away from the dock, the Governor shook off the yawn and dismissed the daydream of his coming breakfast. He needed to focus on his upcoming public appearance.

The main purpose of his St. Croix trip was to attend the afternoon's Transfer Day celebrations, commemorating the anniversary of the sale of the Danish West Indies to the United States.

As the headlining speaker, the Governor faced a difficult task. He would have to strike a delicate balance to avoid offending any of the disparate viewpoints in the crowd.

The event was being held at a restored Danish plantation in the rain forest north of Frederiksted, with several hundred spectators expected to attend. The audience would be evenly split between the Governor's West Indian constituents (many of whom traced their ancestry back to relatives once enslaved by Danish colonials) and a number of Danish tourists (many of whom traced their lineage back to the enslavers).

THE GOVERNOR STROKED his round chin, reflecting on the upcoming festivities. Transfer Day, he mused wryly. He could think of few milestones less appropriate for celebration: the historical convergence of two competing occupiers, neither of which had treated his homeland with the respect it deserved.

The islands were sold to the Americans in 1917, after years of lukewarm negotiations. By the time the transaction was finally completed, the Danes had been trying to unload their Caribbean colony—and its corresponding financial burden—for over fifty years.

The world sugar market had long since declined, rendering the islands' agricultural economy unsustainable. With few viable trade connections remaining between the territory and its European landlord and maintenance costs growing by the month, the Danes had been eager to find a buyer.

American interest in the Caribbean territory was based primarily on its strategic geopolitical value. Given its close proximity to the Panama Canal, the Virgin Islands were seen as a possible site for a future naval station.

The United States waivered on the potential Virgin Islands purchase through several administrations before at last agreeing to acquire the territory for $25 million. An unverified rumor that then-rival Germany had placed a bid on the property was the tipping point that pushed the sale through.

Members of Congress were soon hit with a serious case of buyer's remorse. The speculations over Germany's intentions were at best overstated, if not out-and-out lies. Moreover, days after the sale was completed, the United States formally entered World War I, and the country's foreign policy shifted to focus squarely on Europe. The Virgin Islands' strategic military benefits never came into play.

Meanwhile, the mounting costs for necessary infrastructure improvements to roads, hospitals, schools, freshwater conservation, and sewage treatment facilities caused many in Washington to see the acquisition as a boondoggle.

The hostile sentiments from Congress were relayed down to the islands and quickly reciprocated. Although the Islanders had initially welcomed the U.S. purchase, they soon became disillusioned with their new landlords. Instead of the much-vaunted American democracy the residents had been expecting, they were subjected to continued autocratic rule.

Immediately following the transfer, the U.S. territory was set up under the administration of the navy, with a series of naval officers serving as the appointed governor. Virgin Islanders were given no say in the matter.

Over time, the islands' governance shifted to the Department of the Interior, and a legislative assembly with democratically elected members gradually evolved. But it would be 1970 before the people living in the US Virgin Islands were allowed to choose their chief executive officer. To date, they had no vote in the U.S. presidential election.

THE GOVERNOR FOLDED his hands over his rotund belly and sighed tensely. The mental review of the day's historical backdrop hadn't made him any more enthusiastic about his upcoming speech.

His aide had been working on the address for weeks, and the text had been thoroughly vetted by the Governor's numerous advisors and consultants. He was equipped with the right words; he just had to execute the delivery.

His brow furrowed as he considered the expected audience.

The Danish delegation would be headed by the country's U.S. ambassador and his wife, who had flown down from New York for the event. But while the Danes were sending a top-level diplomat, the official representative from the U.S. government would be notably absent.

The islands' elected congressional delegate had backed out at the last minute, blaming a legislative emergency up in DC. An unpaid intern had been nominated to attend in her place.

Since the VI's representative was allowed only limited participation in the U.S. Congress, the Governor couldn't imagine what contingency could have arisen to prevent the woman's appearance, but he didn't hold the dodge against her.

The Governor chuckled ruefully. He would have gladly passed off his duties to an intern if he'd thought he could get away with it.

THE SEAPLANE PULLED away from the pier and rumbled across the water, slowly gaining lift as it picked up speed. With the plane rising into the sky above Charlotte Amalie, the Governor glanced out the nearest oval-shaped window and looked across at the white-painted Government House on the hill above the harbor.

Beyond the inherently touchy nature of the Transfer Day celebrations, this trip would be fraught by an additional layer of complication, difficulties that he would encounter on an entirely different front. He was leaving his home base, an area where he enjoyed a relatively high approval rating, and headed into far more fractious terrain.

The Governor rubbed his forehead. He wasn't thinking

about the spear fisherman who had been terrorizing the seaplane's water runway in the Christiansted harbor for the past several weeks—although the rogue swimmer was somewhat emblematic of the problem.

The island of St. Croix was a minefield of easily discharged emotions, and the chief executive of the territory was the largest target, both literally and figuratively, upon which to lob complaints.

SANTA CRUZ HAD always been a troublesome place to govern. Ever since 1493 when the native Carib gave a working over to Christopher Columbus and his Spanish crew at Salt River, the island had taken great pride in its orneriness. Its residents had never been amenable to extraterritorial rule, be it French, Danish, American, or Thomasian.

Being the most recent offender, St. Thomas bore the brunt of the current grudge.

It didn't help matters that the bulk of the territory's tourism traffic focused on St. Thomas and, to a lesser extent, St. John.

A popular cruise ship stop and vacation destination, Charlotte Amalie had several blocks in its downtown district dedicated to duty-free shopping, with stores specializing in fine jewelry, watches, and perfume—all located within a short walk of its deepwater port.

In addition to the frequent cruise ship activity, St. Thomas boasted several full-service resorts. A number of commercial flights from the States made the island an easily accessible getaway, so a high percentage of the American tourists flying into the territory booked rooms on the Rock.

A short ferry ride away from Charlotte Amalie, St. John laid claim to a huge national park, whose beaches, most notably the one at Trunk Bay, were ranked among the best in the Caribbean. While St. John had far fewer options for overnight accommodations, it saw a high volume of daily traffic from St. Thomas, both in terms of long-term visitors and day-tripping cruise ship passengers.

Comparatively speaking, St. Croix was an afterthought,

a barely visible line on the horizon, with fewer flights, generally less luxurious accommodations, and limited public-beach access. Seaplane arrivals to the Christiansted harbor were greeted by a towering electrical plant eyesore; commercial flights landing at the island's interior airport couldn't help but fly over the massive oil refinery that dominated the southern shoreline.

Saddled with being both distant and different, Santa Cruz had developed an innate resentment toward its sister Virgin Islands.

If it couldn't be beautiful, it could at least be belligerent.

Crucian voices were among the loudest of those pointing out that the West Indians living on the islands at the time of the transfer hadn't been asked to verify the territory's sale to the United States. Several even likened the subsequent governing arrangement to a new form of slavery. Others used this historical fact pattern to argue for the granting of Native Rights (tax exemptions, land redistribution, and public office requirements favoring those who claimed heritage back to residents from the islands' original transfer).

That the territory's chief executive was now an elected position had done little to temper the perceptions of inequality and injustice.

Indeed, it was not unusual during public meetings—particularly those held on St. Croix—for the Governor to find himself lumped together with his colonial predecessors in criticisms of corruption and ineptitude.

THE GOVERNOR SIGHED with resignation. Of all this, he was well aware. He looked down at his wedding ring. He was, after all, married to a Crucian.

His wife would be joining him at the Danish plantation later that afternoon. She'd flown down a few days earlier so that she could spend time visiting with her family. They would all be dining together that evening.

At the thought of his in-laws, the Governor let out an

audible groan. That was just what he needed to top off the day—a whole clan of contentious Crucians.

He glanced through the plane's side window. It was a short flight, and they would be landing shortly. The first shadows of the Christiansted shoreline were already starting to appear in the distance. Assuming the spear fisherman didn't cause them to capsize upon landing, he would be strolling down the Santa Cruz boardwalk within the next half hour.

The Governor was an easily recognizable figure, particularly when accompanied by his suited entourage. He would likely run into several constituents on his way to his first meeting.

He expected a frosty reception.

~ 40 ~

A Morning's Surveillance

GEDDA STOOD IN the alley alongside the gravel courtyard behind the Comanche Hotel, watching the morning unfold. Her gnarled hands gripped her shopping cart's rusted metal handle as she tracked the pedestrian movements along the boardwalk. Her gaze soon focused on the line of small boats moored off the pier that jutted into the harbor near the sugar mill bar.

The boat tied to the pier's fourth slot rocked in the water as a short man in a green dress peeked out its rear cabin door.

Two curious dachshunds and a bemused opera singer looked on as Charlie Baker crept onto the boat's back deck, trying to estimate how fast he could run the length of the pier, across the boardwalk, and down the path to the Comanche.

With a here-goes-nothing shrug, the cross-dressing contractor set off at a sprint, the hem of the dress swinging at his knees. He slowed near the sugar mill bar, pausing for a brief exchange with the bartender. Then he goose-stepped onto the rough path circling the courtyard.

As Charlie reached the lower edge of the swimming pool, he noticed the old woman standing in the alley, and for an eerie moment, the two exchanged stares.

Gedda gummed the gaps in her lower jawline, sucking on the toothless openings. Her hollowed cheeks sank into her gaunt face; her yellow eyes glittered in the shadows.

Charlie fiddled nervously with the dress's fabric before dropping his gaze and scurrying along the sharp-edged paving stones that led beneath the hotel's pavilion.

Gedda smiled as she watched him disappear down the passageway. Her dry lips parted to release a cackling snort.

In her opinion, he was starting to get the hang of wearing those dresses.

GEDDA HOBBLED OFF down the alley toward the King Street taxi stand where the drivers had begun to gather.

Her left foot dragged across the pavement, a dull scraping sound that, together with the cart's squeaking wheels, amplified the notice of her arrival, but the men paid her no attention. Settling into their folding chairs, the drivers pulled foil-wrapped breakfasts out of paper bags and dug into both their food and the day's gossip.

Gedda's crippled body swayed to and fro as she listened to the drivers' hushed voices, filtering through their commentary for any tidbits of interest.

The Governor's pending arrival was briefly touched upon, generating several jealous remarks about the private limousine service he and his team would be using to convoy across the island to the Transfer Day ceremonies. A few of the men speculated on the whereabouts of Emmitt, who was conspicuously missing that morning, and wondered if the tall Crucian had scored a freelance driving job with the limo company. The suggestion set off another round of grumbling.

The conversation then turned to the cruise ship that had just docked off the island's west shore. There was a fair amount of commiserating about the fickle nature of cruise ship passengers and the unfortunate logistics of trying to lure them across the island to Christiansted. The drivers wondered if the man from Nevis was having any luck picking up riders at the Fredriksted pier. They admitted they would feel foolish if he wound up bringing a full load of passengers to the boardwalk.

With those topics exhausted, the rest of the conversation focused on the morning's chicken count. After several minutes of good-natured ribbing and more than a few crude poultry jokes, they began placing the day's bets.

Gedda waited as the men called out their wagers. Then she smiled knowingly.

Despite their enthusiasm, she didn't think any of the drivers would hit on the winning number, meaning the pot would roll over to the next day.

She suspected the Nevisian driver would still manage to clean them out when he returned the following morning.

HAVING FINISHED WITH the taxi drivers, Gedda meandered out the alley and down the sidewalk toward the national park's green space. After circling the Scale House, she crossed to the boardwalk's eastern terminus. With stiff, stilted movements, she hobbled down the wooden walkway, which was starting to see more action as the shoreline came alive.

The staff at the rainbow-decorated diner had just finished hosing down its concrete floor. The waitresses bustled about, wiping down tabletops and laying new place settings. Several sunburned Danes began wandering sleepily in from the attached hotel for the breakfast service.

A few doors down, the spear fisherman splashed out of the harbor. Carrying his spear and snorkel in one hand, a wire cage holding his early morning lobster catch in the other, he walked down the boardwalk toward a seafood restaurant. The chef, who stood outside negotiating with a group of sailors for a haul of fresh tuna, beckoned to the snorkeler, inviting him to bring the lobster over for inspection.

AS THE SPEAR fisherman strutted soggily past, the sugar mill bartender poured the last bag of ice into the chests behind his counter. Resting his back, he leaned against the mill's coral-rock wall and stared out at the harbor. His soppy gaze centered on a large sailboat and its female captain, a woman with dirty-blonde hair and sun-kissed skin.

His girlfriend was hard at work readying her ship for the day's snorkel tour to Buck Island. She'd kicked off her flip-flops and left them on the dock. Barefoot, she scrambled about the boat, expertly adjusting its sail and riggings.

She wore a pair of cutoff jeans and a loose-fitting top over a bikini swimsuit. As she bent to secure a knot around a cleat mounted to the boat's topside, the shirt slipped off her left shoulder, revealing a nautical tattoo that spread across the center of her upper back. The detailed black-ink design depicted a ship's helm overlaid with an anchor.

The bartender sighed, staring at the beautiful tattoo—but failing to appreciate its significance.

He was but a temporary fixture in her life. She was forever partnered to the sea.

Oblivious to his dispensable status, the bartender reached for a paper cup of coffee and took the last cold swig, swallowing the liquid with lovesick gusto.

He called out cheerfully at the hag as she passed his station.

"Morning, Gedda."

SHAKING HER HEAD at the young man's foolishness, Gedda pressed on.

About a hundred yards away, she spied the Governor's heavy suited figure plodding out of the seaplane hangar. He was accompanied by his ever-present entourage of aides and advisors. Bodyguards flanked the front and rear of the procession, wireless transmitters feeding into their ears, an arsenal of weaponry strapped to their waists.

The boardwalk's morning bustle screeched to a halt as the Governor marched past, a ripple of upturned faces gawking at the territory's senior politician.

There were a number of icy stares, a couple of muttered curses, and a scattering of nodding glances.

Only the spear fisherman stepped forward to offer the Governor a wet handshake.

GEDDA BUMPED HER creaky cart toward the vacant structures near the boardwalk's west end. The dance club's abandoned shell stood disturbingly empty. The coconut boys had not returned the previous evening for their share of the pork chop leftovers from the brewpub. They'd last been seen riding in the bed of Nova's pickup truck, headed for the other side of the island.

After pondering the unoccupied porch steps for several seconds, Gedda parked her cart near a pile of trash outside the club, removed one of the plastic bags from the carriage compartment, and began hobbling back along the boardwalk.

She needed to find a ride to Frederiksted.

~ 41 ~

The Market

KAREEM PARKED HIS car on a quiet side street, a few blocks off of Strand, Frederiksted's main waterfront thoroughfare.

Stepping out of his shiny black sedan, he flicked a button on his keychain to engage the lock and started off down a cracked sidewalk. The peekaboo view of the sea revealed a massive cruise ship anchored beside a sizeable dock that extended fifteen hundred feet into the water. Squinting, he could just make out the clumped masses of hundreds of tiny human figures ambling about the boat, as well as a few smaller clusters that had begun the long walk to the shore.

A good sign for commerce, Kareem concluded as he turned a corner and strolled toward the address for his newest grocery store.

FREDERIKSTED WAS A tiny town, no more than a small village, with less than a thousand people living within its city limits. The main streets ran parallel to the shoreline; most of its economic activity revolved around the transiting cruise ships.

An important cultural marker, Frederiksted was the site

of several significant historical events, milestones that epitomized the island's feisty nature and headstrong independent spirit.

In 1848, the town was the location of a popular uprising that eventually forced the territory's colonial governor to declare emancipation for the entire Danish West Indies. Thirty years later, it was the starting point of the Fireburn riots, a violent laborers' revolt stemming from the onerous terms of post-slavery work contracts. The riots resulted in the burning of much of the town as well as several plantations across St. Croix.

Despite its importance to the island's heritage, modern day Frederiksted suffered from its secondary stature. The town's colonial-era buildings were in a general state of disrepair. Its brick red fort compared poorly with the yellow ochre one in Christiansted. Graffiti marred the exterior walls; water drainage had damaged the structure's interior.

In recent years, multimillion-dollar improvements to the waterfront had created a deepwater port (along with the mammoth pier) to attract passing cruise ships. Unfortunately, that initial effort hadn't been matched with long-term maintenance. Many of the public light fixtures in the shoreline area were inoperable or had pieces missing; parts of the decorative chains that lined the main walkway were broken. The casual observer couldn't help but notice the multiple signs of vandalism and the general sense of slide.

Nevertheless, with the ship in dock, colorful tents displaying all manner of souvenirs and trinkets dotted a pavilion area on the shore next to the dock. A number of hopeful vendors had set out their wares, but so far, the shoppers were few and far between.

A handful of the ship's passengers snorkeled off the end of the pier, and the occasional curious pedestrian wandered down to the vendor pavilion and Strand Street's row of waterfront stores. But for the most part, those seeking to explore St. Croix would take off in taxi vans or on guided tours, quickly leaving Frederiksted behind.

A FEW BLOCKS inland, the narrow streets sloped gently upward. With its jaw-dropping views of the sea, the area could have been a Caribbean gem, but beyond the shoreline's cruise ship facade, the neighborhoods turned steadily seedy. Cracked and crumbling facades were overlaid with overgrown weeds, scattered refuse, and the occasional abandoned vehicle. In the constant island heat, it didn't take long for infrastructure to deteriorate.

Ever the optimist, Kareem viewed Frederiksted as a unique business opportunity. He saw himself at the forefront of the town's transition into a showcase tourist destination. He envisioned pedestrian-friendly neighborhoods with island-themed boutiques, restaurants, a few parks, and even a museum. If only a portion of his planned development was enacted, he reasoned, it would bring about a dramatic economic upturn to the area.

It was against his nature to contemplate a deeper decline.

AS KAREEM APPROACHED the grocery store's gated front entrance, he glanced warily up and down the empty street before feeding his key into the lock of the door's iron-welded fronting.

The Frederiksted store was the newest of his grocery properties. The rest were located toward the center of the island, in the residential regions surrounding Christiansted.

He was excited about his latest venture. He'd negotiated an excellent deal on the building's lease, and it had taken only minor refurbishments to ready the space for use.

Granted, there had been several muggings and a few shootings in the area since the shop opened. The security alarms that monitored the building's perimeter were triggered on a nightly basis, and his employees had recorded more than the usual number of shoplifting incidents.

But despite these drawbacks, the surrounding community had responded well to the new store, appreciating its convenience and variety of goods. There was little direct competition within Frederiksted's underserved neighborhoods. The local police had stepped up their patrols, giving at least the impression of increased security, and with a high turnover of merchandise, the shop's profitability had already exceeded that of his other locations.

Feeling smugly satisfied with his investment, Kareem pulled open the door and stepped inside. The potential safety issues were well worth the risk, he thought, recalling the latest balance sheets.

AFTER RELOCKING THE door, Kareem began his morning inspection. He walked the aisles, checking that the goods on the shelves were in order, dust free, and optimally positioned.

As he surveyed the store, the click of an automatic switch signified the start of the building's air-conditioning unit. A low humming noise was soon followed by a blast of cold air, which funneled out of a metal grate mounted on the ceiling.

Kareem looked up, noting with approval the machine's power and efficiency. He'd had excellent service from the company that leased him the equipment. The man with whom he had originally set up his account had been promoted, so most of his contact had been with the replacement representative, but he still found himself occasionally thinking of the original installation manager—if for reasons other than air-conditioning.

Kareem stared up at the ceiling vent, reflecting.

He credited Adam Rock with helping him meet Mira.

HIS INITIAL REVIEW complete, Kareem slipped behind the cashier counter and into a small office. After hanging his suit jacket in a closet, he removed an apron from a peg on the wall near the door and strapped it around his waist.

The staff would begin arriving in the next ten minutes;

the shop would be cooled and officially open for business within the hour.

Kareem turned to gaze at a pegboard mounted above a small but neatly organized desk. Wanting to ensure a successful launch of the new facility, he had been working in the Frederiksted store for the past month. Since he had temporarily moved his home office to this back room, he had taken a few minutes to personalize the space.

Several pictures had been pinned to the pegboard, most of them depicting members of his family. There on the top left was Elena, with her curly pigtails and mischievous green eyes. Adjacent was a photo of Hassan, striking a serious pose that conveyed a maturity well beyond his tender years.

His stepchildren, a teenaged girl and boy, occupied a third photo. Even in the still shot, Kareem could sense the reserve in their eyes.

At the center of the collage, Kareem had pinned a picture of his wife. Mira wore a dark cloak over her shoulders, and a veil covered the top of her head, but the black fabric had been pulled back around the edges of her face, revealing her high cheekbones, pale skin, and distinct American features.

As Kareem stared at the center picture, the confidence he'd felt upon entering the store began to slip away.

Much as he tried to distract himself with his business duties, he couldn't help but worry about his secretive spouse—and what she'd been up to the night before.

~ 42 ~

Pack Your Bags

MIRA WAITED UNTIL she heard Kareem's car backing down the driveway; then she peeked out the villa's front window for a last look. She watched through the blinds as her husband carefully reversed the car into the street and turned it toward the community's gated exit. Pressing her forehead against the glass, she caught a quick glimpse of his head and shoulders before he drove away.

As the vehicle disappeared into the morning's humid haze, a light moisture glistened in her eyes—the effects of a wistful good-bye, but something less than a fully formed tear.

Mira sighed tensely, wishing for a cigarette.

This was not a step to be taken lightly. She was leaving a man she'd lived with for almost ten years, terminating a marriage that had been, for the most part, peaceful and strife-free.

A moment of reflection was in order.

Glancing up at the arched ceiling above the window, she thought of all the things she was giving up: the beautiful home, its lavish furnishings, and the five enormous walk-in closets.

Then she smiled, surprised at her utter lack of regret. Those items no longer held any allure to her.

The seclusion and stability had had its benefits, but she'd grown bored of the restrictive lifestyle. Her constant trips to Christiansted and the neighboring islands were proof enough of that. As for poor Kareem, she'd lost interest in him long ago.

She was ready to turn the page and enter her life's next chapter.

SHAKING HER HEAD, Mira wondered why it had taken her so long to make the break. Her second marriage had lasted almost twice as long as the first. A great deal of inertia, she supposed, had built up over the last decade.

Yet once the dam began to crack, water began seeping through, and it wasn't long before the entire wall crumbled.

The plan for today's departure had come together suddenly. She had made the decision after just a few minutes' deliberation. But the restless mood and the need for change had been growing for months.

Looking back, she could trace the first inklings of the transition to the fiasco with Charlie and the sequence of events triggered by her oldest daughter.

She sighed, remembering. The girl had caused her no end of trouble.

Mira was lucky that her contact at the seaplane terminal had alerted her to Charlie's booking last Thanksgiving. It had taken every last ounce of her creativity and wile to quash her daughter's shenanigans, but she had managed to negate the crisis and, in the meantime, exacted a modicum of revenge.

At the mental image of her ex-husband clad in a green dress and heels, Mira's smile broadened into a triumphant expression.

That was all over now, she thought with a chuckle. In just a few hours' time, she and her four children would be leaving this island.

After this adieu, Mira had no intention of ever coming back to Santa Cruz.

ELENA SPRINTED INTO the room, hollering at full voice. "I'm not going to school today. I tell you, I am not going . . ."

"No," Mira interjected, turning away from the window and stepping briskly toward the kitchen. "No, you're not." Her gaze moved from Elena to the other children, who were still seated at the breakfast table. "None of you are."

All four looked up at her in startled puzzlement as she clapped her hands together and instructed energetically.

"Each of you, pack a bag. Just the essentials. Your toothbrush and a couple changes of clothes. Maybe a toy or two. We'll be getting on the seaplane, and they have strict luggage limits."

After a moment of stunned silence, Hassan was the first to speak.

"Where are we going?" he asked, his face evoking a serious inquiry.

Mira had anticipated this response.

"It's a surprise," she said with a wink. "You'll have to wait to find out."

Hassan was not placated. "What about Pappa?" he asked, perplexed. He pointed at the door. "He just left for work."

Mira pursed her lips. "He'll be joining us later," she replied, assuring herself that this was a necessary lie.

"But . . ." Hassan sputtered.

"You ask too many questions, dear," Mira said, gently patting him on the head. Then she snapped her fingers. "Chop-chop. You all had better get moving."

As the seated children rose from their chairs, Mira gave her oldest daughter a meaningful look.

"No funny business. We're leaving at noon."

~ *43* ~

An Early Departure

WORDLESSLY, THE TEENAGE girl joined her siblings in the wild rush to pack for the surprise seaplane trip. As she hurried down the villa's tile-floored hallway, she felt her mother's eyes upon her back, a sharp piercing stare. With great relief, the girl slid into her bedroom at the end of the corridor and shut the door.

Not wasting any time, she quickly changed out of her pajamas and into a T-shirt and shorts. Kneeling in front of her closet, she dug through a pile of rumpled clothing until she unearthed a loaded backpack. The bag had been ready for quite some time, just waiting for this moment to arrive.

Mira may have only recently decided to leave Kareem, but her oldest daughter had been planning her escape for months.

SCOOPING UP THE pack, the girl stood and turned to take a last look around the bedroom she'd occupied for almost ten years.

Her gaze paused on a white-painted dresser with flower-decorated knobs. The surface was cluttered with a teenager's typical trinkets: pastel-colored notepads, pens with plastic cartoon figures affixed to the ends, hair barrettes, and an assortment of cheap jewelry. None of these items caused her to linger.

She turned toward a twin bed whose length was pushed up against the far wall. The sheets were still unmade, and the bright-pink comforter was crumpled into a heap at the foot of the mattress. On the floor below lay a matching pink throw rug whose plush fabric was topped with a scattering of books and a mismatched collection of shoes.

The room's decor had been picked out almost entirely by her mother. Few of the furnishings held any appeal to the daughter.

Pink isn't even my color, she thought with disdain as she snatched a colored pen from the dresser and slid it into her backpack.

A MIRROR HANGING on a nearby wall caught the girl's reflection as she surveyed her soon-to-be-abandoned belongings.

The teenager bore a far closer resemblance to her father than her mother. She had inherited Charlie's sturdy, short-statured build; Mira's delicate, refined features were missing or had yet to develop. The girl's hair was a wild tumble of brown curls, cut into a pixie style that she wore loosely clipped in a barrette—that is, she did when her head wasn't covered by the community-regimented black scarf.

The daughter tossed her head indignantly. Unlike her mother, she had never seen any benefit to the community's confining dress code. She felt as if she had spent her whole life hiding beneath a cumbersome black cloak.

That was another element of her past that she would not miss.

HER GOOD-BYE COMPLETE, the girl crossed to the window by the bed. Scooting over the rumpled sheets, she wrapped her hands around the window frame's bottom edge and shoved upward, creating a three-foot opening.

Glancing furtively at the bedroom's closed door, she tossed her backpack through the window and watched it fall to the ground. With grunting effort, she slid her body through the hole and eased herself over the ledge.

She was just about to release her grip when she heard her mother's distinctive footsteps tapping down the hallway outside the bedroom.

The girl sucked in her breath as the steps drew nearer. If she were caught now, it might be weeks before she got another chance. She needed at least five minutes of lead time before her mother discovered her disappearance.

Dangling over the ledge, she listened as the footsteps stopped—and then pivoted toward the master bedroom. The diminishing *clap* was soon muffled by the closing of yet another door.

Exhaling, the daughter grinned an impish smile—and let go of the ledge.

AFTER DROPPING TO the ground behind a row of bushes, the girl hefted the backpack onto her shoulders. Then she reached beneath the nearest bush for a small satchel that contained several items she'd retrieved earlier from one of her mother's closets.

In addition to a packet of money from her mother's secret stash, the items included the girl's cell phone, which her mother had banned from her possession after the events of last Thanksgiving.

Clutching the satchel to her chest, the teenager slipped through the greenery, rapidly moving away from the villa and into the forest surrounding the community's compound. Seconds later, she uncovered a moped that had been hidden in the underbrush. Hopping on, she cranked the engine and sped off toward Frederiksted.

She was determined to at last meet up with her long-lost father.

This time, there was nothing her mother could do to stop her.

The Note

THE GREEN DRESS bouncing as he chugged up the stairs, Charlie finally reached the top floor of the Comanche Hotel. At the end of the hallway, he turned the key in the lock to room seventeen and pushed open the door. Dashing inside, he quickly scanned the room for his belongings.

Given the number of visits he'd made to the place since last Thanksgiving, the layout was painfully familiar.

There was the triangular-shaped ceiling, the wooden floors, the windows cut into the roofline . . . and the distinct aroma of Mira's sweet perfume.

Choking, Charlie sucked in his breath, trying not to inhale any of the scented air. Despite the failure of his mask equipment to prevent his most recent incapacitation, he was still suspicious of the flowery fragrance.

He marched across the room to the bed, where his clothes had been folded and neatly stacked next to the pillow. His worn combat boots were on the floor by the nightstand. The shoes stood side by side, in perfect formation, as if patiently awaiting his return.

Charlie scrambled out of the green dress and quickly pulled on his camo shorts. He slid a hand into his rear pocket, confirming the location of his wallet. Scooping up his ponytail holder from the nightstand, he wrapped the elastic band around the back length of his hair. He re-strapped his watch to his wrist and checked the reading on its face.

He'd have to hurry if he was going to make his flight to St. Thomas.

This was typical of his recent run of luck, he thought as he threw his T-shirt on over his head. The seaplane was one of the few modes of transportation in the Caribbean that, weather permitting, actually kept to its schedule.

Popping his arms through the shirt's arm holes, he reached for his baseball cap, the last item of clothing on the bed.

But as he scooped up the cap's brim, he uncovered a small envelope that had been tucked beneath.

His name was written in pink-colored ink on the envelope's front side.

"Charlie Baker," he read out loud, puzzling. He felt certain this wasn't Mira's handwriting.

The envelope crinkled as he wrestled open the flap and slid out the sheet of paper folded inside.

After skimming the paragraphs written on the paper, he sat down on the bed, instantly forgetting the impending seaplane departure.

He put on his cap, fiddling with the brim as a stunned expression settled across his face.

He reread the note, slowly this time. Then, he folded the paper and returned it to the envelope. Standing, he slid the envelope into his front pants pocket next to the return plane ticket and thoughtfully rubbed his chin.

"Guess I'm not headed home this morning after all."

~ 45 ~

The Entourage

THE GOVERNOR WIPED his hands together, trying to remove the fishy smell from his handshake with the spear fisherman.

"Hand cleaner, sir," his aide offered, quickly reaching into his coat pocket for a plastic vial.

"Thank you, Cedric," the Governor said with a sigh. He held out his hands while the aide squeezed a dollop of alcohol-formulated gel into his palms.

The Governor made a sour face as he squished the slippery substance between his fingers.

"The things I do for this job."

HAVING RID HIMSELF of the worst of the fishy aroma, the Governor strolled down the boardwalk toward the open-air diner on the first floor of the coral-pink hotel, the location of his first meeting, and meal, of the day.

As usual, he was surrounded by his entourage. Such was the nature of his office. He rarely found himself alone.

It was a strange, often claustrophobic, existence, one to which he'd never truly adapted. He couldn't escape the constant presence of others, some looming, some furtive, some filled with nervous energy.

His life lacked a certain stillness that he feared he might never regain.

THE NERVOUS ENERGY belonged to Cedric, the Governor's eager assistant.

A trim, well-dressed individual, Cedric was the only person the Governor had ever known who could keep a starched shirt and tailored suit unwrinkled in the humid island heat. He was neat, efficient, and ruthlessly organized.

While not in any way small in stature, Cedric's medium build was dwarfed beside the Governor's bulky frame, which is where he hovered—seemingly day and night.

Cedric was the Governor's right-hand man. He kept track of the politician's endless appointments and carefully managed the logistical details of every engagement, but that was only a minor part of the aide's duties.

Having closely studied local politics for the last ten years, Cedric was a walking encyclopedia of both substantive public policy issues as well as the thorny political nuances that underlay even the most banal of administrative decisions. He could provide a succinct micro-summary on any given topic, rattling off relevant names, figures, and statistics at a moment's notice—and he was often asked to do so in the minutes before the Governor entered a meeting.

As a natural outgrowth of his detail-oriented character, Cedric was the designated worrier of the team. It was a role the Governor was happy to delegate; he'd grown heavily dependent on the young staffer's ceaseless updates and reminders.

The Governor had enough on his mind these days, he reflected as he gazed at the empty and abandoned lots along the boardwalk, much more global concerns that demanded a great deal of his mental focus. Sometimes, he felt as if the fate of the entire territory were resting on his shoulders. And so, in an odd way, Cedric's fretting and anxiety gave the Governor a much-needed sense of peace.

He chuckled to himself. At this point, he was helpless to navigate breakfast without Cedric's guidance on each food item's caloric intake, fiber content, and blood sugar impact.

CEDRIC WAS THE only member of the entourage whose presence the Governor truly welcomed. The rest, he could easily live without—and that included the lumbering shadows of his bodyguards.

The Governor found it impossible to tell the beefy men apart. He'd long since given up remembering their names. He simply called them all Brutus.

The security shifts were manned in pairs. While the faces changed every few hours, the mercenary bodies always remained the same: men with thick, solid hands that looked as if they could chop through concrete, bulging chests that appeared capable of deflecting bullets, and steely, unemotional eyes that made the Governor worry that if an enemy were to offer the right incentive, they might be swayed to turn against him.

The Governor risked a timid, sideways glance at the closest bodyguard. The man stared grimly ahead, his gaze sweeping the horizon for potential threats.

On his next step forward, the Governor veered slightly toward Cedric. Suppressing an inner shudder, he glanced down at his watch, wondering when the next shift would take over—and knowing that the next team of Brutus and Brutus would be just as intimidating as the one that came before.

AS MUCH AS the Governor disliked the bodyguards, he loathed the last contingent of the entourage even more.

The remaining seats on the seaplane that morning had been occupied by members of the Governor's cabinet. Given Transfer Day's high profile within the territory, almost all of his appointed staff would be attending the afternoon's event.

The lone exception was the Lieutenant Governor, who, following protocol, had stayed behind on St. Thomas. He had been allowed to move from his adjoining office space into Government House while the rest of the cabinet was off-island.

The Governor rolled his eyes. They'd been gone just over an hour, but the man was probably already passed out on the carpet in his office. Despite Cedric's efforts to secure the main liquor cabinet, the Lieutenant Governor always managed to find a way to open it, particularly when left unsupervised. After this two-day trip to St. Croix, they would have to completely restock the bar.

Other than his proclivity for fine rum, the Lieutenant Governor was harmless enough, especially compared to the rest of the lot.

The Governor cast a second sideways glance, this time directed at the motley crew of conniving backstabbers and hangers-on who made up the rest of his cabinet. The members of this troublesome group were the bane of his existence and, in truth, far more likely to do him harm than a rogue bodyguard.

With a wistful sigh, the Governor envisioned the day when he would retire from public office and give all of these unsavory characters the heave-ho.

He watched as the cabinet members fanned out across the boardwalk, eager to squeeze in their own round of meetings prior to the departure of the official convoy to the restored plantation on the west end of the island where the Transfer Day ceremonies would be taking place.

With a grimace at the nearest Brutus, the Governor ran his hands across his plump waistline and turned to Cedric.

"Right, then. Where're we headed for breakfast?" He rubbed his stomach. "I'm starving."

~ 46 ~

The Stakeout

"I GOTTA TELL you, Currie. I'm so hungry right now, I could eat my right arm off."

Mic sat on the floor of a boarded-up house in downtown Frederiksted, leaning against a grimy wall, gripping his slim—and loudly rumbling—stomach. Currie knelt beside him, staring through a crack in the front window's outer covering. From there, he had a perfect, if narrow view of the grocery store across the street.

"I can't stop thinking about those pork chops we missed last night," Mic moaned. "I've eaten them in my head so many times, you'd think I'd be stuffed already."

He closed his eyes, recalling the imagined meals.

"First time, I had them grilled, medium-rare with a nice ring of seared fat around the edge." He nodded his head, humming his approval. "Next, I ordered them dipped in beer batter and dunked in the fryer." His eyes cracked open, and he pointed a slender finger at the ceiling. "Those were quite tasty, my friend. A highly recommended preparation."

He smacked his lips as if savoring the fictional food.

"Then, for variety, I tried them slow cooked and slathered with barbecue sauce . . ."

"Stop it, Mic. You're killing me," Currie cut in, exasperated by the stream of images.

No sooner was the phrase out of his mouth than he realized his poor choice of words.

The pair exchanged somber stares and then fell back into silence.

MIC AND CURRIE had spent a long night in the boarded-up house. After Nova dropped them off there the previous evening, they'd been tasked with keeping watch on the grocery store across the street until the proprietor arrived to open it for the day's business.

Theirs was no longer a voluntary assignment. The gun from the truck's front seat had been put to full intimidating use. When the pickup arrived in Frederiksted, Nova had parked behind the house and forced them inside at gunpoint. They'd been locked in the building, without food or water, for the duration of the evening.

Just a half hour earlier, Nova had returned with their final instructions. The door was now unlocked, but he was monitoring their position from a hidden location somewhere nearby. He'd been clear about the ramifications should they fail to follow through on their mission.

"You'll do exactly as I tell you—or else," he'd said, waving the gun from one man's chest to the other.

Ever inquisitive, Mic quickly piped up. "Or else what?"

Currie gulped as Nova glared menacingly at his friend. Then the bully aimed the gun at Mic's thin neck.

"Or else you'll end up like the last fool who dared to disobey me," Nova said, jerking his head toward a heap of discarded clothing in the far corner of the room.

Mic shuffled over, nudging the pile with his toe. His face suddenly flashed with recognition.

"What? You did in Frosty?" he sputtered, incredulous.

Then he turned to look back at Currie. "You know, I always wondered what happened to that dude."

MIC RESUMED A low-level muttering about his pork chop fantasies as Currie continued to monitor the grocery across the street.

The store had obviously been recently renovated. It was the newest-looking establishment on the block, if not the whole of Frederiksted. The walls were painted bright green, and crisp white edging detailed the sparkling-clean windows. The protective metal cage surrounding the front door showed no signs of wear or rust.

Mustering his limited literacy skills, Currie studied the banner stretched across the store's roofline. The bold-typed English words were underlined with smaller font of curving Arabic text.

Currie leaned away from the splintered sill and rubbed his stubby chin.

"Well, Mic. We've really stepped in it this time."

EVEN WITH HIS geographic range restricted to Christiansted, Currie had picked up on the recent increased immigration of Middle Eastern nationals to St. Croix—as well as the related objecting undercurrent. Despite the Muslim community's self-imposed seclusion, its growing numbers were beginning to draw attention.

The group's primary interaction with the rest of the island was through its expanding commercial enterprises. A sizable portion of the grocery stores and gas stations on the island were now owned and run by a prominent Saudi clan.

Currie had overheard numerous conversations about the topic on and around the boardwalk, among the shopkeepers, the taxi drivers, the refinery workers, and the local fishermen— none of it positive.

However, no faction viewed the matter more grievously than his fellow West Indians, who saw the Arabs' economic success as unwanted—and unwarranted—competition.

Currie thunked his chin worriedly.

He suspected he and Mic were about to become unwitting casualties in this brewing societal conflict.

A MOTION ON the street brought Currie's attention back to the storefront. Cramming his face against the crack in the window, he watched a well-dressed Saudi man approach the store, unlock the front gate, and step inside.

With his eyes, Currie followed the man as he walked through the shop, inspecting the shelves and occasionally pausing to straighten the merchandise. After a few minutes, the man appeared satisfied with the setup and disappeared into a rear area, separated from the showroom.

Wiping the sweat from his brow, Currie pulled back from the window and glanced down at a timepiece Nova had strapped onto his wrist.

They were to wait until eleven o'clock, broad mid-morning daylight, to make their move.

With a cruise ship docked three streets over and the Governor entertaining his Danish guests at the Transfer Day ceremonies less than a mile to the north, he and Mic had been ordered to walk into the store and rob the cashier.

Currie shifted his weight, wrestling with his conscience. Yes, they had been known to steal an odd item or two, but they typically took things that no would ever notice were missing: a spare fishing net with a couple of holes in it from the dive shop, a stained dish towel from the brewpub's laundry pile, or a couple of coconuts from a grove of trees in a nearby residential neighborhood.

Of course, according to Mic, that last category wasn't really theft—they were *liberated* coconuts.

Currie managed a weak smile as his gaze fell to the revolvers lying on the floor beneath the window.

They were unloaded, which was just as well. Neither he nor Mic knew how to use a gun.

Unfortunately, Nova was supremely adept with weaponry, Currie thought with a nervous gulp.

He wiped the sweat from his brow and returned his attention to the crack in the window.

He'd gotten them into a real mess, and they were running out of options.

A GASTROINTESTINAL GURGLING from the floor interrupted Currie's concentration.

"That was me eating oven-roasted pork chops," Mic offered by way of explanation.

"Can you try to focus?" Currie replied sternly. "We're in a lot of trouble here."

"I don't want to die on an empty stomach."

With a despondent sigh, Mic raised himself to a standing position. He wandered back across the room to the discarded clothing and bent over to inspect the pile.

"Do you think Frosty left behind anything good to eat?"

‿⸞

A FEW BLOCKS over, an unmarked van pulled into the pavilion area on the shoreline next to the Frederiksted pier. After a short pause, an old woman limped out of the side passenger door. The van sped off, leaving Gedda standing on the curb.

She'd made the journey from Christiansted using the island's informal transit system, which operated at a level beneath the licensed taxi drivers, who mostly catered to tourists, refinery workers, and the occasional businessman.

Manned by privately owned vehicles, the unofficial transportation network stopped at designated pickup points across the island. While unmarked, the spots were well known to locals. It was an efficient means for residential passengers to get around the island, and the fare was less than one-tenth the price charged by the regulated taxis.

Her left leg dragging across the pavement, Gedda crossed the main thoroughfare and began hobbling up the sloping side streets toward Kareem's grocery store.

She hoped she wasn't too late. She didn't want to miss all the action.

~ 47 ~

A Power over Men

CHAOS REIGNED IN the bedroom shared by Elena and Hassan.

Lampshades had been turned askew, and toys were strewn from one end to the other. Half of the clothes hangers were turned sideways on the closet rod; the rest were scattered randomly across the floor. A white-painted dresser stood with a portion of its drawers pulled open, while others had been completely removed and were resting on the floor.

The place was totally upended. Clothes had been flung in every direction. The Winnie the Pooh wallpaper—firmly attached to the underlying plaster—was the only feature that appeared untouched by the tornado.

A pair of suitcases lay open in the middle of the mess, but few items had been added to their compartments.

The source of all this destruction stepped out of the closet to perform a dance in the center of the room, a whirling dervish maneuver that involved the flinging of additional clothes, for visual effect.

Elena accompanied her jig with a tune she'd made up for the occasion. The only words to the song were "I am not going to school today."

MEANWHILE, HASSAN SAT on the edge of his bed, a concerned look on his face. He held his favorite teddy bear in his arms, the one item he was determined to bring along on the trip. He had otherwise ceded control of his suitcase to his sister.

There had been a disturbing lack of detail about their upcoming excursion, Hassan mused. Their mother had been far too vague about their intended destination. The situation was causing him great unease.

What if the Comanche didn't know where to find him?

As Elena finished her dance routine and shifted her efforts to a less energetic form of mayhem, Hassan crossed his short legs, one over the other, and repeated the question that had been troubling him from the outset of his mother's sudden trip announcement.

"But—*where* are we going?"

His sister tossed her head informatively.

"I'll tell you where we're going, Hassan. We're going to a place called"—she threw her arms wide as if holding a banner—"this is not a school!"

She tossed a sundress into the air to emphasize the point. Hassan ducked the dress on its downward trajectory.

"But—*how long* are we going to be gone?"

"The longer, the better," his sister replied. She bent toward one of the dresser drawers that had been laid out on the floor. "Better take lots of underwear."

Pondering, Hassan reached through a pile of clothing to uncover the night-light closest to his bed. Unplugging it from the wall, he carefully set it and the teddy bear inside his suitcase.

DOWN THE HALLWAY, inside the master bedroom, a much calmer scene was unfolding. Mira walked slowly across the tile floor, quietly contemplating her pending departure.

She had dozens of things to do before the taxi van came

to take them to the seaplane hangar, including her own bag to pack, but she needed a moment to focus her thoughts.

Even for a woman who was prone to impulsive action, she found herself feeling a little overwhelmed by her recent decision. It was no small feat to swoop out of town with four children in tow.

They would keep the luggage to a minimum, she reminded herself. That would simplify the process. There would be plenty of time to buy new things once they were situated in their next household.

And besides, she thought as she glanced across the room, she didn't want to carry any unnecessary remnants of this life into the next.

Her gaze paused on a framed photo sitting on the dresser. The shot had been taken at the reception for her second wedding. She and Kareem stood, hand in hand, beaming at the camera, while sparkling confetti fell through the air around them.

She stared at the just-married-Mira's face, a ten years younger version of her current self. Then she shifted her focus to the mirror mounted above the dresser.

Time had done its best to wear her down, but she'd kept its forces at bay. Expensive face cream had helped to fend off wrinkles. Regular hair-coloring treatments had covered up the few gray strands that had crept into her golden-brown locks.

Her third wedding photo wouldn't look that much different than the second, she concluded proudly. She still possessed the mystique of beauty.

Mira returned to the photo, this time looking at Kareem. The picture had captured a gleam in his eyes, a shine of pure bliss. He was about to marry the love of his life. At that moment in time, he clearly considered himself to be the luckiest man on the planet.

Mira smiled smugly to herself.

She had always had a power over men.

~ 48 ~

Santa Cruz

AS MIRA STOOD in the villa's master bedroom, confidently assessing her middle-aged looks, her future prospects, and the regret-free end of her second marriage, she let her thoughts drift momentarily to concern.

Despite her self-averred powers of persuasion over the male gender, things hadn't always worked out the way she'd planned.

She had miscalculated once before.

MIRA WAS STILL a young girl when she learned how to turn male brains to mush. With her sweet smile and bewitching green eyes, no toy or doll was beyond her reach. There was no treat or special privilege she couldn't finagle. Even the most sensible, discerning men fell under her spell.

As she grew older, she refined her skills, perfecting her techniques. Simple gestures, she discovered, could have a profound impact. A casual flirtation could yield hefty indulgences.

With her maturing expertise, the bounty from her bevy of male suitors began to pile up: fine clothing, fancy dinners, expensive salon treatments, and—her most prized category of present—high-end shoes.

By the time she met Charlie, Mira had thoroughly mastered the art of male manipulation. Having sampled a merry-go-round of boyfriends, she was on the hunt for a permanent mate. She picked him out of the (albeit limited) crowd of northern Minnesota's available bachelors and set her sights on reeling him in.

In the successful building contractor, Mira had found the perfect husband: a malleable man, pliant from head to toe, with plenty of resources to meet her fashion and accessory needs.

At the outset, it seemed like a good match. Mira had Charlie pinned firmly under her thumb. He occasionally squirmed from the pressure, but he never really complained. For five years, he catered to her every whim, no matter how frivolous or expensive.

Mira thought she had Charlie safely secured—until the day she ran up against a force more magnetically mesmerizing than herself.

Santa Cruz.

FROM THE GET-GO, Mira and Charlie's trip to St. Croix was an unsettling anomaly in their Mira-centric relationship. Charlie wasn't one for spontaneity, and he rarely made substantive decisions without first consulting his wife.

This behavior hadn't come about by accident; it was the intentional result of years of Mira's careful guidance and training.

So the day Charlie came home from work and announced he'd booked a Caribbean vacation, her surprise was one of far more shock than pleasure.

What had come over him? What could have inspired such an abrupt purchase?

Mira tried to dismiss her unease as she packed her bags and ushered the children onto the plane. But the moment the family landed on the island, her intuition started ringing out alarm bells.

Her control had begun to loosen. Her plodding puppet was starting to cut his strings.

THROUGHOUT THAT WEEK of family vacation, Mira's anxiety only grew.

It was as if the tropical climate had planted some rogue independent spirit inside her previously compliant husband. He was missing—or ignoring—all of the obedience cues that had once been so effective.

Just after breakfast on the first full day of their stay, Mira paused by the concierge desk at a counter that displayed pamphlets detailing the resort's onsite spa offerings. Contemplating a luxurious day of pampered massage while Charlie watched the kids, she gazed longingly at the display, draping her elegant arm across the counter as she sighed loudly to draw her husband's attention.

But Charlie merely walked past with their daughter riding piggyback on his shoulders, their young son toddling on the ground, gripping his father's hand.

Ten feet later, Charlie turned and nodded for his wife to follow.

"Come on, Mira," he called out enthusiastically. "We'll be late for the Buck Island snorkel sail."

CHARLIE'S SPUNKY STREAK was more than a one-day burst of initiative. Throughout that week on St. Croix, he continued to organize all sorts of island-themed adventures for the family. Almost every day, they were busy with one activity or another—and Mira's extensive bag of tricks failed to have any influence on the decision-making process.

"Hey, hon," he announced one morning while Mira was lying in bed, dreaming of a quiet day at the pool. "I've booked us on a rain-forest tour. Get this, they'll take us in jeeps over to the other side of the island, and then in the forest, we'll stop at a farm with beer-drinking pigs."

"You did what?" she exclaimed, immediately pulling herself into a sitting position.

Charlie grinned, misconstruing her mortified stare. "I know. Where else are we going to see a bunch of pigs drinking beer?" He grabbed her hand and pulled her up from the bed.

"They drink it right out of the can!"

THE MOST STUNNING turn was yet to come.

They were headed for the airport, the long week—to Mira's view—finally over, when Charlie voiced the fateful proposal.

"Mira, hon, what do you say—why don't we move to St. Croix?"

Her throat clenched as her jaw fell open. She gripped the handle to her suitcase, wordlessly apoplectic in her refusal.

No. Absolutely not. Had he gone completely mad? The protesting thoughts flooded her head.

Then Mira saw the look on his face, and she swallowed her objection.

She had never met a muse more dazzling or beautiful than herself, but she recognized the symptoms.

She had been bested.

By an island.

~ 49 ~

The Lean-To

THE MOVE TO St. Croix powered forward under its own steam, sweeping Mira along with it. She had no time to regroup, no workable strategy to defeat it.

Charlie put the Minnesota house on the market as soon as they returned home from the vacation. Mira tried to sabotage the first showing, leaving the children's toys and other random articles scattered about the place—to no avail. The property fell almost immediately under contract, as if even the real estate gods were conspiring against her.

With the closing date rapidly approaching, the family began a mad dash to prepare for their permanent transfer to the Caribbean. They could only afford to ship a fraction of their furniture, so Charlie sold the heaviest pieces through adds in the local paper. Mira watched, tears silently streaming down her face, as some of her most treasured possessions marched out the door under the care of new owners, never to be seen again.

The contents of the kitchen cabinets were similarly pared down. Only a small collection of essential dishes and appliances would make the trip. The rest, they auctioned off at a yard sale or donated to charity.

Each day, more pieces of Mira's life were broken away, scattered to the wind.

The voluminous walk-in closets emptied as cardboard boxes swallowed up what remained of her belongings. Everything she knew, the home she had carefully assembled, the material fixtures that had framed her existence, were quickly dismantled.

At the end of the month, Mira climbed into Charlie's pickup truck for the bumpy ride from Minnesota to Miami. For more than seventeen hundred miles, the family drove south, their two screaming kids crammed into the cab's rear seating area. Hot and harried, they finally arrived at the tip end of Florida's peninsula.

Holding her daughter's hand, Mira watched the truck roll onto a shipping vessel for the last leg of its voyage.

It was too late to turn back now.

She would have to begin again.

AS SOON AS they arrived on St. Croix, Charlie rented a car to drive them out to their new island home. Eager to get the transition under way, Charlie had insisted they move forward with the real estate transaction while still in Minnesota, so they had purchased the property based on the realtor's descriptions, sight unseen.

About fifteen minutes east of Christiansted, Charlie steered the car off the main road and parked it in a gutted gravel driveway next to a rusted mailbox that was only halfway attached to its mounting post.

Mira sat stiffly in the front passenger seat, hoping against hope that this wasn't the right address and that he had simply gotten lost. But alas, Charlie bounded out of the driver's-side door, providing the dreaded confirmation.

"Can you believe it?" he'd asked jubilantly. "Look at this place. What a steal!"

Mira could still remember the sight of Charlie in his combat boots, tromping across the cactus-strewn lot, pacing off an area for an in-ground swimming pool.

Distant waves crashed in the background as her husband climbed up onto the roof of the lean-to and excitedly described all of the building's wonderful renovation possibilities.

Mira had looked out across the bleak acreage, numb with shock.

It had been so much worse than anything she could have ever imagined.

THE LEAN-TO WAS located on a large plot of land not far from Point Udall, a pillar-stone marker on the easternmost rim of the island and, consequently, the United States. The house's cracked front porch looked out across a blustery landscape, the most inhospitable place Mira had ever seen.

While St. Croix's northwest quadrant featured lush rain forests, here, the arid environment supported only low lying brush, dotted with a variety of cacti and yucca plants. A nonstop wind further blunted the rugged terrain.

In those early days, Mira had spent hours on that porch, staring at their dry, parched acres and, beyond, the Caribbean Sea, which stretched out, flat and forbidding, for as far as the eye could see.

She had hated that sea—hated its lapping shorelines, its white-capped waves, and its deep alluring blue. The mere sight of it caused her to seethe with anger.

But even worse than the water was the island it surrounded. Santa Cruz.

She blamed that rotten spit of land for everything that had been taken from her: her well-ordered life in the States, her perfect two-plus-two family, and her precious walk-in closets.

Most of all, she hated it for seducing her husband and turning him against her.

FOR WEEKS AFTER they moved into the lean-to, Charlie came home tired and frayed, his every nerve pinched with stress.

He had always been a quiet, serious man, but never had he turned so completely inward.

It was disconcerting for Mira, becoming so secondary in importance, subject to his struggling business—and worse, this wretched island. She was used to performing against a blank landscape, not being overshadowed by it.

She had once been in love with Charlie, or at least in love with the thought of him. But with each passing day, her resentment grew, and her feelings toward him became increasingly muddled.

During the long hours while her husband was at work, Mira started gathering up the kids and slipping into town. The three of them spent hours walking along the Christiansted boardwalk, playing in the buildings outside the old Danish fort—anything to escape the ghastly crumble of the lean-to.

It was on one of those outings that she encountered Adam Rock, then a junior sales rep for his air-conditioning company.

Rock had suggested a way for her to gain some financial independence. It had been his idea for her to set up the clothes shopping service for the Muslim community's women. And it was his connections within the community that had led her to the villa the night she first met Kareem.

MIRA LIFTED HER suitcase onto the bed and began filling its compartment with clothing. Her face, which had darkened while remembering all this sad life history, regained its optimistic smile. She tamped down the niggling questions at the back of her mind.

She had made the right decision, she thought with assurance.

She could trust Adam Rock.

Ten years ago, he had helped her find a solution to her problems—he was doing the same now.

~ 50 ~

The Breakfast Meeting

THE GOVERNOR PAUSED in the middle of the boardwalk, waiting for his aide to brief him on their first meeting of the day.

"So, Ced. Who's our lucky breakfast date?"

Cedric riffled through a clipboard stacked high with handwritten notes and computer printouts relating to the day's itinerary, his demeanor unusually flustered. His brown skin took on an anxious pallor as he looked up at his boss.

"Ahem, sir," he replied with a gulp. "You're meeting with a high-level executive from an air-conditioning company. He's one of their top salesmen." He glanced down at his notes for clarification. "In the Caribbean region."

"Cedric," the Governor asked, exasperated. "Why in the name of all that is good and holy am I meeting with an air-conditioner salesman?"

The aide blanched further. "His name is Adam Rock, sir." He tilted his head suggestively, as if insinuating a hidden meaning.

The Governor's brow furrowed.

"Adam Rock?" He shrugged his broad shoulders. "Never heard of him."

"It's about that . . . that other matter, sir," Cedric replied uncomfortably.

The Governor immediately snapped out of his complacent stance.

"I thought we had that resolved," he said sharply, leaning toward the aide to shield his voice.

One glance at Cedric's worried face told him differently. Clearly, the matter had become un-resolved.

"Oh."

The Governor paused, wondering which of his scheming cabinet members had outmaneuvered him—and which one he would pass the blame to if the underlying imbroglio came to light.

"How unfortunate."

～

THE CRAB LIVING in the boulders at the edge of the rainbow-decorated diner looked up as the hostess led a group of five men, four of them imposing plus one smaller by comparison, toward the back of the seating area.

The Governor's bodyguards peeled off for the counter by the bar, where they could both eat and monitor the perimeter, while the three remaining men greeted each other, formally shook hands, and then moved toward the crab's table.

From the safety of his boulder, the crab ogled up with interest at the Governor, his assistant, and the air-conditioner salesman.

The waitress took the men's orders and returned minutes later with orange juice and coffee. An uneasy chitchat floated back and forth across the table as the men sipped their drinks. In the crab's assessment, the purpose of the conversation was more for the men to size up one another as opponents than to convey any substantive meaning.

Before long, plates arrived, piled high with food, and the trio began to eat.

Generous expense accounts and nonstop business meals had given the Governor and the salesman sizeable girths.

The pair dug into their food, edgily eying one another like a pair of torpedo-shaped fish angling for the next piece of raw meat. The nervous pecking of the aide explained his trim physique.

Midway through the meal, the salesman paused, wiped his mouth with a napkin, and took a long slurp of coffee. Then he put forth his proposed quid pro quo, tossing it across the table as if it were a lure on a line, tethered to a barbed hook. The Governor glanced over at his aide, seeking the smaller man's counsel, before grudgingly agreeing to the salesman's pitch.

The breakfast ended shortly thereafter. As the party disbanded, the crab crept cautiously out from behind his boulder.

He couldn't help thinking that the two large men who had been sitting at his table were far more fearful predators than the tarpon lurking in the nearby lagoon.

~ *51* ~

A Change in Plans

IN ROOM SEVENTEEN of the Comanche Hotel, Charlie Baker laced up his boots, gathered his backpack, and prepared to leave. Still pondering the note that had been hidden beneath his cap, he tossed the green dress and shoes into a trash bin and started down the maze of stairs to the hotel's first floor.

The woman at the front desk raised a skeptical eyebrow as he approached her station.

"Ready to check out?" she asked stiffly.

He shook his head, still marveling at Mira's cheek, once more leaving him with the bill after dumping him unconscious at the fort.

"No, I'm going to need to stay another night," he replied. Then he paused, reflecting on the handwritten note. "Is it possible for me to keep the same room?"

A FEW MINUTES later, Charlie tromped down the boardwalk toward the seaplane hangar, giving the warped boards an extra *thump* with each stride. It was a relief to have his feet back inside his heavy-duty combat boots. His arches still hurt from being crammed into the high-heeled shoes while he was unconscious.

Outside the rainbow-decorated diner, he passed a pair of heavily armed men surrounding a suited gentleman he recognized as the territory's governor. He gave the armed men an extra four feet of cushion space as he circled around them; then he continued down the boardwalk and turned in to the seaplane hangar.

Beyond the security gate, he could see the plane floating at its dock. Passengers were already dumping their luggage into the bins for undercarriage storage and climbing up the gangplank into the plane's narrow cabin.

"You're just in time," the attendant monitoring the gate said as Charlie approached the service counter. "I didn't think you were going to make it."

Charlie shifted his backpack to his left shoulder and leaned over the counter. He recognized the attendant as the man he had seen pushing the luggage cart on his arrival the previous afternoon.

"I've got to reschedule. Can you book me on a flight out tomorrow?"

The attendant looked down at his computer screen. After scrolling through a few pages and punching several buttons, he replied, "Yes, it looks like I can seat you on the flight leaving at the same time in the morning." He cleared his throat. "For a small fee."

As Charlie reached for his wallet, the attendant glanced up mischievously. "Did you find the woman in the green dress?"

The man grinned at the blush rising on Charlie's cheeks.

"I heard she was walking around town less than an hour ago."

~ 52 ~

Bert

CHARLIE EXITED THE seaplane hangar, eager to put as much distance as possible between himself and the mocking baggage clerk. Striding up the boardwalk, he pulled the note with the pink writing from his pocket and once more read the message, studying the address listed near the bottom.

"I've got to get to Frederiksted," he muttered, tapping the note against his leg.

The taxi drivers who parked along King Street next to the park seemed like his best option. Charlie proceeded up the walkway toward the taxi stand, but halfway along the shoreline, he paused at the line of boats docked across from the sugar mill bar.

It's worth a try, he reasoned with a shrug.

As Charlie strode down the pier, Umberto emerged from his boat's galley holding a cup of coffee.

"Hey, Bert," Charlie called out. "You got a ride?" He grunted a clarification. "I mean, other than the boat?"

The opera singer flinched at the nickname, but if it bothered him, he didn't voice a complaint.

"Where do you need to go, Mr. Baker?" he asked politely.

"The other side of the island," Charlie replied, jerking his head toward the west. "Place just north of Frederiksted."

He folded the letter over so that Umberto could see the address.

Umberto read the information and then gave Charlie a curious look.

What an odd little man, he thought. First, there was his bizarre escapade at the Danish fort. Now, he was following pink handwritten instructions toward Frederiksted. What could possibly explain this strange sequence of events? The opera singer couldn't help but be intrigued.

"Hop in," he said. "I can take you to the cruise ship dock. It'll be about a mile's walk from there. You can walk or catch a cab on the Frederiksted side."

Charlie took a wide step away from the boat, nearly falling off the pier in the process. "Oh, that's okay. I'll just take a taxi from here." The mere idea of motoring to the other side of the island in the small watercraft made his stomach turn green.

He glanced up at the sky. A dark ribbon had begun to form across the eastern horizon. The approaching rainstorm would only add turbulence to an already sure-to-be bumpy boat ride.

"No, no," Umberto entreated, waving Charlie onboard. He lifted his lawn chair from the rear deck and folded it up. "I insist."

Warily, Charlie shuffled back across the pier to the boat. Gripping Umberto's outstretched hand, he stepped over the boat's railing and onto the deck. He was immediately greeted by the two wiener dogs, whose tails wagged as if welcoming an old friend.

Umberto quickly untied the moorings and lifted the securing lines from the pier. He reached into his pocket for a pair of keys and jingled them in the air.

"Andiamo?"

With a resigned shrug, Charlie assented and followed

Umberto through the boat's galley to the steering compartment at the front.

"All right, let's go."

As the boat puttered out of the harbor a few minutes later,
Charlie looked over at the opera singer and asked weakly,
"You got a bucket?"

~ *53* ~

The Danish Ambassador

FARTHER UP THE shoreline on the northeast side of Christiansted, the Danish ambassador and his wife were finishing a late breakfast. Surrounded by starched white tablecloths, gilt-edged porcelain, and silver place settings, the pair sat on a verandah at a luxury resort, one of St. Croix's finest accommodations.

The resort's restaurant was positioned at the highest point of the property. A line of arched openings had been cut into the length of a wall, providing an expansive view of the sea.

With a rolling multi-acre golf course, numerous tennis courts, its own private beach, and a full-service spa, the resort was a favorite for weddings, honeymoons, and anniversary getaways. A carefully crafted veneer created the convincing facade of a tropical paradise.

Highly regarded in the travel industry, the resort was regularly featured in advertising targeted to North American audiences. Through the years, it had even been featured in numerous public radio sweepstakes for local stations throughout the United States, including northern Minnesota.

After a week of pampering at this prestigious locale, it

was not uncommon for vacationers to consider a permanent move to the island.

THE AMBASSADOR LAID down his fork and neatly wiped his mouth with a linen napkin. He gazed out at the panoramic shoreline, taking in the sweeping view of the sea. A pristine beach ringed the water's edge, the sand framed on its opposite side by a border of carefully manicured greenery. Blurred in the distance, he could just make out the quaint buildings of downtown Christiansted.

A recent appointment, the Danish politician was making his first trip to his country's former island colonies.

He was a pale powerful-looking man with a square jawline and thick gray hair streaked with shiny strands of silver. Suitably distinguished for his position, he was dressed in a three-piece suit, silk tie, and hand-stitched leather shoes.

Crooking his pinky finger, the Ambassador picked up his morning cup of tea and politely sipped the last swallow of the warm brown liquid. The day was off to a marvelous start, he thought with a reserved sigh.

His wife noted the subtle signal. They had been married for more than twenty years. Throughout the length of that time she had devoted herself to being an expert companion. Her husband, she sensed, was ready to depart for their day's activities.

A similar age as her spouse, the wife had a slim build, feathery gray-brown hair, and a delicate bone structure. She wore a simple yet classy dress of a muted color, belted around the waist. It was paired with panty hose, sensible heeled shoes, and a string of pearls. Her role was to complement her husband, not to outshine him.

She swallowed the last piece of melon on her plate and looked across the table expectantly.

"Is it time, dear?"

The Ambassador had already gauged the hour from a clock mounted on a nearby wall. Nevertheless, he angled his wrist and gently tugged back his sleeve to check his watch, a jewel-encrusted, multi-armed Swiss contraption.

"I'm afraid so. Such is the life of a traveling diplomat." He gave his wife an indulgent smile. "There's no rush, sweetheart, but I believe the driver will be here any minute now."

SHORTLY THEREAFTER, THE Ambassador and his wife strolled out through the hotel's front reception area. Mural-painted walls evoked a romantic Mediterranean air, a theme that continued through the lobby to the tiered stone fountain in the middle of the circular front drive.

The property had originally served as one of the island's oldest sugar mill estates, and remnants of that era were still readily apparent, most notably in the truncated windmill tower just off the main entrance.

Since the conversion, the hotel had hosted numerous high-profile diplomats and politicians along with several famous athletes and Hollywood entertainers.

This week, of course, the rooms were filled with a high concentration of Danish guests in town for the Transfer Day celebrations.

As the Ambassador and his wife crossed the lobby, they paused briefly to chat with some fellow Europeans who were admiring the hotel's art and decorations. But the husband soon ushered his wife down the polished steps to the front drive.

The ride from the airport the previous evening had been through darkness. He was eager to get his first daytime view of St. Croix.

EMMITT SAT IN a black sedan in the resort's pull-through driveway, waiting for the Ambassador and his wife to emerge from the reception area.

He'd been called in at the last minute to substitute for the scheduled driver who had come down sick. Over his regular taxi driver shirt and slacks, he wore a borrowed black jacket that was two sizes too big. He'd only recently managed to get his name added to the chauffer company's roster, and this was his first official gig.

As Emmitt tapped the steering wheel, admiring the stitching on the leather cover, he spied his likely clients descending the resort's front steps.

The pair looked almost regal as they approached the fountain in the center of the drive. The Ambassador raised his hand and issued a well-practiced wave, the motion apparently meant to signal the driver.

"That had better be the Ambassador," Emmitt muttered under his breath as he opened the driver's-side door.

"I can't imagine anyone else would be parading around like that."

EMMITT CLIMBED FROM behind the wheel and stepped forward to make his greeting.

"Mr. Ambassador, sir," he said, trying to effect a professional manner despite the loose coat flapping about his waist. He nodded toward the woman. "Missus Ambassador."

The Danish pair appeared not to notice his ill-fitting jacket—if they did, they were too polite to let on.

Emmitt opened the door for the wife and then rushed around the car to do the same for the husband.

"How long will it take us to get to the plantation where they're holding the festivities, Emmitt?" the Ambassador asked as he slid into the rear passenger seat.

"Not more than a half hour, sir. I shouldn't think."

"We have some time before the event then," the Ambassador replied cheerfully. "Can you give us a little tour on the way? Show us a bit of the island. My wife and I have never been here before."

"Certainly, sir," Emmitt said, swallowing uneasily. He'd been given strict orders about the route he was to take to the plantation, but as he glanced in the rearview mirror at his distinguished passengers, he sensed he was following the right protocol.

At least, he hoped he was. After a week of chicken-gambling losses, he needed the money from his new driving duties.

THE SEDAN SOON reached the outskirts of Christiansted. Emmitt kept the car's speed as close as possible to the twenty-five-mile-per-hour speed limit, hoping that the Ambassador and his wife wouldn't notice the potential detour.

Emmitt had no intention of stopping in town. So far, he had managed to keep his freelance employment a secret from the other drivers, and he wanted to keep it that way for as long as possible. He could just imagine the jeers he would receive when they found out.

But as the car passed a sign marking the outer city limits, he heard a suggestive throat-clearing from the backseat.

"Christiansted? That's the main town, isn't it? Why don't we take a quick swing through there, Emmitt?"

"Of course, sir," Emmitt replied dourly.

Maybe the King Street taxi drivers would all be taking a mid-morning coffee break, he thought, and the alley would be empty.

Emmitt sighed wearily.

That seemed highly unlikely.

AS THE SEDAN crawled through Christiansted's regular morning traffic, Emmitt slunk low in his seat, pulled his cap down over his forehead, and kept his eyes fixed firmly ahead.

Despite his efforts at disguise, it was impossible for Emmitt to ignore the men in the alley rising from their fold-out chairs to stare at him. There was no getting around it now; his cover was blown. As the sedan entered the King

Street curve, the phone in his front shirt pocket began to vibrate with incoming text messages, but before he could turn off the device, the Ambassador's wife screamed from the backseat.

"Oh! Watch out for those chickens!"

Emmitt mashed down on the brake, narrowly avoiding an energetic youngster that had jumped out in front of its mother. The hen and her line of chicks strutted safely around the sedan's front wheel—as the men in the alley eagerly leaned forward to count the surviving number.

"That's the old Danish Fort there across the park, isn't it?" the Ambassador asked, less concerned than his wife about the poultry's welfare.

"My, it's an impressive building," he said, patting his wife's knee. She was still turned sideways in her seat, looking back at the chickens. "It really gives one a sense of the past, doesn't it?" He called up to the driver, "My wife had ancestors stationed at the fort, back in the day."

Emmitt gripped the wheel a little tighter, and a few tense lines formed around the corners of his mouth. This extra driving job was quickly turning out to be more than he had bargained for.

"You should take the tour while you're here," he managed to say in an even-toned voice.

"They'll give you plenty of information about your ancestors."

~ 54 ~

Timing Is Everything

MIC AND CURRIE were growing restless inside the boarded-up house across the street from Kareem's grocery store. It had been a long night without food or water, and the stress of their impending criminal activity was weighing heavily on them.

"Is it time yet?" Mic asked hoarsely, his throat dry.

Currie glanced down at the cheap wristwatch Nova had left with him. They were to stage the holdup at exactly eleven o'clock—or face the consequences.

"No, not yet," Currie replied, his throat similarly parched. He lifted his shirt and wiped it across his sweating forehead.

Mic sighed in frustration. "You know that thing you told me not to talk about?"

Currie gave his friend a reproachful stare. After Mic's umpteenth mention of the missed pork chops, Currie had declared a moratorium on any further food discussion. The topic was simply too painful for words. They were both becoming weak from lack of sustenance.

"I know, I know," Mic said, holding up his hands, palms outward. "But just in case you were wondering." He swung his right arm down to point at his stomach. "I'm still hungry!"

CURRIE STARED WITH intensity at the watch face as he propped himself against the street-facing wall.

"Eleven o'clock," he murmured wearily. "Eleven o'clock."

"Remind me again," Mic said, looking over Currie's shoulder. "I can never get this right. The long hand means the hour, and the short hand means the minute?"

Currie closed his eyes, trying to think. His nutrient-starved brain took a moment to process the statement. He waved his finger in the air, as if manipulating an imaginary clock in his head.

"No, it's the other way around."

Mic stared up at the ceiling, his face contorted with concentration. "So, the short hand means the minute, and the long hand means the hour?"

There was another long pause as Currie puzzled, brow furrowed.

"No, no, you've still got it wrong. The long hand means the minute, and the short hand means the hour."

"Right," Mic said dubiously. Returning his gaze to the watch on Currie's wrist, he tilted his head sideways. "What about the third one?"

"Which one?"

"The one that swings around faster than the others."

"That's the second hand."

"Second to what?"

Currie groaned with exasperation.

"How did you ever get by without me?"

INSIDE THE BOARDED-UP shack, the heat was rising, and with it, the stench from the pile of ragged clothes left by Nova's last victim. Currie's footing grew increasingly unsteady; his head began to swim.

Time was either dragging or racing. At this point, it was impossible for him to tell which.

Nova lurked somewhere outside with his gun, watching

and waiting. They were surely headed to prison for this stunt—assuming they made it out of the grocery store alive.

Currie gulped a dry swallow and once more looked down at the watch. His hands shook, making the watch harder to read, but one of the wand points was clearly approaching the eleven mark.

He sighed in desperation. Their time had run out. They'd better get a move on.

Somberly, he handed Mic the extra unloaded gun. Nodding grimly, Mic slid the weapon into the waistband of his shorts and followed Currie to the door.

Currie turned the rusted handle, half expecting it to still be locked. Part of him would have preferred to stay barricaded in this room rather than embark on the unpleasant task before them.

But with a loud creak, the door swung open, letting in a blinding ray of sunlight.

He looked back at Mic and waved his gun's muzzle toward the opening.

There was no turning back now.

AT PRECISELY NINE FIFTY FIVE, the erstwhile coconut vendors exited the boarded-up building across from the grocery store. Blinking in the bright sunlight, they staggered into the street.

Shielding his eyes with his hand, Mic gazed at the wide array of foodstuffs visible through the iron bars that protected the store's front windows.

"Hey, Currie."

"Yeah, Mic."

"Forget the cash. We're going to steal some food."

~ 55 ~

The Motorboat

UMBERTO'S MOTORBOAT BOUNCED across the water, skirting St. Croix's north coast on its way toward Frederiksted. The opera singer stood at the wheel, his hair whipping wildly off his forehead, his cutoff T-shirt flapping in the wind.

The two dachshunds lay calmly on the floor at their master's feet, their tongues lolling out of their mouths. Even as the boat ran across waves that caused it to rock dramatically up and down, the pair looked completely relaxed.

The boat's fourth passenger was not faring nearly as well.

A few feet away from the dogs, Charlie crouched queasily beside a plastic bucket. His face had lost all color; every lurching roll brought him closer to losing the contents of his stomach.

Suddenly, a strange sound rose above the rumbling of the motor.

Charlie looked up, incredulous.

Umberto had begun to sing.

Another rolling pitch brought him back to the bucket.

"I should have taken the taxi."

CHARLIE'S CHURNING STOMACH caused him to miss the entrance to Salt River, and he was still bucket-occupied when they motored past scenic Cane Bay. During a short window of intestinal stability, however, he surfaced long enough to see St. Croix's rocky northwest shoreline, the most inaccessible portion of the island.

Umberto stopped singing to point out Maroon Ridge, the rugged area where, during the colonial era, runaway slaves had hidden in caves and other secluded encampments to escape recapture. A number of the fugitives set sail from the treacherous coast in hopes of reaching the freer territories to the north.

Charlie managed an appreciative nod at the historical information—and at the temporary pause in Umberto's singing, the latter of which, unfortunately, soon resumed.

Turning, Charlie stared at the foaming line of waves that trailed behind the boat. The sun was still bright overhead, but dark clouds had filled the eastern horizon. The spreading mass billowed across the sky, as if the weather were chasing after them, saving up its ammunition of moisture to pound upon their heads.

"Wretched Santa Cruz," he muttered to himself.

And with that thought, Charlie returned to his bucket.

"WE'RE ALMOST THERE," Umberto hollered down to his prostrate passenger as the boat finally rounded St. Croix's northwest curve and headed south toward Frederiksted.

Gripping the railing, Charlie pulled himself into a standing position.

The rocky landscape had softened into a sandy shoreline, along which a road could be seen, circling the island's edge. Not far down the coast, the road forked, sending off an inland branch down a mahogany-lined thoroughfare that disappeared into a thick forest.

As the motorboat approached the tiny town, the behemoth cruise ship docked at the pier grew larger in size, dwarfing the adjacent structures. A metropolis on water, the smooth white walls rose up like a mobile skyscraper.

Umberto scaled back the engine as the boat entered the shallow water, a minnow in the shadow of a whale. He peered up at the cruise ship, his focus narrowing on the security personnel patrolling its outer perimeter.

"I'm afraid they won't let me pull up to the pier," he mused, searching the beach for an alternative place to dock.

"You get this thing anywhere close to land, and I'll jump out and swim for it," Charlie replied, emptying the contents of the bucket over the side into the sea.

UMBERTO GUIDED THE motorboat as close as he dared to the Frederiksted shoreline. Then he flipped a ladder over the boat's side. Reaching for his backpack, Charlie waved good-bye.

"Thanks for the ride, Bert." He gripped the railing and swung a foot over onto the ladder's top rung.

"It was my pleasure." The opera singer smiled apologetically. "More mine than yours, I'm afraid."

With a grimace, Charlie clambered the rest of the way onto the ladder. He looked down into the water, sizing up the depth.

"We can wait for you?" Umberto volunteered. He found himself more and more intrigued by the activities of this strange little man.

"Not necessary," Charlie replied swiftly. He took a step lower, easing his booted foot into the water.

"You're meeting someone?" Umberto asked, trying to prolong the conversation.

Charlie shifted his weight uncomfortably before answering. "My daughter."

"She's the one from the note?" Umberto prodded.

Charlie grunted affirmatively. "She asked me to meet her at the Transfer Day ceremonies."

He released one hand from the ladder and reached into his pocket for his wallet. Unfolding it to access the contents, he removed the faded photo, tattered around its edges, of two children posing in front of their just finished plates of key lime pie.

"She's the one on the left," he said, holding it out for the opera singer to see.

Umberto raised his eyebrows.

"She's awfully young to have written that note."

Charlie fiddled with the brim of his cap. "She's a lot older now than when that picture was taken."

He sighed, anticipating the coming recrimination. "Ten years older."

UMBERTO AND THE dachshunds watched as Charlie waded through the water, holding his backpack and wallet over his head. He eventually slogged, dripping, onto the beach. As he reached the side of the road, he shook out his lower half, wiggling one leg after the other in the air. Flapping the wet sides of his pants, he squished the residual liquid from his boots.

Then he pulled down on the brim of his cap and set off toward the Danish plantation, leaving a trail of wet boot prints behind him.

Umberto tapped his chin, trying to imagine the story that had led the stocky man to that day's bizarre events.

After a moment's reflection, he issued his assessment.

"Fascinating."

~ 56 ~

Into the Jungle

CHARLIE MARCHED NORTH along the shoreline road, quickly reaching the outskirts of Frederiksted. He kept to the shoulder on a path of gravel and dirt, the finer particulates of which caked his boots before drying and falling away, leaving a dusty brown residue.

A couple of shabby beach bars lined the seafront, each one surrounded by several rotting plastic chairs, most of them upended. Discarded beer bottles and other random pieces of refuse lay strewn about the weedy stretch of sand, an uninviting entrance that discouraged all but the most intrepid bar patrons.

Past a couple of boarded-up cinderblocks, the road ventured into a desolate no-man's land. An endless expanse of blue water took up the space to Charlie's left; the dense greenery of the wild interior filled in the right. An increasingly dark, brooding cloud mass swirled above.

About half a mile out of town, Charlie veered inland on the mahogany-lined road he'd seen from Umberto's boat. His combat boots steadily drying, he left behind the sea and braced himself for the murky unknown awaiting him inside the jungle.

A NUMBER OF vehicles drove by as Charlie plodded along in the shade of the mahoganies. Each transport was loaded with passengers for the festivities at the plantation down the road.

He found himself looking up at each passing car, bus, or van, wondering if one of the faces peering out the side windows belonged to his daughter.

She'd been a young girl when he'd last seen her. Physical features changed so dramatically as children grew older, he hardly knew what he was looking for. He couldn't help but wonder if he would be able to recognize her.

Even worse, he worried, what if she didn't recognize him?

Given the steady flow of traffic on this otherwise lightly traveled road, the event was going to be jam-packed. How would they ever find one another in a crowd of people?

With a sigh, he continued on, resolute despite his growing list of concerns.

It felt like he had been waiting an eternity for this moment, for an opportunity like this to arise.

He would know soon enough if it was yet another hoax.

As a boisterous school bus rumbled past, he tried to be optimistic.

"I just hope I don't end up wearing another green dress."

TEN MINUTES LATER, the road began a series of sweeping turns, leaving behind the tall mahoganies. With the landscape barrier removed, the jungle closed in on the pavement, pushing Charlie closer to the lane of traffic.

After a few near collisions and several surprised honks, Charlie rounded a corner and found himself within sight of the entrance to the Danish estate. The turn-in was marked with colorful balloons, flags, and several brightly painted banners.

A line of school busses waited with other cars to enter the already filled parking lot. Harried volunteers worked to direct the newcomers into an empty field that was accommodating the overflow.

Hiking up the hill into the estate, Charlie quickly found himself immersed in a festival atmosphere. There were politicians in suits, Danes in tropical linen, and young children dressed in costumes designed for an upcoming performance of traditional dance. He would have suffered from sensory overload, even if he weren't trying to pick out his daughter from the mix.

He stopped to stare at a group of teenage girls wearing blue-and-white school uniforms. Several of them had light skin and dark brown hair, but as he studied each face, none struck him as familiar. But then again, he couldn't be sure. It was an impossible task, he thought grimly.

A sturdy West Indian woman noticed him lurking near the girls and gave him a stern stare.

Charlie shrugged sheepishly. "I'm looking for my daughter."

"What does she look like?" she asked suspiciously.

"I wish I knew."

WITH THE CROWDS milling about him, Charlie pulled the note from his pocket. Once more, he scanned the pink handwriting. His daughter had given him no instructions about how they were to meet up once he arrived at the Transfer Day celebrations.

After listing the address to the Danish plantation, she'd ended the letter in a simple sign-off.

"Hope to see you soon. Love, Jessie."

~ 57 ~

Missing

"JESSIE!"

For the second day in a row, Mira found herself calling out for a missing child.

After packing her own suitcase, she had decided to make the rounds to check on her children's progress. She stood at the entrance to her oldest daughter's bedroom, peering inside.

There was no sign of Jessie—or for that matter, any ready-to-go luggage—but the window by the bed stood suspiciously open.

"Jessie!" Mira tried again, half hoping the teenager would step from the closet or pop out from behind the door.

There was no answer. The room was disturbingly still.

Sighing tensely, Mira slid across the unmade bed and stuck her head through the window. In the dirt five feet below, she spied the unmistakable imprints of Jessie-sized footprints. The bushes closest to the house had a few broken branches, creating a narrow trail leading into the forest that surrounded the gated subdivision.

"Jessie!" she called once more, but this time she didn't expect a response.

Mira pulled herself back inside the house. Grabbing a pillow from the bed, she threw it across the room in frustration.

Her oldest daughter had run off to find her father—again.

JUMPING UP FROM the bed, Mira paced back and forth across the room, trying to figure out where Jessie might have gone.

She glanced at her watch. It was almost ten o'clock. The day's first seaplane had already departed. Charlie should be well on his way to St. Thomas by now.

"Good riddance to him," Mira muttered as she began searching the room for a clue to her daughter's whereabouts.

She quickly rummaged through the piles of clothing in the bottom of the closet as well as the various boxes and books stuffed beneath the bed. Then she shifted her attention to her daughter's white-painted dresser. The furniture's flat top was covered with an assortment of accessories and trinkets. There were hair ribbons, barrettes, little plastic figurines, and, hidden beneath a package of envelopes, a pad of pink paper.

Mira scanned through the items, dismissing each one until she reached the stationery. Fishing the pad of paper out of the stack, she held it up to her face, tilting it to look across the paper's horizontal surface.

She could just make out the impressions left from a ballpoint pen, which had pressed through from the (now missing) sheets above.

Ripping off the paper, Mira returned to the window. She leaned across the bed to place it in a ray of direct sunlight and squinted at the writing.

The bulk of the text was indecipherable, with pressthroughs from previous letters commingling on the page, but the first line had been written on a previously clear space. The words confirmed her suspicions.

"Dear Charlie Baker . . ."

Mira wadded up the paper and tossed it on the floor next to the pillow.

"I should have never let that girl out of my sight."

MIRA RACED ACROSS the hallway and banged on the closed door to her older son's room, desperately hoping he hadn't left with his sister. She was fairly certain Jessie hadn't shared her father-finding mission with her brother; the two weren't very close and rarely spent time together. Nevertheless, she let out a sigh of relief when she heard her son's distinctive shuffle approaching on the tile floor.

A moment later, the door swung open to reveal a teenage boy, a few years younger than his eldest sibling. Short and scruffy, a baseball cap covered his dark brown hair, which he wore in a long cut, the bulk of it tied back in a ponytail at the nape of his neck.

Mira tried to ignore the similarities, but she couldn't help thinking that he looked more and more like his father every day.

Yawning, the boy held up a small duffel bag, as if anticipating a question about whether or not he was packed for the trip.

"That's all you're taking?" she asked, incredulous. "We won't be back"—she cleared her throat and added the false clarification—"for a very long time."

He shrugged. Since turning twelve, this had become his most frequent response to questions. He had been mute so long, Mira had almost forgotten the sound of his voice.

"Jack, have you seen Jessie?"

He gave her another silent shrug.

"Did you see her leave?"

He moved his shoulders in an emotive half shrug, as if to say that he couldn't be held responsible for his sister's wanderings.

"Do you know where she went?"

This time, all she received was a blank stare.

"All right. Well, be ready to go in . . ."
She stopped speaking as he turned and shut the door.

TEENAGERS WERE EVEN more difficult to deal with than ex-husbands, Mira thought wearily. At this moment, she was in no position to order a grounding or any other punishment—and she suspected her son knew it.

It was going to be far more difficult to leave her second husband than it had been the first.

As she walked down the hallway to the bedroom shared by her two youngest offspring, she sucked in a deep breath, trying to steady her nerves. The taxi van would be here in two hours to take them to Christiansted, where they would be catching the afternoon seaplane to St. Thomas. She would check in on Elena and Hassan and then figure out how to corral Jessie.

The door to the first room on the long hallway was slightly ajar. As she neared, Mira could hear playful shrieks and giggles emanating from within. Those sounds, combined with the telltale crunch of bedsprings, indicated that this pair might need some assistance getting their things together.

She had no idea how much assistance.

As Mira pushed open the door, a flying shirt hit her square across the face.

Once she'd cleared her vision and taken a look at the scene inside the room, she let loose a full-throated howl.

~ 58 ~

Jessie

MIRA'S OLDEST DAUGHTER drove her moped onto the grounds of the refurbished Danish estate, weaving around the cars waiting at the entrance. Following the pointing directions of a frazzled Transfer Day volunteer, she motored to a stop beneath a tree next to several other two-wheeled vehicles.

Jessie pulled the key from the ignition and gazed down at her machine. None of the others in the parking lineup, she thought proudly, was as lovingly restored as hers.

She'd taken on the project all by herself. A mechanic down the street from the family's villa had kindly loaned her the necessary tools. Secondhand manuals and instructional videos from the school library had provided technical guidance. Using those resources and her own ingenuity, she'd rebuilt the moped's engine on her own.

The gas-powered bike had proved to be an invaluable resource during her frequent late-night outings through her bedroom window and, more recently, in her efforts to track down her father and lure him to St. Croix.

Jessie gave the worn leather seat a soft pat as she joined the other Transfer Day arrivals in the walk up the hill toward the estate house.

The childhood keepsakes she'd left behind in her room that morning had given her only momentary pause. She had discarded those items without worry or concern.

It would be far tougher to ever part with her beloved bike.

TWIRLING THE MOPED keys in her hand, Jessie wandered toward the main event area. A series of white tents had been pitched in the grassy lawn in front of the estate house, creating shade from the sun or, more likely, given the dark clouds moving in, protection from the coming rain.

Volunteers unloaded metal chairs from a trailer and unfolded them beneath the tents. A wooden podium had been rolled to the front of the covered seating space; a microphone mounted to the podium was in the process of being connected to a series of speakers.

At the opposite end of the lawn, just below the rise of the hill, still more volunteers were setting up for the post-ceremony lunch. Workers hefted metal pans out of transport vans and arranged the food trays on brackets that allowed for tiny Sterno burners to be slid underneath.

The lunch prep had been positioned out of the direct line of sight of the ceremony seating, but the fragrant smell of numerous home-cooked West Indian dishes floated across the lawn. Only a strong westward wind would keep the tempting odor from tormenting the audience through the morning's political speeches.

IN BETWEEN THESE two end posts, Jessie mingled with the growing Transfer Day crowds, searching for Charlie Baker.

A few months ago, she'd had only a blurry mental image of her father, unreliable for purposes of picking him out of such a packed group of people. Recently, however, she had tracked down a photo of him in the online records of an island newspaper. As part of a series of stories on St. John's construction boom, a local journalist had written an article featuring one of Charlie's work sites. The piece was a few years old, but the accompanying black-and-white picture had clarified Jessie's childhood recollections.

As she sifted through the colorful sea of faces outside the plantation's estate house, she knew exactly for whom she was looking—an advantage that she had carefully maintained over her father.

His last image of her was as a five-year-old girl.

In her note to Charlie, Jessie had intentionally left out any details about her current physical description or how they were to connect with one another at the Transfer Day celebrations. She wanted to leave herself plenty of maneuvering room should she decide to bail at the last minute.

Her father was an unknown entity, of whom she had only distant memories—most of them involving key lime pie.

She grinned to herself. The frozen dish at the diner on the boardwalk was still her favorite dessert.

Nevertheless, the fast-melting concoction didn't provide the type of foundation upon which to build a tower of trust.

GROWING UP, JESSIE had spent a great deal of time wondering what had become of her biological father. His abrupt departure from her life had left her with innumerable, often troubling questions. She would lay awake at night, trying to make sense of his sudden exit—as well as his continued absence.

She pursued the issue with her mother, but Mira's vague and misleading answers did little to quash her daughter's growing curiosity.

So, like the moped engine, Jessie had taken it upon herself to investigate the matter.

THINKING BACK TO her childhood, before she was old enough to attend the community school, Jessie remembered that she and her brother had often accompanied their mother on trips to the Christiansted post office.

In each instance, Mira would enter the post office and

walk down a wall filled with rows of tiny metal doors until she reached one at the end of the bottom row. Using a key from her purse, she would open the door to access a long narrow box.

Mira would then remove a packet, which she would immediately open and, upon checking the contents—Jessie recalled this part distinctly—smile serenely.

After the post office stop, her mother would usher the group around the corner to a Christiansted bank. There, Mira removed a check from the packet and deposited it with one of the clerks.

Jessie had puzzled, in particular, over this second detail. Why would her mother choose to do business with a bank in town—and not with the financial institution set up by the Muslim community, where her stepfather served on the board of directors and where each of the children eventually registered individual savings accounts for their weekly allowance and other odd job earnings?

Her mother, Jessie eventually concluded, had a secret bank account that her stepfather likely knew nothing about.

~ *59* ~

The Walk-In Closet

THE PREVIOUS FALL, Jessie spent weeks searching the villa for her mother's stash of hidden records and correspondence. It was a lengthy, drawn-out process. The search times were limited to rare windows of opportunity in the afternoons when Jessie was home from school and Mira was away on errands.

Mira and Kareem's living space had long been declared off-limits to the children, so that became Jessie's logical target area. Through the years, she and her siblings had explored every other inch of the house. If her mother had concealed something within the home relating to her separate bank account, it had to be located beyond the doors to the master bedroom, likely in a spot where Kareem wouldn't accidentally stumble across it.

Mira's many walk-in closets were the easy point of focus.

Over the course of several hunting sessions, Jessie waded through endless hangers of clothing: blouses, skirts, and dresses of every imaginable color, fabric, and length.

A tomboy at heart, she couldn't begin to understand her mother's fixation with fashion. She plowed through several windowless cubicles without coming across a single item that even remotely struck her female fancy. More important, she failed to identify any clues to her mother's secret life.

At long last, Jessie reached the closet at the far end of her mother's boudoir, a room devoted entirely to shoes. Row upon row of racks displayed her mother's size-seven sandals, flats, heels, and boots—all of them, in Jessie's opinion, impractical for island wear.

On the wall behind the racks, stacks of empty shoe boxes rose almost to the ceiling. It was a daunting task, but Jessie began a methodical review of each individual box.

One by one, she fished the box out from its column and lifted the lid to check the interior contents. Then, to make sure she didn't inadvertently disrupt her mother's organizational system, she slid the box back into its specific slot.

Jessie cycled through the first twenty boxes, finding all of them empty. She was about to dismiss the rest when she noticed a green square on the upper left of the stack that appeared slightly out of alignment with the others.

As soon as she lifted the box from its column, she knew she was onto something. It was noticeably heavier than the previous containers, its cardboard edges more worn. The contents shuffled as she tilted it toward her.

A quick peek beneath the lid confirmed her suspicions.

"Now, we're getting somewhere," she had sighed with relief.

THE GREEN BOX, along with several of those surrounding it, contained a trove of data. In the ensuing weeks, Jessie returned to the shoe closet multiple times. On each occasion, she gathered more information.

Ever since her parents' divorce, her father had been sending child support payments north to Minnesota. Her mother had apparently convinced the local postmaster there to re-package the letters and forward them to her on St. Croix. All this time, she realized, her father had been under the impression that they were living up in the States.

As Jessie read through nearly a decade's worth of correspondence, she grew increasingly angry. How could her mother not have passed on the birthday cards, the little Christmas packages, and the endless requests for pictures and phone calls? How could she have deprived her daughter of access to her father, who, it turned out, was living just a short distance away?

And then Jessie paused, reflecting on a more perplexing question.

How could her father have let her mother get away with it?

SO IT WAS with wary caution that Jessie set about devising a way to contact Charlie.

She located his business listing using the Internet on a computer at her school—her online access at the villa was restricted and closely monitored. Then she sat on Charlie's contact details for days, pondering how best to use the information. She stared at her father's cell-phone number for so long, it became permanently committed to her memory.

It was the discovery of the St. John newspaper article that finally pushed her to action. After seeing her father's grainy black-and-white image in the article's attached photo, she decided on her first approach.

Posing as her mother, she called Charlie's phone.

When the man's voice answered on the other end of the line, it took every bit of self-restraint for her not to shout, "It's me, Daddy."

But she kept to her script, inviting him to meet up with the family on St. Croix for Thanksgiving.

IT HAD BEEN a brilliant plan, Jessie reflected as she stood in the middle of the Transfer Day crowds, watching a group of Danish tourists head toward the estate house for a tour.

But even the most cunning strategies could be derailed by unexpected interventions.

Jessie hadn't counted on her mother being such a skilled tactician.

~ 60 ~

Nova

JUST OVER A mile south of the Danish plantation, the tiny town of Frederiksted put its best foot forward to greet the cruise ship docked at its pier.

Despite the dark clouds looming in the sky, several artists set up booths along the shoreline pavilion and optimistically laid out their goods. Strand Street shop owners threw open their doors, hoping to catch a passing day-tripper or two.

At a diner a half block inland from the pier, a worker unfolded a sandwich placard on the sidewalk, touting the day's breakfast special.

Inside the diner, a well-toned man with a beautiful face plopped down at a counter in front of a plate piled high with bacon, eggs, sausage, and potatoes. Sides of buttered toast and fruit salad ringed the plate, along with a tall glass of fresh-squeezed orange juice and a mug of hot coffee.

Nova leaned back on his stool and loosened his belt, preparing to dig into one of his favorite meals.

He sighed with contentment. His day was off to a fabulous start.

LIFE WAS GOOD for the man known around the island as Casanova.

Lady Luck, it seemed, had always favored him. From birth onward, fortune routinely fell into his lap, opportunity crossed his path with frequency, and success was achieved without effort.

He lived a life of reckless confidence, pushing beyond both legal and societal limits. He had no need for caution or restraint. Nothing could harm him.

He was untouchable—by flying bullets, jealous girl-friends, or the futile attempts of the police to restrain his growing criminal empire.

Despite the serious matter on his schedule that morning, he was relaxed and fully at ease.

Nova smiled up at the waitress bashfully watching him from the opposite side of the counter as he scooped his fork into the heap of scrambled eggs. He gave the girl a sly wink, a thank-you for the extra-large portions on his plate.

And, of course, he was laying the groundwork to ask for her phone number on his way out the door.

JUST AS NOVA stuffed the loaded fork into his mouth, his cell phone signaled an incoming call. A thumping reggae ringtone blasted into the diner, disrupting a pair of cruise ship day-trippers at a nearby table.

Swallowing, Nova brought the phone to his lips. "Hello?" he mumbled through the remaining food in his mouth. He reached for the orange juice as he listened to the speaker on the other end of the line.

After a few seconds, he cut in impatiently. "Stop your worrying. Everything's fine."

He glanced up at the clock on the diner's back wall. "The patsies are in place. It'll all go down at eleven."

IRRITATED BY THE interruption, Nova hung up the phone and returned to his breakfast. He dove into the sausage, slicing off a chunk of the spicy meat and stuffing it into his mouth.

He thought briefly of his two psychological captives in the boarded-up house around the corner. Mic and Currie had been half-starved and desperate when he'd checked on them earlier that morning. He chuckled. That was just the way he wanted them. At any rate, those two would be out of their misery soon enough.

Nova had left the door to the house unlocked—he didn't want to chance being seen in the vicinity of the place in the minutes before the two men tried to hold up the grocery store. He wasn't worried about the pair running off. The coconut boys were scared silly. They weren't going anywhere until the appointed time.

All Nova had to do was sneak around to the rear of the store and wait for Mic and Currie to bungle their way inside. He tapped the sidearm strapped to his left ankle beneath his pants leg. Once they set the robbery in motion, he would finish things off with his newly acquired, soon-to-be-disposed-of pistol.

He scooped up a mouthful of potatoes.

But first, he was going to enjoy his breakfast.

~ *61* ~

Pork Chops

KAREEM STOOD IN the center aisle of the Frederiksted grocery store, discussing stocking options with a West Indian woman who he was training for the shop's management position.

After screening through several applicants, the woman had been by far the best candidate for the job. A smart, practical individual, she was earning a degree from the local college while raising two young children.

In the week since her hiring, Kareem had been impressed by her dedication and motivation. She always arrived at work a few minutes early, and during her shifts, she constantly bustled about the store, never needing prompting or oversight.

His star employee, however, appeared to be distracted that morning. He couldn't figure out what was wrong with the woman. The store had been open for just over an hour, and there had been only light foot traffic, so it wasn't a case of circulating customers diverting her attention. Something else, it seemed, was drawing her focus from the matter at hand.

"I thought we might expand the variety of boxed cereal,"

Kareem said, trying again to capture her interest. He pointed at a line of packages. "My charts indicate a high turnover rate on this brand over here. If we moved it up to an eye level shelf and added a few more varieties, I think we might see a profit increase."

"Hmm-mm," she replied absentmindedly.

Kareem had just about given up on the discussion when he noticed his employee looking over the aisle toward the street.

Following her gaze, he saw two scraggly-looking men scurrying toward the store's front door.

The pair looked haggard and hungry. Kareem sighed, empathetic.

And then his eyes narrowed in on the black metallic object the shorter one carried in his left hand.

MIC AND CURRIE scurried across the street, nervously looking up and down the block for signs of Nova. Their captor's unseen presence was sorely felt—despite the fact that he was still seated at the diner eating breakfast a few blocks away.

Believing that Nova's bullet-filled gun was aimed squarely at them, the frightened pair dared not point their feet anywhere other than the grocery store's entrance.

"He's watching us," Currie muttered, gripping the unloaded weapon in his sweating left hand.

"I can feel his eyes on me," Mic agreed with a skin-shaking shudder.

The vibrating motion was more than Mic's loose-fitting shorts, resting on his slim hips, could take. His gun slipped from the waistband and clattered to the ground, skidding across the pebble-strewn asphalt.

The clanging sound of metal on rock echoed through the morning air.

The coconut vendors froze in their tracks, paralyzed with fear. The men stared in horror at the errant weapon lying on the far side of the street—then they slowly raised their line of sight to the shopkeeper standing in the grocery store doorway.

Trembling, Currie waved his shaking gun at Kareem. He opened his mouth to speak, but no words came out. He couldn't bring himself to make the demand. He didn't have it in him. He wasn't cut out for armed robbery.

His partner had no such qualms.

Mic's hoarse voice hollered across the ten-foot distance.

"Give us all of your pork chops!"

KAREEM TOOK IN a deep breath and issued a calm smile. He didn't discount the danger of the situation, but he and his security team had handled far worse. He'd pressed the alert button on the cashier counter on his way to the front door. A number of armed guards and, hopefully, the police, would be arriving within minutes.

In the meantime, he sensed he might be able to defuse the confrontation on his own.

Cautiously, Kareem raised his hands in front of his chest, a submissive gesture.

"Please, gentlemen. I do not wish you any harm." He nodded at the sign above the storefront. "But this is a Muslim-owned store. We do not sell pork."

Mic sighed, crestfallen. Then his eyes lit up with the inspiration for another request.

"What about French fries?"

Currie slapped his forehead with his free hand and muttered grimly.

"We're doomed."

FROM AN ALLEY at the end of the block, Gedda watched the encounter between the shopkeeper and the coconut vendors with amusement. She giggled to herself, pleased that her boardwalk friends had inadvertently avoided a Nova-masterminded annihilation. Their inability to tell time had given them a full hour's jump on their tormentor.

As sirens wailed in the distance, she turned back toward the shoreline and began hobbling to the main road. She would have to get a move on if she was going to make it to the Transfer Day ceremony in time for the speeches.

~ 62 ~

The Chicken Charm

THE NEVISIAN TAXI driver finished skimming the day's newspaper and folded it neatly on the surface of a picnic table located on the Frederiksted shoreline near the cruise ship pier.

He hadn't found any new information within the daily's pages, but, then again, he hadn't expected to. He had picked up the paper only out of boredom.

Draining his second foam cup of coffee purchased from a kiosk by the pavilion, he gazed out at the cruise ship and the ring of snorkelers swimming at the end of the pier.

"Worthless interlopers," he said with a despondent sigh.

He reached into his pocket and pulled out a wrinkled dollar bill and a handful of change. As he counted out coins for a third cup of coffee, the radio in his van began to crackle.

"Hey, Nevis, you catch any fish yet?"

Jumping up from the table's bench seat, the driver returned the money to his pocket, hurried over to the van, and reached through the open front window for the radio's receiver.

"Emmitt, man. Don't jinx me." He tossed the receiver

through the window and slid into the driver's seat. "It's early yet."

A third voice joined the conversation.

"Emmitt—where you at? You still driving around in that Cadillac?"

A defensive grunt came from Emmitt's end of the line. "Get off my back, Seymour." He groaned bitterly. "I'm sitting in it right now, waiting for the Ambassador and the missus to finish their walk along Cane Bay. Then I'm taking them on to Transfer Day at the Danish plantation."

"Hey, Emmitt, how come you never drive me around in that nice-looking car of yours?"

"Can it, Seymour."

The man from Nevis broke in. "Say, Seymour. How're my chickens doing?"

Emmitt voiced his immediate objection. "Nevis, you can't place a bet if you're not working the alley. That's the rule."

"Keep your knickers on, Emmitt. I don't have any money in today's game. I placed an informational bet. No money on it, just my pride. I didn't want my chicken karma to run cold."

Emmitt smacked his disapproval. "I don't like it. Not one bit."

Seymour sniped back, "And I don't like you parading around town all hoity-toity in that slick sedan. Nevis, what was your number on the chickens?"

The driver gazed out his cracked windshield with a smile. He'd been the outsider of the group since his arrival six months ago. It was nice to hear the other drivers beat up on someone else for a change.

"I talked to Lady Jemima this morning before I left," Nevis said slyly. "She assured me she'd keep five of her brood."

Seymour made a satisfied popping sound with his mouth.

"Nevis, that chicken done led you astray. I'm watching her strut across King Street right now, and all I can see is four little birds behind her."

Nevis tapped his worn steering wheel, his fingers drumming out a casual cadence.

"Check your eyesight, Seymour. I'm certain she'll have five."

There was a shuffling of footsteps as the drivers in the alley scurried to confirm the count. Finally, Seymour returned to the mike.

"Curse you, Nevis."

Emmitt blew out a frustrated sigh.

Nevis grinned triumphantly.

"You all should be nicer to my Jemma."

THE MAN FROM Nevis reached up and tapped a trinket hanging from his rearview mirror. A flat piece of metal crudely forged into the shape of a bird swung back and forth on its beaded chain. He watched the trinket sparkle in a flash of sunlight that had broken through the clouds. His chicken charm had never failed him.

"'Course, you could help me out here with some riders," he admonished the iron bird.

Just then a loud banging sounded against the van's metal siding, the thunderous pounding of four human hands desperately trying to open the passenger door.

Startled, Nevis dove behind the steering wheel. Then he peeked up, confused, as a fistful of dollar bills flew through his driver's-side window.

"Please, sir, you've got to give us a ride."

Nevis poked his nose up far enough to see two men reflected in his left-side mirror. The terrified pair looked vaguely familiar. He was pretty sure he'd seen them around the Christiansted boardwalk.

Another wad of cash was tossed over the window ledge.

Grimacing up at the chicken, Nevis flicked the control button for the passenger-door's lock and said steadily, "Okay, boys, hop inside."

Mic and Currie scrambled into the back of the van. Currie leaned toward the driver, his face ashen with fear.

"We need to get off of Santa Cruz—as fast as possible."

Nevis sputtered his objection. "Does this look like a boat to you?"

"Please, sir. You've got to get us out of here. He's going to kill us."

~ *63* ~

Unmet Friends

EMMITT JUMPED OUT of the air-conditioned sedan and rushed around to open the rear doors for the Danish Ambassador and his wife, who had just returned from their stroll along Cane Bay.

"Did you enjoy your walk, sir?" Emmitt asked politely, trying not to notice the sand on the bottom of the Ambassador's shoes as the man stepped into the car. There went yet another rule from the handbook that had been broken that morning.

"It was fabulous, Emmitt," the Ambassador replied with a pleasant smile. "Just fabulous."

Emmitt returned to the driver's seat and quickly set the car in motion, pulling back onto the road from the shoulder where he'd been parked.

He checked his watch. Grimacing, he pushed down on the gas, sending the car zooming along the north shore. There wasn't time for any more stops, no matter how many throat-clearings or verbal suggestions emanated from the car's backseat.

If the Ambassador arrived late for his speech, this would likely be Emmitt's last sedan-driving gig.

NOT FAR PAST Cane Bay, the shoreline grew rocky and steep. Quickly rising, the road twisted into a series of hairpin turns. As the sedan gained altitude, white foam could be seen on the waves crashing against the boulders below.

Emmitt clenched the steering wheel, racing around the sharp corners as fast as he dared.

The Ambassador appeared not to notice the increased speed.

"If you don't mind, Emmitt, I'd like to practice a little bit of my speech," he said cordially.

Emmitt leaned into another tight turn. "Not at all, sir."

"The title is 'A Stranger Is Just a Friend That You Haven't Yet Met.' It's based on a quote by the famous American entertainer Will Rogers."

His focus trained on the road, Emmitt issued a noncommittal grunt.

"The idea is to capture the historical connection between Denmark and the Virgin Islands," the Ambassador continued. "To encourage a renewed friendship between our two countries."

"Hm-mm," Emmitt replied, tensely checking his watch. The car had just summited the top of the hill and made the turn south. If he kept up their pace, they might still get to the event on time.

"I think there's a great opportunity here to increase our business and tourism ties, close the distance between us." Beaming broadly, the Ambassador tapped the top edge of Emmitt's seat. "And turn strangers into friends."

THE AMBASSADOR CONTINUED to practice his speech as the sedan sped toward the western terminus of Centerline Road.

"This is Frederiksted," Emmitt announced curtly, breaking into a momentary pause in the backseat colloquy. As the sedan circled the waterfront, he scanned the shoreline, hoping to find an empty taxi van parked by the pier, waiting for riders.

He let out a muted grumble when he saw that the picnic table where the drivers regularly waited was vacant.

The Ambassador looked up from his speech notes. "What's that, Emmitt?"

"I said, 'It's looking like a good cruise ship day, sir.'"

THE SEDAN POWERED up the shoreline north of Frederiksted and soon turned on the inland road leading to the Danish estate. Emmitt breathed a sigh of relief at the sight of the last straightaway before the curving entrance.

"Those are mahoganies, aren't they?" the Ambassador asked, pointing out his window at the tall trees lining the road.

Seeing Emmitt's nod, he leaned toward his wife. "I read that the native mahogany is a slow-growing tree, which creates a dense wood. They make fine furniture from it throughout the Caribbean."

"That's fascinating, dear," she replied in a placating voice. She tilted her head inquisitively as she stared out the window. "What about that elevated pipe running along the other side of the trees, Emmitt? It must have been quite a bit of work to put that together. Was that used for irrigating the cane fields?"

"Yes." Emmitt answered succinctly. There was a long moment of silence as he considered his next comment. He had made it through the discussion of the soldiers at the Danish fort, the Ambassador's upcoming speech, and numerous other sensitive political issues without offending his clients.

But on this last point, he felt compelled to speak. It was a matter of personal pride and defiance.

"My ancestors helped lay that pipe."

"You see, Emmitt," the Ambassador chimed in. "Look at how much you and my wife have in common. Just over the course of this car ride, I feel like we've gone from strangers to friends."

~ 64 ~

Fled the Coop

NOVA DRAINED THE last sip of orange juice from his glass and pushed away from the counter at the Frederiksted diner. Patting his full stomach, he reached into his pocket for his wallet. He pulled out several bills and placed them next to his now-empty plate, leaving a hefty tip for the cute waitress, who had written her phone number on his check.

Pleased with the prospect of a future date, he glanced up at the clock on the diner's far wall and headed out the door.

He had just enough time to get into position.

FIVE MINUTES LATER, Nova slunk into an alley that passed behind the rear of the grocery store. He looked carefully up and down the narrow passage, but the area appeared empty. With one last glance over his shoulder, he stepped into the store's rear doorway, pulled a black cotton ski mask from his pocket, and tugged it on over his head.

Bending to one knee, he pulled up his pants leg and slipped the pistol from its ankle holster.

Still in his crouched position, Nova placed an ear against

the door and listened for an indication that Mic and Currie had approached from the front.

The shop inside was silent.

Nova waited for ten long minutes, but the alley remained quiet—and the stifling mask grew hotter and more uncomfortable. Despite the cloud cover overhead, beads of sweat began to run down his cheeks, soaking the cotton fabric.

Finally, he yanked off the mask. Cursing, he banged the side of the weapon against the doorway's concrete stoop. The coconut boys had either chickened out or lost track of time.

Either way, Nova thought, bitterly thumping the gun against his thigh, he was going to inflict a beating.

NOVA STORMED AROUND the building and across the street. No longer concerned about being seen, he tromped over to the boarded-up house and pounded his fist against the front door. The splintered wood panel slammed inward, revealing its unoccupied interior.

Charging inside, Nova quickly confirmed that Mic and Currie were gone.

He was going to have to take care of this job on his own. His face darkened into a pitch-black rage.

"You two had better start running," he muttered furiously. "I'll cover every inch of this island if I have to, but I'm going to track you down. You'll rue the day you crossed Casanova."

JUST A FEW miles north, a beat-up taxi van with a cracked windshield and a chicken-shaped trinket swinging from its rearview mirror drove along the coast. The van rumbled over a rutted road that ran beside the edge of the impenetrable rain forest. Several minutes earlier, the vehicle had passed the mahogany-lined turnoff for the island's interior. It was headed toward even more rugged territory: the island's northwest coast.

Dark clouds swirled the sky as the van reached the end of the road and came to a stop. Two men jumped out the passenger-side door and sprinted headlong into the brush.

Arms and legs flailing, Mic and Currie managed to orient themselves onto a narrow trail, a mostly forgotten path leading to the shoreline below the island's historic Maroon Ridge.

Branches reached in from either side, grabbing at their clothes, scratching their hands and faces. Sharp rocks tore into the calloused soles of their feet. Their muscles burned as they gasped for air.

But neither man dared slow his pace.

They were running for their lives.

~ *65* ~

Transfer Day

THE GOVERNOR CLIMBED reluctantly out of his air-conditioned limo and lumbered toward the white-tented area in front of the Danish estate house, where the Transfer Day ceremonies would soon be starting. A greeting line of local dignitaries waited for him beneath the tents, each one eager for their chance to hobnob with the territory's chief executive.

With Cedric hovering by his elbow, the Governor began the obligatory round of handshaking.

"Maddie Nelson, chairperson of the Landmark Society," Cedric whispered as they approached a tall West Indian woman in a yellow dress and a matching flowered hat. "That's the organization that put all this together."

"Miss Nelson," the Governor boomed with confidence. "You've done a wonderful job on today's event." He motioned at the surrounding crowds. "What a great turnout."

After a polite thirty-second exchange with Miss Nelson, the Governor turned to greet the next person in the receiving line. Cedric leaned in with his briefing.

"Jackson Hayes," the aide said quickly. "Ran for one of the legislature's St. Croix seats in the last election. Missed the cutoff by two hundred and fifty six votes. Likely to make it into the senate next go-round."

"Mr. Hayes," the Governor gushed, warmly clasping the man's hand. "So good to see you. You should stop by Government House next time you're over on the Rock."

Mr. Hayes was allotted a full minute of chitchat before Cedric ushered the Governor toward a ruddy man in a three-piece suit.

"Gerard Kohlschreiber, one of the refinery plant managers," Cedric whispered. He paused and added cautiously, "There are rumors that the company has plans to shut the place down."

Scowling testily, the Governor muttered under his breath, "Over my dead body—"

But he cut off his rant at the sight of a burly man with a boyish face who had just strolled into the tented area.

"What's *he* doing here?" the Governor asked through a clenched teeth smile.

Cedric peeked over his boss's shoulder to see the air-conditioning salesman lumbering through the covered seating area near the podium.

WHILE THE GOVERNOR worked the VIP line—and tried to ignore the presence of Adam Rock—other guests participated in guided tours of the estate house.

The stone building no longer functioned as a primary residence, but the place had been carefully preserved, with family heirlooms, antique furniture, and black-and-white photos presented in carefully roped-off displays.

Charlie Baker fell in among a dozen elderly Danish women who were following a docent into the first-floor living area. Having searched for his daughter on the festival grounds without success, he had decided to try the estate house.

As Charlie looked in vain for a dark-haired teenaged girl, he found himself swept from the living area into the kitchen. The tall women packed in around him, blocking his view. Some of them towered almost twelve inches over the rim of his baseball cap. He stood on his tiptoes, trying to see over the tops of the shortest gray heads, but he was unable to make out much beyond the rack of pots and pans shelved across the upper far wall.

"Uh, excuse me, ladies," he said as the crowd shifted to the next room. "I think I'd better try to find the exit."

His meager pleas were either not heard or not understood. With the docent and the women chattering in their native Danish tongue, his voice was lost as white noise.

Charlie tried to turn back toward the entrance, but another set of similarly tall and verbally incomprehensible women had filled in behind his group. There appeared to be no easy way for him to duck out. Sighing with resignation, he shuffled forward as the women funneled up the central staircase.

A HALF HOUR later, Charlie emerged from the tour's end point, breaking free of the Danish women as soon as he cleared the threshold of the house's back door. He stretched his arms and rubbed his shoulders, relieved to be free of the interior's claustrophobic confines.

Midway through the tour, he had managed to maneuver to the front of his group. While he hadn't been able to interpret any of the docent's discussion, he had seen more than his share of teacups, homemade toys, and faded Danish photos. As for elaborate lace doilies, he had received a lifetime's worth of viewing.

Shaking his head, Charlie stepped into a small garden that wrapped around the rear of the house—none the wiser on the estate family's history, but far closer to his daughter than he'd been in almost ten years.

~ *66* ~

A Near-Miss

JESSIE SLIPPED THROUGH the thick forest behind the Danish estate house, quietly circling to the small garden where the tour terminated. After following her father to the house's front entrance, she had decided to hang back when he entered with the group of Danish women.

She stared up at the two-story stone structure, waiting for Charlie to reappear. Over the past centuries, the building had survived the tropical extremes of humidity, hurricanes, and drought. Today, she mused as yet another large group exited, the house was weathering an onslaught of an entirely different nature.

The place was literally crawling with Danish tourists.

AS THE MINUTES dragged by, Jessie maneuvered behind a blind of wide palm fronds. From this concealed position, she had a clear vantage of the garden.

An endless parade of pale and pinkened Danes continued to file out of the estate house, but there was no sign of Charlie. If the women's appreciative tones were any indication, the cultural exhibit was a great success, but she couldn't imagine what her father was doing inside all this time.

Fearing he had retreated out the front door, Jessie was about to return to the other side of the house when Charlie finally leaped through the rear doorway. Quickly separating himself from the rest of his tour group, he threw his arms in the air, as if he'd been liberated after a lengthy confinement.

She suppressed a giggle at his antics and took a tentative step forward. She was now at the edge of the greenery, cloaked by a layer of leaves, but within easy earshot of her father. She wanted to speak, to alert him of her presence, but she hesitated.

She watched as he adjusted his baseball cap and tugged on his ponytail to straighten its knot. Then he reached into his pants pocket and pulled out the note she had left for him in the attic room at the Comanche.

This was the moment for which she'd been waiting. All of her scheming from Thanksgiving to March had been aimed at creating just this type of scenario. Despite her mother's continued foiling of her attempts, she had persevered.

At last, there he was, only a few feet away, searching for her as if he hadn't spent the last ten years in complicit abandonment.

But still she held back, studying his face as he reread her pink-ink handwriting. He looked up and stared into the dense forest, almost as if he sensed her presence.

Then, scowling in frustration, he jammed the paper back into his pocket.

As Charlie crossed to the side of the garden, passing within inches of her hidden location, she couldn't quite bring herself to call out to him.

Jessie stood silent in the trees as he exited through the gate and walked away.

A NARROW STRIP of greenery formed a permeable barrier between the estate's manicured grounds and the wilds of the island's northwest interior. The teenage girl lingered in the leafy border region, one foot planted on civilization's outer rim, the other drifting dangerously close to the jungle's hazardous realm.

Jessie rested her hands on her hips, pondering which path to take next.

She had left the villa that morning with no intention of returning. After everything she'd learned about her mother over the course of the last several months, she was determined to sever all ties with Mira. She had pinned her hopes on reuniting with her father and living with him on St. John.

But now, she wasn't so sure.

As she considered her options, the surrounding vegetation curled forward, stealthily moving in on her. The edge of the storm swooped down toward the plantation, sending a gust of wind through the trees. Branches began to bend and sway, twisting toward the lonely teenage girl as if they were acting under their own volition.

It's the Goat Foot Woman, Jessie thought with a nervous smile, recalling the fairy tale she'd passed on to her half sister.

"If you leesen, you can hear hur, creak-ing through duh trees . . . crackeling een duh branches . . . rust'ling through duh leaves . . ."

Another gust caused a tree carrying dried pods of seed to rattle and shake. The commotion masked a set of approaching footsteps, a human's flat-soled tread matched with a goat's rigid cloven hoof.

The sight of the errant girl hiding in the greenery had drawn a treacherous creature into the woods. The opportunity of an isolated prey presented a lure so tempting, he was powerless to resist. The plastic prosthetic had been discarded at the forest's edge, allowing the beast to traverse the rough terrain with a goat's nimble traction.

While unaware of the advancing peril, Jessie somehow felt a growing sense of unease. Anxiously, she drummed her fingers against the riveting sewn into the waist of her shorts. As the breeze swirled through the forest, she found herself murmuring the words she'd taught Elena.

"Hur spirit's oldah dan dah jumbies . . . oldah dan dis island . . . oldah dan tyme eet-self."

The creature moved with stealthy expertise, rapidly honing in on his target. Despite having eaten a large breakfast at the rainbow-decorated diner earlier that morning, he was ravenous for something more substantial, more fulfilling—like the chewy cartilage of human toes.

Jessie continued the mantra, her lilting voice rising with the wind.

"She wuz here 'fore dah Danes, 'fore dah French, 'fore dah first Spanish slave tradas. She wuz wit duh Car-ib at Salt Reev-ah when Christ'pher Columbus came a-shore."

An involuntary shiver raked through her body.

"Dah Goat-foot Wo-man, she helped dem Car-ib carve up a man from dat Spanish crew. They strung 'eem up ova a fire an' cooked 'eem on a stek."

The creature's eyes seethed with intensity as he closed in on his meal.

"Tha's where she first gut duh taste fer hoom-an flesh."

A strong hand reached out for the girl's shoulder, the muscular fingers curving in anticipation of the soft human form . . .

But a sigh of intense disappointment shook the forest.

The grip fell inches short as Jessie stepped from the bushes and followed her father out the garden's side gate.

~ *67* ~

The Writer

RAINDROPS BEGAN TO spatter against the white tents stretched across the front lawn of the Danish estate house. Undeterred by the approaching weather, the Transfer Day attendees gathered beneath the tented cover and settled into the rows of metal foldout chairs. The crowd was ready for the ceremonies to begin, if for no other reason than to speed along the schedule to the lunch portion of the program.

The chairs had been arranged as close as possible to one another in order to get the maximum amount of protected seating. Eying the cramped area filling in near the podium, the writer took a seat at the back. She pulled a pad of paper from her backpack and began taking notes on the proceedings, occasionally snapping a discreet photo of the collected politicians and Danish dignitaries.

After an opening performance by a group of high school musicians, the first speaker was introduced. The Danish Ambassador stepped up to the podium and gazed out across the seating area, gaining reassurance from the number of familiar European faces interspersed with those of the skeptical West Indians.

"Ahem," he said, adjusting the mike. "I'd like to begin with a familiar saying. 'A stranger is just a friend you haven't yet met' . . ."

FIFTEEN MINUTES LATER, the Ambassador concluded his speech, receiving enthusiastic applause from the Danes and polite but moderate clapping from the Islanders. A second introduction brought the Governor to the podium for his remarks.

The large man strode confidently to the front of the crowd. As he pulled a typed outline from his suit pocket, he looked across the audience, smiling at several of the attendees.

This was perfectly normal behavior, particularly for a politician, but the writer had the distinct impression that the Governor was also scanning the audience for an unwelcome guest.

After a long moment's scrutiny, the Governor lowered his vision to the lectern. Seemingly satisfied with the assembled participants, he launched into his talking points.

He began with a warm acceptance of the Danish offers of friendship and cultural exchange, lauding the opportunity to promote the islands' tourism industry. Listing several notable Danish landmarks, he recalled his own recent visit to the European country. Left unsaid, but nonetheless conveyed by the Governor's occasional involuntary facial expressions, was the sentiment that Denmark was the most frigid piece of land he'd ever set foot on.

Mindful of the West Indian members of the audience, the Governor then tempered his remarks with a gentle but firm reminder that, as a result of the transfer they were all there to commemorate, the Islanders were now U.S. citizens—entitled to the full array of American privileges and freedoms.

It was one of the few instances in modern times where the benefits of that citizenship had been so assertively championed.

AS THE GOVERNOR continued to navigate his verbal tight-rope, the writer felt her mind begin to drift. Her notebook scribblings grew fewer and farther between. The smell of the food from the cooking area had whetted her appetite, and the repetitive tapping of the raindrops on the white-tent fabric above her head began to nullify even the Governor's strong voice.

The writer gazed across the wet lawn, through the increasing drizzle, to the estate house. She watched as the rivulets of rain followed their well-worn path down the grooves in the building's sturdy rock walls.

Midway into a yawn, she suddenly sat upright, startled by the sight of a suited man staggering out of the nearby forest. She recognized him as the air-conditioner salesman who had abruptly ended their conversation at the boardwalk restaurant the night before. Looking somewhat bedraggled, he stepped into the cover of the estate house's front entrance and bent to tie his left shoe.

The smell from the lunch area must have gotten to him, too, the writer thought as the salesman glanced up toward the covered tent area.

His boyish face bore the distinct expression of hunger.

~ *68* ~

Modern-Day Maroons

MIC AND CURRIE crashed out of the woods and onto a short spit of rocky beach. They had reached one of the colonial-era access points along St. Croix's northwest shoreline, where fleeing Maroons had once met runner boats for transport north to emancipated islands.

There was, however, no boat waiting for the coconut vendors on that particular rainy morning.

Soaked to the skin, Currie collapsed on a rock. In his hand, he held a plastic sack given to them by the grocery store owner. The exterior was covered with water droplets, but the bag's contents had remained mostly dry.

As a reward for alerting him to the far more dangerous threat of Nova's pending armed assault, Kareem had given the men a small donation of cash and a day's provision of food. The thank-you gift, however, was of little consolation to the two fugitives.

"Nova's going to flip his lid when he finds out we ratted on him," Currie panted, still flushed from the hike. "He'll send all his friends after us. We'll have to enter our own witness protection program."

Mic reached for the bag and began digging around inside as Currie continued to fret over their future.

"I've got a cousin over on St. Thomas," he said, slowly regaining his breath. "If we could get over to the Rock, he could hide us up there for a while until things die down."

"We're done for if we ever show our faces on Santa Cruz again," Mic replied glibly. "We'd better just start swimming."

From the sack, he removed a wrapped roast beef sandwich, a bag of chips, and a bottle of water. It wasn't pork chops or French fries, but at this point, he wasn't complaining. He tossed the bag back to Currie.

"But we're not going anywhere until I eat this sandwich." Hungrily, he dug into the wrapper. "This could be my last meal. I'm going to enjoy it!"

TWENTY MINUTES LATER, Mic and Currie entered the water, pushing a large piece of driftwood they'd found on the shore. The abandoned door looked as if it had already traveled a substantial distance on the waves. The paint had long since peeled off, and the corners were rounded from the wear of the elements.

"Are you sure about this?" Currie asked nervously. He was extremely uncomfortable about Mic's plan.

There was a reason Currie generally made the decisions for the pair. Mic's wild ideas trended toward the ridiculous, if not downright foolish. Unfortunately, Currie had been unable to come up with any other options, so he had, at last, relented to Mic's proposal.

"How hard could it be?" Mic replied with a casual shrug. "I'm telling you, this is how they did it in the old days. My granny used to talk about it all the time."

Currie muttered an un-interpretable response.

"What about all this rain?" he demanded as the downpour intensified. "Wouldn't it be better to wait until this storm passes?"

Mic smacked the water dismissively.

"Can you imagine how hot it will be once the sun comes out? I'm telling you, it'll be fine. Let's just get it over with."

Confidently, Mic shoved the door out into the waves. The water kicked up to his narrow waist as he navigated around a large boulder that jutted out from the shore.

With a pleading look at the heavens, Currie splashed in after his tall friend and the floating door.

TWENTY MINUTES LATER, the two men had managed to swim about a half mile from the shore. With the storm dumping torrential rain onto an increasingly heavy surf, the situation had quickly turned dire.

Already at the point of drowning, Mic and Currie struggled to keep their heads above water. The wooden door was long gone, swamped by a crashing wave that had taken them both under. Their arms and legs flailed about as they frantically worked to tread water.

A return to their departure point was out of the question. The rocky beach where they had started was now an impossible distance away.

In between gasps for air, they managed to exchange looks, their well-practiced communication system transmitting a mutual message without the need for words: this was the end.

At least we're going out on our own terms, Currie thought as yet another wave rolled over them. If it had to happen, he would rather die this way than at the hand of Nova or one of his cronies.

With effort, he pushed himself back to the surface, relieved to see that Mic had done the same. They had another couple of minutes left in them, but not much more.

Just when Currie was about to give up, lift his arms, and let his body drop to the watery depths—he heard a man's singing. The words to the song were in a foreign language he didn't understand, but the voice was strangely familiar.

"Is it an angel?" Mic gasped, his dark face paled and waterlogged. He spun himself in a circle, trying to find the source of the sound.

Suddenly, a small motorboat pulled up beside them, and an olive-skinned man in a cutoff T-shirt leaned over the side. The pointed faces of two dachshunds popped up on the railing next to him.

Cupping his hands around his mouth, Umberto called down to Mic and Currie.

"Do you two need a ride?"

~ *69* ~

Luck Runs Out

MASK ONCE MORE pulled down over his face and gun at the ready, Nova turned away from the boarded-up house and strode bullishly across the street toward Kareem's grocery store. It was a brazen move, one improvised on the spot, but he wasn't worried.

He was Casanova.

He didn't need the Coconut Boys. They had been an unnecessary complication that his client had insisted upon. Next time, he thought to himself, there will be no such nonsense. He would see to that.

Finger on the trigger and a slight jaunt to his step, he mounted the curb outside the store's entrance. The dark clouds above began to release their moisture as he surveyed the protective metal gate that had been propped against the building's exterior wall. A sign hanging from the inner glass door read OPEN.

With a last glance at the dampening street, Nova dusted a few raindrops from his shirt and entered the shop.

A bell rang, signaling his presence, but no one stirred inside. The clerk's station behind the cashier counter was empty.

Nova stared briefly at the unmanned register, tempted by its contents, but he didn't stop to check the drawer. He wasn't there for the store's cash. He had other business to attend to.

Nostrils flaring with the adrenaline of an approaching kill, Nova circled the open area at the front of the store, looking down the aisles for the owner. A quick scan failed to reveal the man's location, so he began a more thorough search.

Pacing like a panther, Nova moved meticulously through each row, gliding past shelves of boxed cereal, canned soup, potato chips, and bottled water. As he reached the end of the last aisle, he still hadn't seen the shopkeeper.

There was no reason to panic, Nova thought with confidence. He would find him. It was only a matter of time.

The Arabic businessman who owned the store was well known to St. Croix's criminal element. With his flashy cars, sharp suits, and gold watches, Kareem had long been a target. After years of jealous envy, Nova was looking forward to taking the man down.

The sound of shuffling papers caught Nova's attention, and he spun back toward the front of the store, his eyes narrowing on a private area behind the cashier counter.

The office door stood slightly ajar.

Beneath the mask, an evil smile spread across Nova's face. He crept stealthily around the counter and slunk toward the narrow opening.

KAREEM SAT AT his desk, reviewing notes on a clipboard. He was turned toward the wall, facing the billboard filled with pictures of his family. He appeared not to notice as Nova stepped forward, silently entering the room.

Carefully taking aim, Nova raised the pistol toward the back of Kareem's head. But before he could pull the trigger, a voice spoke from behind his left shoulder.

"Come on in, Nova. We've been waiting for you."

Cursing, he spun around to see a number of policemen

and private security guards standing against the wall by the door. Each one bore a firearm leveled at Nova's chest.

After counting the number of weapons trained on his body, Nova lowered his gun in defeat.

KAREEM JUMPED UP from his chair, visibly relieved that the charade was over.

The mask was quickly jerked from Nova's head as he was disarmed, handcuffed, and pushed down onto the empty seat. The chair was then scooted to the center of the room and ringed with guards.

One of the policemen assumed the role of interrogator. With a beefy hand, he clamped down on Nova's shoulder.

"Come on, Nova, spill the beans," the officer urged, bending over the chair. "This isn't your style. Someone must have hired you to come in here like this. Tell us who, and we'll cut you some slack."

Nova paused for a long moment, as if carefully weighing his answer. Despite the officer's grip, he rotated in his chair, so that he was looking directly at Kareem. Finally, he spoke.

"I was hired to kill Kareem," he said, his voice clear and even as he watched the storeowner's reaction. "I was supposed to pin the blame on the Coconut Boys, but they ran off on me, so I had to improvise."

Nova spat on the floor, clearly irked by the betrayal. "Since you all are here, it looks like they sold me out. They'll regret doing that, I can assure you."

The policeman averted his gaze, not wanting to confirm or deny the last assumption.

Nova noted the policeman's non-response. With a conclusive grunt, he continued. "It wasn't about the money from the register. You guys know I don't need the cash." He paused for an arrogant shrug. "I was just supposed to make it look like a robbery gone bad."

The policeman contemplated this information and then prodded. "So who hired you to do this?"

A smirking grin swept over Nova's face. He may have been caught in the act, and he would probably be spending a few months in jail, but he was going to enjoy this reveal.

"It was a woman," he replied cryptically.

The policeman straightened and exchanged looks with the rest of the security personnel. Kareem leaned on the edge of his desk for support as his head began to spin.

Everyone in the room, it seemed, was holding his breath—everyone except Nova, who looked perfectly relaxed.

"What's this woman's name?" the policeman asked.

Kareem let out a painful gasp as Nova nodded his head toward the picture in the center of the billboard.

"Mira." His white teeth gleaming, he broke into a fit of raucous laughter. Then he returned his gaze to Kareem.

"His wife."

Key Lime Pie

MIRA STOOD ON the villa's front porch, carefully positioned beneath the eaves to keep from being soaked. Through the sheeting water running off the roof, she watched a taxi driver load her suitcase along with those of three of her four children into a van bound for the Christiansted seaplane hangar.

The children were already inside the vehicle, Elena and Hassan strapped into their seats, Jack stubbornly refusing to secure his belt until the last second before departure.

The driver hefted the final piece of luggage into the van's rear cargo area and wiped the rain from his forehead.

"Anything else, ma'am?" he asked, plucking at his wet shirt, which was plastered against his chest.

Mira glanced back toward the house and shook her head. She had taken what she needed; the rest she was ready to leave behind.

Gathering up the folds of the black cloak, she hurried from the eaves to the van. The driver ushered her into the front passenger seat and closed the door.

As the driver hurried around to the opposite side, she smoothed the black fabric that covered her lap. She had decided to wear the cloak and headscarf one last time. The concealment, combined with the deference it commanded, might just come in handy on her way out of town.

The seaplane personnel had seen her come and go on these inter-island flights with regularity. Many of the counter staff appeared uncomfortable with the cloak and its religious implications, and they gave her a wide berth. Given the nature of this particular departure, the fewer questions asked the better.

Once she reached Charlotte Amalie, she could easily discard the cloak's outer layer. Beneath the dark covering, a sleeveless green dress, similar to the one from the previous day, was waiting to make its St. Thomas debut.

Her feet, of course, were adorned in the dazzling green shoes, the same pair she'd worn at the start of her marriage. It seemed only fitting that she finished off the union in similar fashion.

Besides, given the evidence she'd found in her daughter's room, she had to be prepared for the possibility that her first husband was still here on St. Croix.

With a sly smile, Mira clicked her heels together. If Charlie got in her way, she knew how to handle him.

THE WIND WHIPPED the driving rain, lashing the taxi van with concentrated torrents that pounded against the metal roof and overwhelmed the windshield wipers. Puddles quickly grew into small streams that sent swirling eddies across the roadway. With jerks and starts, the van proceeded through the flooded streets, the driver braking frequently to avoid gaping potholes and downed branches.

Elena beamed gleefully out her window, chasing the path of the streaking raindrops with her fingers. She hummed to herself, incorporating the bumps from the road's rough surface into her tune.

"I am not . . ." Bump. Bump. ". . . going to school . . ." Ka-thump. Whomp. ". . . today!"

Her younger brother had yet to match her enthusiasm for the trip.

"Where are we going?" Hassan asked again, his face pinched with concern. "And how long will we be there?"

"It's a surprise, sweetie," Mira replied absentmindedly, her thoughts clearly elsewhere.

"What about Jessie?" he persisted.

This question received a sharper response.

"We're going to pick her up in Christiansted," Mira said firmly, but her pursed lips and clenched hands conveyed the uncertainty behind the statement.

THE RAIN BEGAN to lessen as the van reached the seaplane terminal. The transformation from bleary to bright occurred in an instant. The sun broke through the clouds, casting rainbows over the harbor as it shone down on the Christiansted boardwalk. The driver pulled into a nearby lot, shutting down the windshield wipers long before he parked in the unloading zone.

Mira helped the two younger children out of the van as Jack assisted the driver with the luggage. Soon, the group and their bags were unloaded on the sidewalk outside the seaplane hangar.

"There, you see," Mira said optimistically, shaking the wrinkles from her cloak. "We're off to a marvelous start."

"I'm afraid it's just a temporary clearing, ma'am," the driver replied as she handed him the fare. He glanced worriedly at the eastern horizon, where yet another dark mass loomed in the sky. "The main squall will be here within the next hour or two."

Mira noted the approaching weather and sighed determinedly.

"With any luck, we'll be out of here before then."

AFTER CHECKING THE luggage at the counter inside the seaplane hangar, Mira led the three children down the wet boardwalk toward the rainbow-decorated diner.

"Here," she said, pulling a large bill from her purse.

"Why don't you guys get some lunch while I go look for Jessie."

Elena charged inside, dragging Hassan along with her.

"I want the change," Mira said as Jack snatched the cash from her fingers.

Raising his eyebrows in rebuke, he issued his first comment of the morning. "Babysitting fee."

Mira smiled as she watched a waitress greet the trio and usher them to a table. Elena's commanding voice echoed out onto the boardwalk.

"That'll be three plates of frozen key lime pie!"

IT WOULD BE the mother's last sighting of her children.

~ 71 ~

A Fine Art

CHECKING HER WATCH, Mira bustled up the boardwalk, frantically scanning the area for any sign of Jessie. A few pedestrians wandered along the shoreline, taking advantage of the break in the weather to find a late lunch or an early dinner, but the rain had driven the majority of the island's vacationers back to their hotels and resorts.

Turning at the sugar mill bar, Mira sped across the coral rock path leading toward the Comanche Hotel. The black cloak billowing around her, she hurried past the base of the swimming pool and through the tunnel running beneath the second floor pavilion.

She had only one clear idea of where to search. She wasn't sure what she would do if she didn't find her daughter or some clue to her whereabouts inside room seventeen.

It had taken her ten years to finally decide to leave this island, but she wasn't prepared to give up Jessie in the process.

MINUTES LATER, MIRA swept into the hotel's reception area. She rushed up to the front desk, relieved at the sight of the man working behind its mahogany counter. Her long-serving accomplice had successfully switched shifts with the woman who regularly worked during the afternoon.

"Is he still here?" she panted, breathless from exertion. Given the urgency of the situation, she didn't have time for a typical back-and-forth greeting.

The man seated on the opposite side of the desk leaned toward her conspiratorially. He was a tall muscular man, his dark-skinned face wooden in its near-expressionless features—a stolid match to the Comanche statue standing against the wall near the window.

"He left several hours ago," the man whispered in a deep, barely audible voice. He looked over his shoulder to make sure no one else was listening. After confirming that the reception area was empty, he added, "But he booked the room for another night."

"Number seventeen?" Mira asked, glancing up at the ceiling.

The clerk grunted his assent.

Mira brushed back the folds of the headscarf. "And my daughter?"

"I haven't seen her." He paused and looked once more around the place. "One of the maids saw her leaving the note, the night I . . ." He stopped and cleared his throat. "The night I took your husband to the fort." His rigid forehead wrinkled ever so slightly. "She must have stolen your key."

Mira dug inside her purse and then looked up, nodding. "It's gone."

Wordlessly, the clerk reached into the desk and handed her a replacement set, one green-tabbed key for the second-floor access and a second key specific to room seventeen.

Mouthing a silent "Thank you," Mira swished up the stairs.

The man sat stiffly back in his chair. His white eyes, bulging against the sharp contours of his face, followed her until she reached the second-floor balcony and disappeared around the corner.

AT THE HOTEL'S top attic level, Mira raced to the end of the narrow hallway. She slid the key into the lock, pushed open the door—and let out a sigh of disappointment.

The room was empty.

Her gaze quickly passed over the lace-covered bed, the nightstand beside it, and the antique wardrobe pushed against the tallest wall, all the while trying to think of where her daughter might have gone.

The space was much the way she'd last left it—minus, of course, her ex-husband slumped unconscious on the floor.

She circled the room, looking up at the pointed ceiling and then out through the window to the narrow view of the harbor.

The soles of her shoes tapped quietly against the floor's hard surface, her footsteps instinctively falling in a regular even pace.

Tap. Tap. Tap.

It was a well-practiced pattern, one she'd repeated numerous times over the years. Despite the dire circumstances, she let herself smile at the familiar sound and its steady, mesmerizing beat.

This room—room number seventeen—was where she had learned the fine art of hypnosis.

IT HAD ALL started with Adam Rock. He had given her the first tutorials to help with her personal shopping business, just a few rudimentary mind tricks to get her enterprise off the ground. This attic floor room—hot, stuffy, and isolated—had been the perfect location for the lessons.

She was a natural, Rock had gushed as she quickly learned the basic skills. She was soon ready to try her hand on human test subjects.

The techniques were subtle but effective, easily adaptable to selling air-conditioning or high-fashion clothing, and they had worked like a charm on the cloaked women of the Muslim community.

Her first husband, however, had been a far more difficult target. His fixation with their money concerns had overwhelmed all of her psychological efforts to distract him—particularly from his credit card statements.

MIRA'S SMILE BROADENED into a triumphant expression.

It wasn't until she and Charlie met up again last Thanksgiving, years later and her skills much more advanced, that she'd been able to crack his tough subconscious. She'd brought him to this location, her training ground, for maximum advantage.

She'd been nervous at first, not sure if she could pull it off, but suddenly, there he'd been, crumpled like a wet noodle on the floor.

Each subsequent encounter had been easier, she reflected, laughing as she remembered the third instance when he'd shown up with a painter's mask covering his nose and mouth.

The perfume, the makeup, the fancy clothes—all of that was just a distraction. The whole trick was in the sound.

Now, if he'd worn earplugs, she thought smugly, that might have been a challenge.

Charlie's wardrobe change had been a last bit of subliminal messaging. The green shoes were a symbol of their marriage's dissolution. As for the matching dress . . .

She shrugged as if this explanation was self-evident.

The shoes would have looked silly with cutoff camo pants.

SHAKING HERSELF FREE of the memory, Mira took one last glance around the room.

She had better find Jessie soon. She didn't want to wait for a later flight.

Her plan was to be off the island and well on her way to her new home before Kareem discovered she had moved out of the villa.

~ 72 ~

Delicious

THE GOVERNOR'S ASSISTANT paced nervously across the wet lawn outside the tented area at the Danish plantation, anxiously gripping his cell phone. Cedric slipped into the trees at the edge of the Transfer Day ceremonies, trying to find a location with both privacy and cell-phone reception.

The Governor was heading toward the food line. He only had a couple of minutes before his absence would be noticed.

Come on, he thought desperately. *Don't leave me hanging. I need to know, one way or the other.*

Just then, a buzzing vibration shook his hand.

Cedric read the caller ID and frowned. The digital box carried the abbreviation for the St. Croix police headquarters.

He bit his lower lip. This was not a good sign. Tentatively, he brought the receiver to his head.

"Hello."

"It's Nova."

Cedric sucked in his breath. It was definitely bad news. He looked around the wooded area, checking for potential eavesdroppers, before replying.

"And?" he whispered tensely.

"The Coconut Boys flew the coop. Left it all on me."

Nova's voice sounded oddly calm, considering the circumstances.

"And?" Cedric said with a gulp.

"Cops were waiting for me when I went in."

Cedric pulled at his collar, trying to loosen the buttons cinched around his neck.

"And?" he managed to croak.

"Don't sweat it. I'll be out in six months."

Cedric wiped a sweating hand across his brow. Color began returning to his face.

"Did you give them the fallback story?"

"Well, I had no other choice, did I," Nova replied, issuing the comment as a statement of fact, not a question.

"You did the right thing," Cedric said reassuringly, breathing out a short sigh of relief. "Don't worry. I'll be in touch."

CEDRIC HUNG UP the line and stood in the trees, digesting this update and pondering the implications, for both himself and his cabal of conspirators.

The brazen daytime attack on the Muslim shopkeeper, meant to provoke a destabilizing response within the island's polarized political groups, had been defused.

The mission had changed from governmental upheaval to cleanup and regroup—in the near term, at least. There were other schemes already in the works, and his mind immediately began spinning with possibilities. But first, it was essential that he preserve his position as the Governor's main assistant.

There was only one way to ensure he protected that cover.

Cedric punched a second number into his cell phone.

This call rang in the pocket of another Transfer Day participant, an air-conditioner salesman, who had just sat down at a picnic table, less than a hundred yards away.

ADAM ROCK LISTENED, somberly, as Cedric relayed the news of the day's sabotaged plot. The Governor's coerced assistance would no longer be needed to ensure Mira's speedy departure from the island. The quid pro quo Rock had extracted from the politician at their earlier breakfast meeting had been negated. With Nova in custody and Kareem still alive to ask questions, they couldn't risk the chance that Mira might unwittingly expose their underlying scheme. The potential scandal that Rock had used to extort the favor would be put to another use, later down the line.

Now that Mira had been fingered as the culprit in her husband's attempted murder, she was a loose end that would have to be eliminated.

If only the Coconut Boys had played their part, Rock thought with frustration.

After pausing for a brief moment of consideration, he formulated his succinct response.

"I understand."

Then he stood from the picnic table, leaving the food on his plate untouched, and began walking toward the parking area.

He had hoped things would work out differently with Mira. He had been looking forward to bringing her and her children to his Caribbean vacation home. It was a fabulous estate, located on an isolated island a few hundred miles away. There, they could have started a new life together, a picture-perfect family—albeit one with a few fascinating secrets.

It would have been just him, Mira, and her four—delicious—children.

He tapped the pocket that held his wallet, sensing the weight of the ring still tucked inside. He would be putting that gold band back on after all, he thought ruefully.

Now, he was going to have to do something unpleasant.

But it was sure to be tasty.

Mira had always had such delicate, delectable-looking feet.

~ *73* ~

Familiar Footwear

WITH THE SPEECHES finally completed, the Transfer Day crowds rapidly shifted to the lunch area, forming long lines behind the buffet-style tables that had been set up earlier. The hungry hordes chatted with anticipation, eagerly waiting for their turn at the lineup of heated metal pans.

But for Charlie Baker, the fragrant West Indian food held no allure. The stomach-churning experience of the earlier boat ride, combined with the disappointment of yet another missed meeting, had completely sapped his appetite.

He had scoured every inch of the grounds looking for Jessie, closely studying well over a hundred teenage girls, to no avail. He had been scowled at, frowned upon, and outright threatened for his suspicious leering.

Something had happened to prevent her from coming, or, more likely he thought with chagrin, she had changed her mind.

Dejected, he walked toward the parking lot.

NEAR THE PLANTATION'S front entrance, Charlie spied a taxi van that was about to pull out onto the main road. Waving his arms in the air, he chugged down the hill, flagging the driver.

"Christiansted?" Charlie asked as the man from Nevis rolled down his window.

"Hop in," he replied, cheerfully flicking a chicken charm hanging from his rearview mirror.

Wrenching open the handle for the passenger-side door, Charlie slid the metal panel far enough back on its rusty rollers so that he could climb inside.

The vehicle already held several riders, including a broad-shouldered man with a familiar round face who made room for Charlie on the front bench seat.

"Hello, my friend," the air-conditioner salesman said as Charlie crawled inside and shoved the door shut.

Blinking to adjust his eyesight, it took Charlie a moment to recognize his seatmate from the seaplane. "Hello again," he replied after making the connection.

He nodded a welcome and then wrinkled his nose. A peculiar aroma emanated from the rear seats. Craning his neck to look behind his bench, he found himself face to yellowed, wrinkled face with the old woman from the boardwalk.

Gedda cracked a toothless smile as Charlie quickly returned his gaze to the front.

The van drove off down the mahogany-lined road, trailed a short distance away by a dark-haired girl on a moped.

THIRTY MINUTES LATER, the van pulled into its slot on the King Street straightaway in downtown Christiansted. The last passenger to get in, Charlie was the first one out. After disembarking, he walked around to the driver's door to pay the fare.

The man from Nevis leaned out his front window, making sure to flash each payment to the drivers jealously watching from the alley.

Charlie handed over his contribution and then shuffled to the curb, not sure where to go or what to do next. The rain had temporarily stopped, but he had seen more than enough of the boardwalk's attractions, particularly, he thought with a shudder, the Danish fort.

Charlie was about to head back to the Comanche when he noticed the old woman hobbling away from the van. In her left hand, she carried a worn plastic bag.

His eyes were immediately drawn to a sharp, pointed object sticking out of the bag's open top—the emerald-green heel of a woman's shoe.

"Wait!" Charlie called out, but Gedda only moved faster. Despite her stilted movements, she quickly crossed through the park and set off down the boardwalk.

Perplexed, Charlie chased after her.

He was so engrossed in the old woman's green shoe that he didn't see the teenage girl parking her moped by the Scale House. Puzzling over her father's strange behavior, Jessie followed after him and Gedda.

As Charlie passed the rainbow-decorated diner a few hundred yards later, he similarly failed to observe the three children seated inside eating key lime pie.

~ 74 ~

Treacherous Assistance

AFTER AN EXHAUSTIVE search, Mira finally left the Comanche's attic room. Skirting the edge of the second floor balcony, she took a set of exterior stairs down to the front alley. Feeling increasingly desperate, she sped around the corner to the taxi stand.

She was about to ask the drivers if they'd seen a girl fitting Jessie's description when she heard a familiar voice in her left ear. Adam Rock's deep baritone was soothing and yet, at the same time, strangely unnerving.

"Mira," he said calmly. "I hope you haven't had second thoughts."

"It's Jessie," she replied, spinning around. "She's run off." She threw her hands in the air. "I can't find her."

Rock nodded across the park. "I might have seen your daughter heading toward the fort just a few minutes ago. The girl looked like the one in the picture you showed me the other night. She's about fifteen with short brown hair, right?"

Mira immediately set off toward the park's green space. The salesman chugged after her, trying to catch up, as the skies began to darken with the arrival of the second squall.

By the time they neared the fort's front gates, splattering drops were smacking against the building's metal roof.

Rock listened to the constant, repetitive sound and murmured to himself.

"Perfect dinner music."

MIRA DASHED INTO the fort's sloping courtyard. The brick surface was quickly growing slick from the rain. A scan of the fenced-off area revealed it to be empty. Shaking her head in frustration, Mira looked back at Rock, who had just staggered inside behind her.

"Let's try in there," he said, pointing toward the pyramid of white-painted steps leading into the main building.

Mira nodded her agreement, and the duo slipped and slid their way across the incline and up the short flight of stairs into the protection of the central arched hallway.

Once inside, Mira resumed her search, immediately setting off down the first corridor with Rock closely trailing behind.

The windows to the interior courtyard were curtained with liquid sheets of rain, leaving the unlit corridor dreary and dark. The dampness seeped inward, coating the stone surfaces with a film of moisture. Everywhere, it seemed, there was the echoing staccato of rain.

Mira reached the corner of the building, finding no sign of Jessie. She paused in the hallway, trying to decide where to look next. The narrow stairs to the basement dropped down to her left, while the upper holding cells, including the room where Alexander Hamilton's mother had once been imprisoned, stretched off to her right. She was about to veer toward the latter when Rock stepped beside her.

He reached into his coat pocket and pulled out a pack of cigarettes he'd purchased a few hours earlier. Still in its protective plastic wrapping, the contents had remained dry. Peeling off the wrapper, he slid out a cigarette and offered it to Mira.

"Yes, thank you," she said, smiling weakly as she rolled the slender stick between her fingers.

Rock dug in his suit pockets and fished out a lighter. "Please, allow me," he said as she placed the cigarette in her mouth.

With a round thumb, he flicked the ignition switch and waved the resulting flame beneath the cigarette's paper end.

Closing her eyes, Mira sucked air through the lit embers, causing the tip to glow bright red. A sweet scent enveloped her, as if someone had just spritzed her with perfume. The flowery aroma gradually dissipated, replaced by a slow, even tapping sound—Rock's fingertips drumming in time with the raindrops, amplifying the effect.

A moment later, the cigarette dropped from Mira's fingers. Her knees buckled beneath her, and she swooned, falling backward.

Rock caught her in his arms and gently laid her on the floor.

He gazed down at her feet, encased in the green high-heeled shoes, his eyes honing in on the slender toes peeking out through the opening at the point.

"Oh, Mira," he said with a hungry sigh. "You always had such wonderful toes."

INSIDE THE FIRST floor of the Comanche Hotel, the wooden man sitting behind the reception desk looked up with alarm.

The clerk rose from his seat, as if he had somehow sensed the ravenous zeal of the beast dismantling his victim inside the Danish fort a short distance away.

Reaching beneath the counter, he removed a wooden staff, his thick hands wrapping around the pole in a powerful iron grip. Wielding the crude weapon like an axe, he passed through to the alley, pulled the hood of his jacket up over his head, and lumbered off into the rain.

MINUTES LATER, THE clerk's heavy footsteps tread up the mahogany-lined path leading to the fort. The wet wind swirled through the leafy canopy, whispering down an unheeded warning.

Charging through the front gates, he followed the familiar path across the sloping courtyard and up the front steps into the main building. At the end of the central arched corridor, he turned left down the side hallway, his bulging eyes sweeping the stone interior for any sign of the cloven-hoofed creature and his hapless victim.

An orchestra of dripping water echoed through the dark structure as rivulets of rain ran through the intricate drainage system of gutters and pipes, down to the lower portion of the sea-facing wall where it dumped into the sea.

The deafening noise roared through the brick courtyard as the clerk turned to leave, his clothing soaked—and his heart aching with sadness.

His search had turned up nothing but a woman's green high-heeled shoe.

~ *75* ~

The Reunion

CHARLIE BAKER TROTTED down the boardwalk, trying to catch up to the old woman and her plastic bag of shoes. Rain began to dump out of the sky, sending a cascade of water running off the front of his baseball cap. Shielding the brim, he increased his pace, but Gedda's crippled form soon disappeared in the distance.

As Charlie neared the walkway's western terminus, the hag was nowhere to be seen.

Soaked to the skin, he turned a slow circle. His gaze stopped on the empty lot across from the seaplane hangar, where he'd seen the old woman when he arrived on St. Croix the day before. The area was strewn with trash and several damp chickens, but there was no indication of human activity.

Next door, however, he caught a glimpse of the woman's rusted-out shopping cart parked by the abandoned nightclub.

Cautiously advancing on the structure's concrete shell, Charlie peered through one of the gaping windows. There, in the middle of the dusty floor, lay the old woman's plastic bag, stuffed with a collection of green high-heeled shoes.

After looking over his shoulder, Charlie crawled through the window and shuffled over to the bag. Kneeling, he sifted through the contents, removed three identical pairs of shoes, and set them on the ground.

He selected one from the pile and flipped it over in his hands, studying the sole.

It was a knockoff, a cheap replica of the expensive pair he'd once found in Mira's closet. Holding the shoe against his left combat boot for comparison, he confirmed the size was a rough fit for his feet.

These were the shoes he had woken up wearing after his encounters with his ex-wife—the shoes he had subsequently thrown away in the hotel room trash bin. The hag must have pulled them from the Dumpsters where the Comanche staff deposited their garbage.

Standing, Charlie reset his baseball cap. He stared down at the heap of women's footwear, reflecting on the bizarre encounters they represented.

He'd had his share of wild nights in the Caribbean. He and his fellow expats on St. John had played a number of off-color pranks over the years—but none of those antics had come anywhere close to this.

Charlie stroked his chin, puzzling. He still couldn't figure out why, after all this time, Mira had lured him back to Santa Cruz in the first place. Why had she called, out of the blue, to invite him to the Thanksgiving get-together?

It couldn't have been just to torture him. It made no sense.

HE THOUGHT BACK to the second incident, which had occurred a few weeks after the Thanksgiving episode. He'd returned to St. John to attend to his construction business, but as soon as he could take a break, he'd hopped on a flight to St. Croix. He was determined to figure out why Mira had been on the island and how she had managed to render him unconscious and dump him at the fort.

Not long after the adventurous seaplane landing—the spear fisherman was beginning to ramp up his lobster-hunting activities—Charlie received a phone call from Mira. When Charlie demanded an explanation for their Thanksgiving encounter, she suggested they meet at the Comanche Hotel, where, she promised, she would explain everything.

The same sequence of events transpired.

Charlie climbed the four flights of steps, all the way to the top of the building, and entered the stuffy room at the end of the hallway. Inside room seventeen, Mira stood in a green silk dress and the matching shoes—the shoes that had started it all.

He lobbed outraged questions at his ex-wife as the sweet smell of her perfume swept over him. Her footsteps clicked across the wooden floorboards.

Tap. Tap. Tap.

As Mira drew nearer, his vision blurred. The room began to spin, and he struggled to maintain his balance.

Charlie staggered sideways on the nightclub's concrete floor. He felt woozy just remembering the experience.

And then, suddenly, he recalled one more scene from the room at the Comanche.

He saw Mira's green-clad figure bending toward him, checking his pulse. Her face neared his, and she whispered something to him.

Charlie racked his brain. What was she saying?

His mental image zoomed in on Mira's red-painted lips as they slowly mouthed the message. An un-interpretable murmur gradually clarified into distinct words.

"Charlie," she said softly. "It wasn't me. I didn't call you."

He pulled out the damp letter from his pants pocket and stared at the smeared pink-ink writing, the realization setting in.

"Jessie!" he exclaimed.

Just then, a teenage girl appeared in the doorway. She rushed toward him, tears streaming down her face, arms outstretched.

"Daddy, it's me!"

A PAIR OF yellow eyes rose silently over the windowsill. Gedda's wrinkled face stretched into a gap-toothed smile as she watched the father-daughter reunion.

~ 76 ~

Afoot on St. Croix

THE RAIN SOAKED the Christiansted boardwalk for several hours, the storm lasting into late afternoon. It was a slow day for tourists, and the brewpub opted to postpone their regular crab race for tomorrow's sunnier weather.

Inside the pub's near-empty eating area, an Italian opera singer waited for his "to go" order of pork chops and French fries. Umberto had just gassed up his boat for a short trip to St. Thomas. He planned to leave, with his two extra passengers, early the following morning.

THE NEXT DOOR down, at the sugar mill bar, the writer sat beneath the eaves, listening to the bartender mope about his now-former girlfriend. Earlier that day, the sailboat captain had dumped him for a scuba diving instructor.

"Apparently, this other guy has an apartment with air-conditioning . . ." he moaned despondently.

OBLIVIOUS TO THE rain, the salesman strolled past.

"Never underestimate the importance of proper

ventilation and cooling," Adam Rock mused upon overhearing the bartender's lament.

He continued down the boardwalk toward the seaplane hangar, rolling his suitcase behind him. He had a ticket on the day's last flight out.

Whistling softly to himself, he strummed his ample belly.

For the first time in months, he could honestly say that he wasn't hungry.

AT THE RAINBOW-DECORATED diner, the chef emerged from the kitchen with the day's scraps. Hefting his bucket, he marched up the bridge overlooking the lagoon. He swung his bucket over the railing, but the water remained eerily still. The tarpons' dark shadows circled lethargically, without interest, in the shallows below.

Peering down through the rain, the chef noticed a faint reddish tinge to the water. And then, in the muddy sand at the bottom of the lagoon, he spied the remnants of a shredded black cloak and a woman's green high-heeled shoe.

GEDDA BUMPED ALONG the boardwalk pushing her rusted cart, taking careful note of all these activities.

Not far from the lagoon, she peered inside the restaurant to where Charlie Baker sat eating a slice of key lime pie at a table with four youngsters, two of them his teenage children.

At the sound of the incoming seaplane, the old woman turned toward the harbor, watching as the aircraft circled the shoreline, its pilot scanning the water runway for signs of the spear fisherman's snorkel.

Her voice cackled into the rain.

"Children ain' nuttin but an appetizer."

**THE FIRST IN THE CATS AND CURIOS MYSTERIES
FROM *NEW YORK TIMES* BESTSELLING AUTHOR**

· Rebecca M. Hale ·

HOW TO WASH A CAT

Uncle Oscar was one of a kind. His dusty antiques shop, the Green Vase—nestled in San Francisco's historic Jackson Square district—was like his own personal museum to the Gold Rush–era. Needless to say, I was shocked when he was found dead in his shop, and even more surprised to discover he'd left the venerable establishment to me!

I had no sooner started exploring the shop's fascinating array of curios and novelties—along with my two cats, Rupert and Isabella—than I began to meet a motley crew of Uncle Oscar's former associates, all of whom seemed deeply interested in the shop and its hidden secrets. Before long I learned my inheritance included all sorts of clues Uncle Oscar had left behind—a peculiar key, a trapdoor, a puzzling map . . .

To unravel the mystery, my feline friends and I had to follow a twisted trail of deadly deception that began right in his shop, and led all the way back to the days of the Gold Rush itself . . .

M839T0411

THE *NEW YORK TIMES* BESTSELLING SERIES FROM

·Rebecca M. Hale·

HOW TO MOON A CAT

A Cats and Curios Mystery

When Rupert the cat sniffs out a dusty green vase with a toy bear inside, his owner has no doubt this is another of her Uncle Oscar's infamous clues to one of his valuable hidden treasures. Eager to put together the pieces of the puzzle, she's soon heading to Nevada City with her two cats, having no idea that this road trip will put her life in danger.

facebook.com/TheCrimeSceneBooks
penguin.com
howtowashacat.com

M978T0911

WELL-CRAFTED MYSTERIES
FROM **BERKLEY PRIME CRIME**

- **Earlene Fowler** Don't miss these Agatha Award–winning quilting mysteries featuring Benni Harper.

- **Monica Ferris** These *USA Today* bestselling Needlecraft Mysteries include free knitting patterns.

- **Laura Childs** Her Scrapbooking Mysteries offer tips to satisfy the most die-hard crafters.

- **Maggie Sefton** These popular Knitting Mysteries come with knitting patterns and recipes.

- **Lucy Lawrence** These brilliant Decoupage Mysteries involve cutouts, glue, and varnish.

- **Elizabeth Lynn Casey** The Southern Sewing Circle Mysteries are filled with friends, southern charm—and murder.